I0598371

Searching Among the Stars

by

Vicky Burkholder

Galactic Danger, Book 3

Searching Among the Stars

Cover Art by *The Wild Rose Press, Inc.*

The Wild Rose Press, Inc.
PO Box 708
Adams Basin, NY 14410-0708
Visit us at www.thewildrosepress.com

Publishing History
First Edition, 2022
Trade Paperback ISBN 978-1-5092-4469-0
Digital ISBN 978-1-5092-4470-6

Galactic Danger, Book 3
Published in the United States of America

Dedication

Bob, Misty Simon, Natalie Damschroder, and Victoria Smith for their unwavering support.

As she finished the last of the patches, her suit beeped at her. She was out of air. If someone didn't get to her soon… She gasped as all her systems red-lined. If she kept still, she might have three minutes of air left. Maybe. She tried hard not to panic.

"Cass? Are you all right?" The welcomed and worried voice of Zack Anderson, her partner Ben's friend—and her…what? She wasn't sure what to call him. He wasn't exactly a boyfriend, but there were definitely sparks between them, though she'd only known him just over a year. But as his voice came over her helmet com, she closed her eyes in relief.

"Zack? How…?" She shook her head and answered his question. "One of Ian's shots hit my engines. I'm dead in the water, life support's out, and my suit's almost done as well. Wait, what happened to Ian?"

"We sent him packing."

"What? How? We who? And how are you out here?" She gasped as her air died out. "Can't breathe."

"We're coming. Hang tight."

As Cass fought for every breath, she wondered how he had gotten to her so fast. There wasn't enough time for him to get here from Pointe Noir station since she'd sent out her call.

Dark spots clouded her vision when she saw an angel. And gasped in fresh air.

"Zack?"

"Shh. Just breathe. I got you."

Chapter One

Cassie Brennan clomped through the dark corridor of the derelict spaceship, open doorways on both sides of her. The headlamp from her environmental suit was the only light in the darkness. As she passed each doorway, she looked in, finding what appeared to be quarters with bunks. So far, they'd all been empty of everything but what was fastened down. Unfortunately, she hadn't found what she was looking for. Yet.

" 'Easy to find,' he said. 'You won't have any trouble,' he said. Humpf." Cassie clomped down the narrow passageway.

"You say something, boss?" Delta, Cassie's ship's AI, spoke in her com unit.

"No. Just letting off some steam. Ben said this would be a nice, easy job. It's neither nice nor easy." She grasped a partly open door and shoved as hard as she could, grunting with the effort. "Another bunk room. Stars and fardles, how many crewmen did this ship have? Delta, Ben said the relic should be in what they called their worship room. Any idea where that might be? Have you had any luck getting into the systems?"

"No. And no. Those systems are just too old. Plus, the Throquins really knew how to put security on their systems."

Cass continued through the ship. Holes of various sizes showed where space debris or rocks had hit the derelict. She finally reached the end of the corridor and stepped through the last door. "This might be interesting."

"Would you like some good news, boss?"

Cass stepped past rows of benches toward what looked like an altar. "I could sure use some about now. Looks like this place has been stripped."

"Well, Ben filed the claim—and it's pure. There are no previous liens or ties to the ship beyond what the buyers want you to find. Whatever else you uncover is yours, free and clear."

That made Cass pause and look more closely at her surroundings. Pure salvage claims were rare. Most derelicts had some kind of attachment. She'd bet her next pay that her partner, Ben, hadn't known that when he accepted this job. He'd contracted for her to find a relic from a long-abandoned ship. Cass had assumed the buyer would pay for salvaging the entire ship, but all they wanted was a little statuette? Nice. She looked at the old ship with new eyes.

"Boss, your heart rate just spiked. You okay?"

Cass chuckled. "Yep. This search is now more interesting but definitely not any easier."

She stepped up to the altar and looked back. The room was shaped like a hexagon—six sides with the altar in the middle. The platform appeared to be a large stone slab, pure black, also six-sided. "If I was a priest of some sort, where would I stand? There would always be someone at my back. That doesn't make sense." There was nothing on the altar, so she turned to face one of the walls. Each triangular section held ten rows of benches from wider ones near the walls to short ones near the altar. Each wall depicted a different scene from...what?

The Throquin war? She peered at each one.

"Delta, you recording this?"

"Yes."

"What is your assessment of the scenes?"

"There seems to be a sequence of events. Turn forty-five degrees to your right. That appears to be the first one."

Cass peered at the mural. The painting seemed to be a starscape with a bright spot in the center. "What do you think, Delta? Their version of creation?"

"Perhaps."

Cass followed the scenes around, seeing a point of light grow to a sun, planets, and more. The final scene depicted some sort of biped that she couldn't figure out. The best description she could come up with was a bird-like creature standing on a planet holding its hands up with the sun centered in its palms. "Their god?"

"Makes sense since the statue you're searching for is supposed to look like that."

"So the most obvious place would be in the center of the altar, which is right under a clear dome." Cass studied the altar more closely.

"Uh, boss?"

"Yeah?" She noticed six different colored stones in each corner of the altar.

"Boss, if you're going to find that relic, now would be a good time."

"Delta? What's wrong?" Cass pressed the stones, but nothing happened. Then she looked at each mural and pressed the stones in the order of the scenes. The altar shook, then split apart into six pieces, and a pedestal rose. And on the pedestal was the statuette she was there to find. She loosened the clamps holding the piece down

3

and grasped the figurine before it could float away. "I got the statue, Delta!"

"Great, 'cause we got company and they ain't the kind you ask for tea. Get your butt back here now."

Blasted claim jumpers! How had they found her?

Cass grabbed the statuette and attempted to put the figurine into the bag at her waist, but the darned piece was too big and awkward. She settled for tying the sculpture to her belt. Then she glanced at the stones on the altar and shrugged. "Why not?"

She grabbed her knife and pried the closest one off. The crystal gave off a blue glow, and she bit her lip. "I couldn't be that lucky, could I?" She scanned the area for a box to encase the gem, but there was nothing. Finally, she just shoved the stone in her bag and went after the next one.

"Boss, they're coming in close."

"Delta, are you hidden?" Cass pulled off the yellow one and stuffed the gem in the bag. Then a white.

"As well as I can be. I'm on the back side of the ship. I don't think they've seen me yet, but you have seriously run out of time."

"Fardles." Three would have to be good enough. Reluctantly, Cass stowed her knife, turned off the magnets on her boots, and pushed off, floating through the room to the door. She zipped down the corridor much faster than she had come earlier, arriving at the airlock within a couple of minutes.

"Where are they, Delta?"

"Coming in the port bay now," her ship's AI told her. "Quickest way out for you is the aft bay, two levels down."

Cass scanned the dark corridor, her headlamp

picking out an opening a dozen meters away. She headed there, ducking as a bright light scanned in her direction. She pushed off the wall straight down and came out in a wide-open space. There was one small shuttle sitting there, but from the looks of the broken wings and scattered pieces, the craft wasn't in flying shape. Blast marks blackened the walls and floor of the bay, and a gaping hole showed in the side wall. That and other damage she'd seen told her why the derelict had been abandoned.

"Delta, open your port airlock. I'm going to come in dark and fast. As soon as I'm in, get your tail in gear."

"Aye, boss."

Cass turned off her suit lights, hugged the statue to her chest and made sure her other finds were secured in her bag, scrunched her legs against the side of the ship, and pushed off toward her own vessel just as two beings in jetpacks came around the end of the derelict.

They shot after her, but she beat them to her airlock. Not by much, though, as the door slammed shut. "Delta! Go!"

Cass flattened against the wall as the rumbling underneath her feet told her Delta was putting on speed. As soon as the pressure eased, she set the statue on the floor, tugged off her gloves, and undid her helmet.

"Delta, report."

"They're on my tail. I'm doing my best to evade."

Cass ran for the bridge and slid into her seat. "How many?"

"One ship. Boss, it's the *Dagger*."

"Damn!"

"They left their people behind!"

"Of course they did. Ian doesn't care about them."

Ian McClaren ran that ship. Of all the people to find her, why him? One of the more ruthless claim jumpers in several parsecs. She felt a thud, and sparks flew from wiring overhead.

"Delta! Are you hit?"

"Yes. Trying to reroute systems, but…"

"Give me manual control. You take care of damage. I'll take care of Ian."

The ship shuddered again as Cass took over. Her fingers flew over the controls as she tried to find a spot where they could hide. Cass hated hiding, but better subterfuge than trying to fight the *Dagger*. At the moment, she was outgunned, outmanned, and her ship was damaged.

She didn't have the power to outrun Ian, but maybe… "There!" Cass headed for a nearby asteroid belt. Her little ship, the *Seeker*, was more maneuverable than Ian's bigger one.

"Cassie, darlin', you wouldn't be thinking of going into that belt now, would you? Might make me think you don't want to see me."

Cass barely kept from gagging at Ian's smarmy tone. "Damned straight."

"We could be good together, Cassie. Real good."

Another blast rocked the *Seeker*.

"If we could be so good, why the hell are you firing on me?"

"Just trying to get you to see reason, darlin'. With your record for finding abandoned ships and my resources, we could clean up around here."

"Yeah. You could use some cleaning up." She ducked behind a large asteroid, then shot straight down to a smaller one and tucked in under an overhang. The high tritanium content of the surrounding rock would effectively hide her from his scanners. "Delta, go dark."

"Not without your full suit on."

"Damn it, go dark. I'll get my helmet and gloves." She hated when her AI went all controlling on her. But that's what she'd paid for. An AI that actually thought for itself.

"B…B…boss, we g…g…got a problem."

"Another one? What now, Delta?"

The ship shuddered, then went still. Completely still. And dark. Cass felt her straps cutting into her shoulders as weightlessness set in. That was odd. Usually when she told Delta to go dark, the AI just turned off the main power, not the gravity. And definitely not before she was ready. Cass unbuckled from her seat and floated back toward the airlock and her helmet and treasures. She flicked on her wrist lamp even though she could find her way through her ship blindfolded. But the little circle of light was a comfort.

"Delta?"

Dead air.

"Delta?" Cass grabbed her helmet and clamped the seals to her suit. Delta never went dead. Delta was her right hand out here in the vastness of space. Her companion and more. Yes, she was just a computer and could be replaced, but…she was Delta. "Delta!"

Cass headed for the engine room. What she found hurt her heart. A gaping hole about as big as her helmet marred the smooth outer wall. Liquids bubbled and floated from multiple leaks, and wires hung from the hole. As for the engine, that was also dead, judging from the leaks emanating from the central core.

"Damn it. You will pay for this, Ian! I swear, if it's

the last thing I do, you will pay for this."

Cass dashed back to her workroom and grabbed the largest piece of plasticine she could find and some sealant and ran back to the engine room. She sealed the hole and accessed the control panel, but the damage was done. And so was her ship. Cass was going to have one hell of a story to tell her friends Omar and Katie when she got back.

If she got back.

Shoulders slumping, she went back up to the bridge and toggled on her emergency beacons. "To any ships in the area, this is Cass Brennan on the *Seeker*. Emergency alert. I repeat, emergency alert. I am dead in the water here. Emergency alert." She added in her coordinates and set the signal to repeat. She prayed that anyone other than Ian would hear her call and get her, though at this point, she didn't have much choice. If Ian came, she'd take his *hospitality*, knowing doing so would cost her dearly.

She went back to the workroom and secured the statuette in packing materials and her bag of crystals on a shelf. Then she went down to the engine room and did what she could to patch the leaks and reconnect wires, all the while knowing her work probably wouldn't help, but even a useless task was better than waiting around. Cass blew out a sigh of relief as the emergency lights powered back on. That meant she might be able to get life support back.

As she finished the last of the patches, her suit beeped at her. She was almost out of air. If someone didn't get to her soon... She gasped as all her systems red-lined. If she kept still, she might have three minutes of air left. Maybe. She tried hard not to panic.

"Cass? Are you all right?" The welcomed and

worried voice of Zack Anderson, her partner Ben's friend—and her…what? She wasn't sure what to call him. He wasn't exactly a boyfriend, but there were definitely sparks between them, though she'd only known him just over a year. But as his voice came over her helmet com, she closed her eyes in relief.

"Zack? How…?" She shook her head and answered his question. "One of Ian's shots hit my engines. I'm dead in the water, life support's out, and my suit's almost done as well. Wait, what happened to Ian?"

"We sent him packing."

"What? How? We who? And how are you out here?" She gasped as her air died out. "Can't breathe."

"We're coming. Hang tight."

As Cass fought for every breath, she wondered how he had gotten to her so fast. There wasn't enough time for him to get here from Pointe Noir station since she'd sent out her call.

Dark spots clouded her vision when she saw an angel. And gasped in fresh air.

"Zack?"

"Shh. Just breathe. I got you."

"How?"

"I jetted over to give you some of my air. You should be good until we get you back. You can breathe, but go easy."

She nodded. "How did you get here so fast?"

"You'll see. Now, we might have a bit of a challenge getting the *Seeker*. Ben's ship is too big. He's going to send some drones over and set tow lines. We'll bring the *Seeker* into the cargo bay, then get you both home."

Ben's ship? Since when did Ben have a ship? They didn't have enough funds in their business for a new ship. And repairs on the *Seeker* took up almost all their non-salvage budget.

****

Ben and Zack were waiting for her as she stepped out of the *Seeker* into a large cargo bay, a troubled look on the latter's face as she ripped off her helmet. The normally stale, canned air of the ship—any ship—had never smelled so sweet. Zack took her helmet and gloves.

"Cass?" She heard concern in his voice. "How are you doing?"

"Breathing, which is nice. But my suit is done. Glad you got there when you did. And though I really want to know what you're doing out here and with a ship, I need a drink and a shower, in that order. And here…" She handed Ben the statuette that was the cause of all this trouble. "The payday better be worth what I went through for that thing."

He grinned, and his eyes lit up. "Oh, it is, darlin'. It is. Did you find anything else?" He hefted the statuette into his arms and cradled the piece like a baby.

She'd known Ben since birth—he'd been friends with her parents—and she had been partnered with him for the last seven years. He was the face part of their business. The salesman. She was the muscle.

"Timmons, set course for Pointe Noir," Zack cut in.

"Yes, sir."

Cass stripped out of her suit, hoping Ben hadn't noticed she didn't answer his question about finding anything else. She wanted to keep the crystal finds to herself for the moment. Not that she didn't trust Ben. She did. But…the small crystals she found might be enough to buy her bigger star charts. Her current ones were pretty good, but the sale of those crystals could buy some decent upgrades, and better charts meant a favorable chance of finding her parents. "Who's Timmons?" she asked.

"This ship's AI," Zack said.

"Yeah, about that, where did you get this ship?"

"Not *my* ship. Ben's."

That got a raised eyebrow. "Ben's ship?"

Ben wouldn't look at her, and she knew she was going to get a story—one that probably stretched the truth to the breaking point. "I…borrowed him. From a friend." He strode away from her, and she hustled to keep up, hopping from one foot to the other as she wiggled out of her suit and handed the pieces to Zack. He grinned at her, then winced and waved his hand over the offensive odor coming off her and the suit.

"Hey, better than me not having any air at all. Which I didn't."

"I noticed. Not sure I'd want to breathe this," he teased. "I'll put your suit in the refresher for you and meet up with you and Ben in a bit."

"Zack, what's going on? And why are you here?"

Zack shrugged and shook his head. "He asked me to check out this ship. Next thing I know, we're out here, fighting off that McClaren guy, and you're calling for help. I know Ben's got something going on, but I have no clue what."

That made sense. Ben and Zack had only known each other a few years. Cass didn't know their entire history, but she'd met Zack through Ben, and the two of them had struck up a friendship. Though why Zack and Ben were friends was a bit of a puzzle to her. Ben was a good twenty years older than Zack—closer to her parents' age than hers and Zack's. And Zack was a good engineer who worked on the station and sometimes tended bar for her friends Omar and Katie. But he and Ben had almost nothing in common, so why were they friends? She'd been trying to figure that out almost from the beginning.

After Zack stepped into a side area where they kept their suits, Cass dashed to catch up to Ben. The older man could put on speed when he wanted. "Ben, exactly how much trouble are we going to be in when we get back?"

"None! Honest! I didn't steal the ship. It really does belong to a friend who is not in need of transportation at the moment. So I thought a test run would be a good idea. We're, um, buying this ship."

"Buying it? Exactly how? With what funds?"

His face went red all the way to the top of his bald head, and he wouldn't look at her, which meant he had something going on. Something she probably wouldn't like. "Um, well, actually, we already did…buy it, I mean. On the honor system. As soon as we get paid for this statue, we'll have what we need to pay for this ship and repairs to *Seeker*."

As they headed through the ship, Cass noticed issues like worn flooring, doors that weren't quite shut, flickering lights. She did not want to think how much this old ship was going to cost them. "How did you even manage to get here in this? Not to mention get away from Ian."

Ben stepped into what turned out to be a workroom of sorts. Shelves lined the walls, and a long table stood in the center. He set the figurine on the table. "This ship's got some years on it, but it's in great shape internally.

Just needs some prettying up. And I had a secret weapon that took care of Ian for a while."

"Uh-huh." Cass raised an eyebrow at him. "What kind of secret weapon?"

He blew out a sigh. "A black-crystal-based EM pulse."

"What the hell? Ben, where did you get a weapon like that? We don't have the money for a crystal pulse!"

"That derelict and this statue took care of the costs. The Throquin Conglomerate is ecstatic to have their property back."

"I'll bet." She glared at him. They rarely dealt with the Throquins. They were secretive, war-like, and just not exceedingly nice. Their nearly eternal war with the Rujaz Empire had affected several surrounding systems for hundreds of years. There was now a demilitarized zone between the two factions, and Pointe Noir sat directly in the middle. But a bad war made for good hunting when you were talking salvage. Cass's parents had been in cargo and salvage, and she'd grown up in the business. So she kept going when the ship they were on disappeared…and she kept hunting. Hoping that the next derelict might lead her to them. No matter what she found, she just wanted to know. Seven years was a long time to keep hoping, but she refused to give up the search for the *Phoenix*.

"Which way's a berth?" She noted that Ben didn't give her the name of the ship, just the AI, and wondered about that, but was just too damned tired to care at the moment. Ben was wiry thin with twinkling blue eyes and old enough to be her father, and sometimes acted more like one than any she'd known since her own had disappeared on the *Phoenix* seven years ago. He'd worked with her folks from before she was born, and when they disappeared, he stepped in to help her get her feet back under her. He was her best friend, and she trusted him more than she did anyone else—up to a point. He was also an expert manipulator and knew just which buttons to push for her to do what he wanted. But she loved him and usually went along with his harebrained schemes. She did the research and physical work while he schmoozed the clients for the business. On occasion, like this, Zack joined them. Zack was a wiz with electronics and ships' systems. And she actually liked having him around. He was often the only one who could get Ben to back off of some of his wild schemes. But he was frequently in demand for his expertise, so she didn't get to see him as often as she would have liked.

Ben peeled away some of the plasticine surrounding the statue and let out a whistle. "What a beaut, isn't it?"

To Cass, the figurine just looked like a big bird of some sort with outstretched wings. Pretty, yes, but not nearly as interesting as the crystals she'd pried from the altar where she'd found the piece. "Yes. Cabin?"

He motioned in the general direction of left. "What else did you get?"

Cass thought about her bag. "I have a hold full of good cargo for the station that I picked up before you called me for the statue job."

His eyes brightened, and he grabbed her and kissed her on the cheeks. "This is going to be our best payday ever! I'm going to log this in. Delta has your inventory?"

"Hey, lay off my girl," Zack said as he joined them.

Cass felt a warmth zing through her. *His girl*? Okay, they'd dated a few times, but they weren't serious. Were they? She studied Zack. Though she wouldn't mind.

Maybe.

Ben laughed as he released Cass, then sobered. "I'm sorry about *Seeker*." He grasped her shoulder. "We'll get her back. Go get cleaned up. I got this."

Cass nodded. "Thanks. Zack, cabin?"

"Right this way, my lady." He held out his arm and escorted her through the ship. "We have to take the lift up two levels to the main deck. Crew's quarters, recreation, galley, and medical on that level. Bridge is one more level up."

"This is quite a ship."

"Yeah. I haven't gone over all the systems yet, but everything seems sound, just a little worn around the edges." He stopped at a cabin. "This one's yours. I'm next door on the right, and Ben is across the corridor in the captain's cabin."

"Of course."

"I ordered you a beer and some snacks. I'm heading back to the engine room. Give me a call if you need me." He palmed open the door for her. "The AI is Timmons."

"Thanks." She touched his face. "And I do need you. Just not right now."

Cass went in and let the door swish shut. Why had she said that? Yes, he was important to her, but… She shook her head as the catering unit beeped. She took her drink and a plate holding a sandwich and chips out and studied the room. The space was easily double the size of her cabin on the *Seeker*. To her left, behind a half-wall, was a soft bed on top of storage cabinets. The rest of the cabin contained a small sofa, two upholstered chairs, a table and two wooden chairs, a desk, shelves, and an entertainment screen. A wide porthole behind the sofa gave her a view of space beyond. The cabin was comfy, if a little worn around the edges.

"Hello, Timmons?"

"Yes, ma'am? How may I be of service?"

"You may call me Cass."

"Thank you, Cass."

"Can you give me the specifics about yourself?"

As Cass continued toward the bedroom area, Timmons reeled off the dimensions, capacity, power, and more, impressing Cass. The craft might not be much to look at, but it had some impressive stats. "What is the name of the ship?"

"The *Crimson Raider*."

She stopped and looked up at the ceiling. "Wow. You're the *Raider*?" Everyone had heard of the *Raider*. And its crew. They were ruthless...jumping salvage claims all over the sector until Ian McClaren came in and took over. But she had a vague memory of...she didn't know what. "Timmons, who were your original owners?"

He named a crew that was no longer in this sector, but she was sure they weren't what she was trying to remember. "Did you have other owners?"

"Yes. Would you like me to list them?"

"Yes, please."

He ran down a long list. Cass recognized most of the names, but the last owner of record was just a business name.

"Timmons, who owns the MTW business?"

"I'm sorry, but that is not in my database. Would you like me to search for the information?"

Interesting. "No. That's fine. If you don't mind my asking, what happened with you?" She figured she'd get Delta to do the search for the company once she had

Delta back online.

"Time. And younger, fleeter ships. And too many security people out here now. My original crew decided to move on. Since then, no one owner has lasted more than a few months."

Timmons almost sounded like a sad human in that moment, and Cass felt a little sorry for him, though she wondered why no one lasted with him. What was wrong with the ship? Old, yes, but still serviceable from what she could see. "Yes, but you just took out Ian McClaren's ship. Not many can claim that."

"I just finished what your Delta started. But thank you." The door to the fresher unit slid open as Cass got near, and lights came on.

"Wow. This is nice. Timmons, have you managed to get Delta back?"

"Delta is…not at her best, but I was able to communicate with her. I've already got bots working on some of the damage. We will be arriving at Pointe Noir in four hours jump time. Jumping in five minutes."

"Timmons?"

"Yes, ma'am?"

"Can you refresh my clothing while I clean up?"

"Yes, ma'am. I believe you will find everything you need in the fresher area."

"Thank you." Cass went into the little room across from the foot of the bed and sighed happily. In addition to toilet, sink, and shower area, there was an actual small soaking tub as well as a clothing refresher. She shed her clothes, dumped them in the bin and set the controls, then went to the shower.

Ten minutes later, clean and dressed in refreshed clothes, she headed for the bridge. Cass hated to be jealous, but she was. Her little ship was a wonder, but this one…wow.

Cass found Ben settled in the pilot's seat on the bridge, so she sat in the copilot's spot. "Hey, thanks for getting me out of that situation with Ian. And for picking us up. Where's Zack?"

"He's still down in the engine room doing whatever he does. Are you okay?"

"Yeah. What do I need to know?"

"With that statuette and the salvage claim filed on that ship, we will have a really nice payday coming. One that will help overhaul this baby and *Seeker,* giving us two good ships for our salvage and cargo operations. We'll use the *Seeker* for smaller ones and this one for big hauls. *Raider* has a specially shielded cargo bay that we can use for any cargo that might be problematical. We've never been able to do that before."

"Sounds good. If we manage to get back and if your buyers give us what they promised and if—"

"Oh. We had to change direction for a bit. We have to deliver that statuette first. I'll set the coordinates."

"Wait. They're not meeting us at the station?"

"I just got a message from them a couple minutes ago. There was a change of plans. We're meeting at the second moon of Kilner. It'll be fine. No worries."

He turned to her, a serious look on his face. "Cass, girlie, you know I love you like my own kid, don't you?"

She frowned at him. "Yes."

"And that I'd never do anything to hurt you."

"Of course not. Or not on purpose." She grinned at him, then stopped. He wasn't smiling back at her. "Ben? What's this about? Are you all right?"

He shook his head, then gave her an impish smile. "Yeah. I'm good. Like I said, no worries."

Which was exactly why Cass was worried.

Chapter Two

"Did you recheck the coordinates?" Cass asked as she studied the empty planetoid beneath them. The moon was habitable but barely. Readouts said there had once been a crystal-mining base there, but the place had been abandoned years ago when a catastrophic mining accident forced the closure.

"Multiple times. And so did Timmons and Delta. And you."

"And me," Zack said as he joined them. "Ben, can I see the message they sent?"

Ben frowned at him. "Why?"

"Are you sure you got them right from the buyers?"

"Yes. I mean, I think. I mean…"

"Bennnn?" Cass glared at him. "Yes or no? Did you get the coordinates right?"

He rubbed his head. "Well, I mean, this is where the latest notice said to meet them."

Cass got a sinking feeling in the pit of her stomach. "And you're certain the contact came from the buyers?"

"Maybe? I mean yes. I'm sure." He wouldn't look at her, which set that stomach feeling roiling.

"Not unless the buyers are someone called the MTW Conglomerate," Zack said.

"Timmons! Get us the hell out of here! Now!" Cass yelled.

"Coordinates?"

"Anywhere! I don't care. Just go! Away from them!"

They took off just as a blip showed up on their screens. "Look, Cass. That could be them." Ben pointed at the blip.

"And that could be McClaren or one of his thugs. Timmons, ID on that ship?"

"The ship is the *Sword's Edge,* owned by Ian McClaren."

She was right. A McClaren ship. "Blast it. How many ships can one pirate have? Go! All speed! And pray they didn't see us!" She turned to Ben. "Do you have any more of those secret weapons you used on the *Dagger*?"

He shook his head. "No. Wish I did, though."

Sweat dripped off Cass as their ship ducked behind the planet and headed in a direction away from the other ship. Thirty minutes later, she felt like she could finally breathe. "Okay. Timmons, how far to Pointe Noir station now?"

"Six hours standard. Though I assume you wish to avoid any further encounters with the McClarens?"

"Definitely. And if you can figure out how he keeps finding me, I'd love to know."

"I'm afraid I do not have enough data to answer that question. But to avoid areas he has been known to frequent, we would need an extended detour. Delta and I have mapped a promising route, but the distance is significantly longer. According to our calculations, you will miss your deadlines for the cargo you are carrying."

"Figured as much. But I don't have any time-sensitive materials there. I'll let my buyers know. I'd rather not jump for such a short distance. Show me star charts for this area. Let's see what's out here." Even in Ben's ship, Cass was the one in charge of navigation. Ben could get lost finding his way from his bed to his bathroom.

Ben rose from his seat. "I'm going to go find out what kind of repairs Delta and the *Seeker* need."

Cass gave him a side-eye. Ben was acting really strange…and for Ben, that was saying a lot. "You sure you're okay?"

"Yeah. Just need to stretch my legs a bit. Besides, you got this. See ya." He took off at what for him was a fast clip.

"Okay." Cass really wanted to know who the MTW Conglomerate was, but she was fairly certain she knew. The owner had to be Ian or one of the McClarens. That family had their hooks everywhere. But who had sent Ben those coordinates and why? She could make a guess or three, but Ben wouldn't work with Ian. The star diagrams came up on Cass's screen. There wasn't much. A couple uninhabited planets, a weak star, another nasty asteroid belt…

"Cass? You think something's wrong?" Zack asked.

She sighed. "I don't know. Just a feeling I have."

"Yeah, well, I've got one too. I might not know Ben as well as you do, but I'd say he's got five aces up his sleeve. At least." He swiveled back and forth in his seat at the communications station. "Any interesting objects outside?"

"Not much to look at."

"Okay. I'm going to go check on some of the systems I haven't looked at yet. Give me a yell if you need…um…me."

She chuckled when his face turned red. But she let

him off. "Will do. Thanks. And thanks for the food and drink earlier. They were just what I needed."

"Well, that and the shower you must have taken." He grinned at her, and she blew him a raspberry.

"Go get to work." She enjoyed bantering with him. No hassles, no expectations, just…what? Friends, yes, but more too. She just wasn't sure what yet. And she didn't want to get tied down to anyone while she was still searching for her parents. That much was certain. So…for now…fun. But that was all.

Shame her heart didn't quite agree with her brain.

Zack gave her a jaunty salute. "Yes, ma'am. Right away, ma'am."

They were less than three hours out when the proximity alert beeped. Cass, who had been napping in her seat, sat straight up. "Timmons, report. Are the McClarens after us again?"

"Negative. Though this appears to be a ship, the configuration is larger than any object in my databases."

Cass's heart sped up. A device larger than known? How could that be? And who? A blip could mean a lot of things from an abandoned wreck to a ship in trouble, or just plain trouble. "Can you give me details?"

"Not at this time. They are on the extreme edge of my sensors."

She toggled on the com unit. "Hey, Zack."

"Yeah?"

"Any way you can bump up the sensors? We have a blip but too far away to see much."

"I'll do what I can. Give me a couple."

Cass peered at the screen as the image went from almost invisible to just blurry. "That's all you can get?"

"At this range, yes."

"Timmons, how far off is that?"

"Twelve hours at standard speed. Would you like me to change course?"

Cass chewed her lip. A detour like that would add a day travel time plus time to check out what was there. That would really put her over her cargo deadlines. Plus, she wasn't sure what kinds of supplies Ben had laid in.

"If that is a ship in trouble, we are obligated to offer assistance," Timmons pointed out.

"Yeah, and if the ship's been abandoned, we might be able to put in a claim." Another one. Multiple claims in one trip would be unusual but not unheard of. She clicked her com. "Ben? Zack? You there?"

"Yep," they both answered.

"Mind a little detour?"

"What you got?" Ben asked.

"Might be a ship in trouble. Or a derelict. Or take a guess."

"We're kind of low on supplies. I wasn't planning on a long trip. How long a detour?"

"Maybe a day. Maybe more."

"Emergency rations it is. Go."

"I'm good down here," Zack said. "Engines are humming, and we've got plenty of fuel."

"Okay. Will let you know."

That's what Cass loved about Ben. He trusted her instincts without too many arguments. And Zack was starting to give her that same trust. Plus, he was darned good with systems, even better than Ben.

"Timmons, set course for that blip, but engage security fields." She might be curious, but she wasn't stupid.

Her salvage and cargo work paid for these little

trips, but if she were honest, she enjoyed the salvage work more. She'd been born into the job, raised on the hunt. Doing the research was especially fascinating to her. Finding derelict ships that had been abandoned or even small stations or hollowed-out asteroids piqued her interest not just for what she and Ben could sell or use, but for their historical value.

For a really good historical find, Ben often reached out to museums or societies, turning their discoveries over for a small finder's fee. There were also times when Cass left a site behind because of dangerous situations, disputed claims, or other reasons. Like when she'd found an entire family—including a tiny baby—frozen for all eternity on a doomed ship. She'd notified the authorities and set warning beacons around that one even though the ship had valuables that would have paid for a couple of months on Pointe Noir station. The surviving family—if there was one—could have the spoils. She wasn't heartless.

She collected salvage sites the way other people collected jewelry or artwork. Especially if the find was left over from the Throquin-Rujaz wars. Those derelicts were worth their weight in credits.

Her heart pounded with excitement as they headed for the blip. Standard speed was incredibly slow compared to faster-than-light, but FTL was difficult to control on short hops. Faster-than-light was meant for longer distances. "Timmons, if we do an abbreviated FTL jump, could we cut the time down?"

"That's a really short jump. We might overshoot."

"So you can't?" She wasn't above appealing to an AI's ego, even if he was digital.

"Of course I can."

Cass almost laughed at Timmons's snooty voice. "Set the drive and go."

Her stomach clenched with nerves. Two months ago, she'd followed a blip and found a ship with failed life support. Of the fifty crew, only a handful were still alive—barely. Cass had taken them aboard only to discover they were pirates who'd just raided another ship and killed the crew. Thanks to the *Seeker's* sticky fields and sleepy meds, Cass had made her way back to Pointe Noir—where she received a considerable bounty for the criminals. Still, she'd rather not do that again. You never knew what you were going to find with a dead ship, but space was big, and there weren't many people out here willing to help others, so she did what she could. Within reason.

Ten minutes later, they came out of FTL speed almost on top of the blip. As she'd feared—and hoped— it was a ship. A huge ship. She could easily park the one they flew in one of the bays and have room left over for a fleet. The design was an elongated teardrop with four wings evenly spaced around the middle and tapering back to beyond the tail point. Cass admired the sleek shape.

"Timmons, go dark and silent and let Ben and Zack know."

"Done." The lights, communications, and most of the power turned off. She kept an eye on the sensor readout. So far, no one was scanning them. "Timmons, scan for any life signatures."

"I do not detect any. Nor do I sense any environment or active power beyond a beacon sending out a weak signal. I didn't even hear it until we got here."

"Some sort of automatic one?"

"Unknown. The signature is not in any of my databases. Or Delta's. Nor is the power system."

That was even odder. "Any indications of other ships in the area?"

"No."

Cass's heart rate soared, and she chewed her bottom lip in excitement. "Any indications of active weaponry or other no-no's?"

"Negative."

"Any claiming beacons?"

"The same."

Cass grinned as Ben and Zack joined her. "Timmons, send out a quick contact ping."

She studied the ship as much as she could. "She's bigger and sleeker than any ship in our databases."

"Agreed. Not even the Throquins or the Rujaz have vessels like this," Ben said. The Throquin Conglomerate consisted of at least a dozen star systems. The Rujaz almost as many. So both had access to a lot of different types of ships. But both were also secretive almost to obsession about their records and history.

"Timmons, Delta, any idea where this might be from or how old she is?"

"Historical records and sensor readings indicate the ship may be as old as three thousand years," Delta replied.

That took Cass by surprise. "Any idea how long the ship has been abandoned?"

"Not exactly," Timmons said. "Our scans show that the hull is heavily pitted and scored, so probably an extremely long time."

"Give me outside lights, and let's take a look-see," Cass said. "And bring our interior back to life."

The outer spotlights came on, highlighting the derelict. They slowly circled the find, checking all over. On the far side was a hole nearly as big as the *Seeker*, which would have killed all systems and meant that there couldn't be anyone alive inside. They also saw other indications of damage, both large and small.

"Are you sure there aren't any pirates around? No McClaren ships?"

"All sensors are silent, even on the *Seeker's* extended range. We are alone."

Cass grinned. "So how did this get out here, and why has no one found it?"

"Hypothesis," Timmons said.

"Yes?"

"While in FTL drive, we passed through an extensive asteroid field, possibly the remains of a small planetoid that broke up. It is feasible the ship was hidden by that."

"Or that it had even landed on the planetoid at one time and was kicked out here when the moon or whatever broke up," Zack added.

"So how did we see it?" Cass asked.

"Maybe a shift in position," Ben said. "If the ship was on a planetoid that broke up, there should have been more damage."

"I'd like to get a closer look," Cass said.

"Your suit has barely been recharged," Ben pointed out. "You won't have time for much more than a quick trip. Are you sure such a short trip is worth the trouble?"

"For a closer look at that baby? Yes." She couldn't tamp down her grin. The researcher in her wouldn't allow her to give up this chance. "I promise, just a few minutes. I can't leave now. Timmons, set buoys and claim beacons, and mark the coordinates." She headed out for the airlock.

"I'll go with you," Zack said. "I'll meet you at the lock."

Cass nodded.

"Delta asks if you want to file the claim," Timmons said.

"Not yet. Tell Delta to do the preliminary research. I want to explore whatever this is some more before we let anyone else know the coordinates." Cass took her suit from the locker. The unit hadn't yet finished cleaning and replenishing the air. For a closer look at that ship, she'd put up with the ripe smell. This could be the greatest find she'd ever had. "Make sure to do complete scans."

"Yes, ma'am. Delta and I have completed our pairing. She will make sure our scans are up to your specifications."

"Thank you." Cass met Zack at the airlock but noted he didn't have a suit on.

"Thought you were coming."

"Can't. My suit's developed a leak in one seal. I'll need time to repair the hole." He checked her seals. "You're good to go." Zack hooked her tether to the wall. "Be careful. And don't take too long." He stepped back and closed the inner door, allowing her to open the outer one.

"Yes, sir. Eeny, meeny, miney…" Cass headed for the lowest portion of the hole. Careful not to touch the jagged edges, she clicked on the magnetic settings on her boots and settled onto the floor of what looked like an engine room, but not like any one she'd ever seen. What she did see, though, had her gasping.

"Cass? You okay? Your heart rate and respiration just took a huge spike," Zack said.

"I'm fine. I just discovered something wonderful. You are not going to believe this. You're both going to love me forever, and that's all I'm going to say." She gazed at the sparkling piece of red crystal in front of her. Nearly as big as her fist, the rock would be enough to power a ship this size or a small space station. From what she saw, the crystal was probably once part of the engine system but, except for some wires, had been thrown clear by whatever hit the ship. She looked around for tools to retrieve the gem with. The red crystals were as rare as water on the sun and cost more than a small planet to own, but if she could get the piece…

They were in high demand by everyone for their power, but they were lethal to touch with bare skin. Though the scientists didn't know what the issue was, everyone who'd ever touched one was dead from some new kind of radiation poisoning that was deadly within hours of contact. Even in her suit, she was risking a lot, but sometimes risks were worth taking. She discovered a tool kit of sorts in a corner and went to work. "Come to momma, baby."

"Cass, your cameras aren't working. Are you all right?" Ben asked.

"Yes. Probably just a glitch." Caused by the red?

She was careful to keep the red in the shielded container, taking the entire contraption with her. Then she sealed that in a case she found in a storage closet. She had a red crystal.

Delta's voice beeped over her com. "Boss, you are out of time. If you don't get moving now, you'll be out of air soon. And by soon, I mean now."

"Fine. I'm on my way." Reluctantly, Cass looked around. She really wanted to spend more time exploring this place, but… She sighed and headed for the opening. Back at the ship, Cass kept her suit on as she pressurized the airlock. She wasn't taking any chances with the red. Zack met her at the lock, giving her a puzzled look.

"Cass?"

She shook her head and waved him off. "Stay away from me. Contamination. Ben, set course for home." Zack backed away, but not far enough to suit her. She opened the container far enough for him to see inside. His eyes went wide as he backed away.

"That ship's quite a find!" Ben said over the com. "We'll be drowning in credits from historians alone!"

She could hear the excitement in his voice and felt the same. "Don't tell him," she mouthed to Zack. He cocked his head at her but nodded.

"Hold?" he mouthed back, and she nodded. He led the way, opening doors and giving her space.

"Boss?" Delta's voice came through her helmet as Cass headed for the secure hold Ben had told her about. "Is there a reason you're still suited? I don't detect any life support issues with the *Raider*, but I do detect odd readings from you. Care to let me in on the secret?"

"Not just yet." She stowed her new find in a second sheltered container Zack got out for her, sealed that one, and headed out, peeling off her suit as she went. Cass set her suit in a decontamination regen unit, then headed for her cabin, Zack close behind.

"Cass! That's a bloody red! Are you okay?"

"Yes. I was careful."

"So why not tell Ben?"

She sighed. "I don't know. But I'd like to keep this

just between us for a bit if you don't mind."

"You're the captain."

That made her snort. "Only when I'm on the *Seeker* and doing salvage." They reached her cabin. "I'll get a shower."

"Make it two. That was a dangerous stunt you pulled, getting that red."

"I took every precaution. I think I'm good. No problems yet."

"Will you let me check you over in the med unit when you're done?"

She shook her head. "You know as well as I do, if I got zapped, you can't help me. If I didn't, there's no point then either." She reached out, then dropped her hand before she could touch him. "I'll be fine, Zack. Relax. I'll see you on the bridge."

He sighed and nodded. "Fine. Just tell me this. Do you often take chances like you did here? I mean, we already had to rescue you from Ian. And now this. You worry me."

She chuckled. "Get used to the feeling. This is what I do. I'm a salvager. Salvage and danger go hand in hand."

"Quite the life you lead."

"Yep. See you above."

"Yep." He backed away, and her door shut. Thirty minutes and two showers later, she was dressed in clean clothes and headed for the bridge. Ben sat in the captain's seat, and Zack was at a monitoring station on the lower level. The bridge had two levels with a captain's seat on the upper one and four stations below and in front of that. A large view screen covered the front of the bridge, and she stared at the ship they had found.

"I set out buoys and have the coordinates locked in and have the claim filled out, just not filed yet," Ben said as she stood beside him.

"Good. I don't want Ian getting hold of this one before I have a chance to look her over more thoroughly. Ben, that ship is unbelievable."

"Agreed, but…"

Cass recognized the *we-don't-have-time* tone in Ben's voice. "I know. I know. But stars, I really want to look more thoroughly."

"So do I, but I want to get that statuette to the buyers and unload the rest of the cargo. With what we have already, we can afford to upgrade both ships and mount a real salvage operation for a change."

Cass still wasn't sure about Ben's buyers. There was something hinky going on there, but he was correct in that they needed to get moving. "You're right. I hate it, but you're right." Cass peered at the ship as it faded from view, her heart thumping wildly.

Ben touched her arm. "We'll be back. I promise you."

"I know."

"Zack, you have an incoming call," Timmons said.

"Who from?"

"The contact is blocked, but the origin is from Jovani."

Zack gave Ben a puzzled frown. "Wonder what this is about."

"Might as well go see," Ben said.

"Put them through to my cabin," Zack said.

"Yes, sir."

"I need to check on some stuff too," Ben said as he rose. "Cass, you can have my seat."

"Thanks." Cass relaxed against her seat as the men left, and she thought about the find and what she had stowed in the hold. She also thought about Zack. She'd never felt so comfortable with anyone like she did him. She loved Ben like a father, but Zack…he filled a hole in her she didn't know was there.

Cass was going over her inventory when the emergency klaxons went off and the gravity fields failed, along with a lot of other systems. If not for her belt, she'd be floating in midair. Again.

Chapter Three

Zack sat at the desk in his cabin. "Okay, Timmons, put them through."

He recognized the face of the man on the screen but knew him only as Ty. Ty was one of those people you went to when you needed information and couldn't go through legitimate channels. "Hey, Ty. What do you have for me?"

Zack glanced at Ty's surroundings. The small room looked like it should be condemned. The plasticel covering on the tabletop was peeled and scratched and was flanked by two mismatched chairs. Behind that was an unmade bed. Trash littered the furniture and floor, and a bare window showed the blinking lights of a low-rent bar.

"Got some of that data you were looking for."

"Send all the info to the account I set up."

"Already done. File's called Z-10."

Zack checked his email and found the file. "Got it. Thanks. Any highlights?"

"Yeah. You were right about who went after your family. But not for the reasons you thought. They were after the mineral rights. Your family held the deeds."

"Mineral rights?"

"Yeah. Seems there's a good-sized crystal vein under where your house was."

Zack hung his head. The stupid caves where he and

his brothers used to play. "So he killed my folks just to get to the crystals?"

Ty shook his head. "No. Not him. Not who you think. Someone else, but they're all in the same business."

"The MTW Conglomerate."

"Yeah. The file I sent you has all the particulars." He glanced around wildly as Zack heard a knock at Ty's door. "Hey, hate to ask this, but I need to disappear. Don't know what you got me into, but it's getting hot here."

Zack touched a few keys. "Credits are in your account."

"Thanks."

He signed off, but not before Zack saw Ty's door slam open and two men storm in just as Ty went out the window. He hoped Ty would be okay and thanked the man as he read the file. As he thought, the McClarens were behind the attack on his parents' farm. The McClaren family had a lot of branches, and every single one of them rotten to the core. Oh, sure, they looked legit from the outside, but dig a little under the surface, and you found a lot of nastiness. And Ben was deep in with them. What he couldn't figure out was why? As far as Zack knew, Ben didn't have any family connections to the McClarens. So why work with them?

That was what Zack was trying to find out through Ty. He'd been searching for answers for two years. And the only lead he'd had was a conversation overheard in Omar's bar one night. A blurb about Ben Knoble doing a job for the McClarens. One that had gone bad.

Bad was right. Both of Zack's parents were killed. His younger brothers both badly injured. Zack swore he'd get even but so far hadn't been able to find solid evidence. That didn't mean he would stop looking. But Ben definitely bore watching. What he couldn't figure out was Cass.

He put security seals on his files, just in case. He didn't have time right now to look into every file Ty had sent him, but as soon as he could, he would. Meanwhile, there was Cass. Ben was Cass's friend, but so far, none of his searches had turned up a connection between her and Ben's dealings beyond their salvage business. And Ben seemed genuinely fond of her.

Zack had no trouble understanding that. He was growing fonder of her as well. She was strong, intelligent, and beautiful. But she did like to take a lot of chances. He thought about the red crystal in the hold. A lot of chances.

Zack was heading back to the bridge when the entire ship went dark, and he started floating. "What the hell?"

Chapter Four

"Delta! Timmons! What just happened?" Cass
yelled as she grabbed her seat harness and strapped in.
Zack floated in and joined her.

"All systems are dead," he said.

"I noticed. Including Timmons and Delta."

Zack's hands flew over the console, but every
system was dark. Except for emergency lighting, they
had no power at all. And even that was flickering.

"Zack?"

"You'll know as soon as I do. Where's Ben?"

"Here," Ben said as he floated in. "Any ideas?"

"Not yet. Ben, check life support," Zack called to
him.

Cass accessed the com, bringing up whatever she
could find, which wasn't much.

The view out the forward screen showed them to be
in the midst of an asteroid field. A massive one. And they
had no control over the ship. "Damn. How the hell did
we get here?"

Sweat beaded her face and slicked her hands as Cass
attempted to get the engines working before a rock the
size of a large house hit them.

"Zack!"

"I see it!" He kept working. "Try thrusters!"

Cass did, thanking all the gods and goddesses who
watched over spacemen—and Zack—as she slung

around the mountain, using its gravity to thrust her away. Unfortunately, that put them in the path of dozens of other rocks. "Okay, new plan. Land on one of the asteroids. And then figure out what's going on."

"Agreed," both men said.

Cass used the thrusters to push away from the huge rock to one only slightly smaller and touched down hard enough to jar her teeth. "Sorry!"

"What the hell happened?"

Zack had engaged the emergency backup systems—which should have come on automatically—and Cass relaxed a little when she felt a tiny breath of air coming from the vent.

"Life support minimal but functioning," Ben said.

"What else do we have?"

"Very little," Zack said. "Looks like we were hit by some kind of an EM pulse."

"You think? But from where? And why? That derelict didn't have any claim markers. Plus, some of our systems are still intact. A true EM would have fried them all. Could the attack have been Ian again?" Cass ducked instinctively as a small asteroid zoomed too close for comfort. "Okay. So, possibly a weird EM pulse. Ben, are you sure you didn't have another secret weapon? One that maybe went off and caught us?"

"I didn't! Honest."

"Okay. That means no air, no lights beyond minimal manual, and the temperature is going to get extremely cold and fast," Zack said.

"Suits. Now," Cass demanded. "Zack, is yours fixed?"

"Good enough for here."

Cass nodded, unbuckled her belt, and floated toward

her cabin with Ben just ahead of her and Zack behind. When she got to hers, she checked the levels on her suit readouts. The sensors on the close-fitting suit showed half power. That would have to do. Several long minutes and choice words later, she was sealed in, breathing decent air, and her feet once more on the floor. This was getting repetitive—and really old. She met Ben and Zack in the corridor, and they checked each other's suits and connections. "You head for the engine room. I'll be on the bridge," she said to Zack. "Ben?"

"Engines with Zack."

She nodded and plodded off in the opposite direction of the men. Once on the bridge, she checked each system. All were in top order, just dead.

"Zack? What's the word?" she asked over her suit com.

"The word is, we're dead in the water. No power. Not even thrusters now. Our landing took them out. And the *Seeker's* out too. Pairing her with the *Raider* took out both systems."

"Damn."

"Yeah. We need help, but without communications, there's no way to let anyone know."

Cass chewed her lip. She had that crystal she hadn't told Ben about, but could they make the piece work? Should they? After all, the crystal was a red. Illegal to have without special permissions from multiple entities. Ben would have a fit. That was a definite. But if they didn't use the crystal, they were as good as dead. How could she not use what she had? The argument went on in her mind even as she headed for the cargo bay. "Time for *my* secret weapon," Cass muttered. "Give me a minute. I might have a solution. Zack, can you meet me in the hold?"

"Are you thinking what I think you are?"

"Do we have a choice?"

"Not really. Problem is, can we make your solution work with our systems?"

"What are you two talking about?" Ben asked.

"Give us a couple, and you'll see," Cass said as she headed for the hold. Once in the bay, she pulled out the hexagonal crystal—sparkling red—in her helmet light. She quickly closed the shielded box as Zack joined her. "What do you think?"

"That we're both crazy, but we don't have a lot of choices."

Cass nodded and strode to the engine room, Zack beside her. They met Ben on the way out. "It's no use, girlie."

"Maybe." She held out the box and opened the lid. She didn't need to see his face to know what he was thinking.

He stared at the crystal, then backed away. "What the effing hell, Cass! What are you doing with a red? You didn't touch that, did you?"

"No, I didn't touch it. Give me a little credit. I found this on that last ship we discovered. Can we use this to get some power?"

"Zack, you knew about this?"

"Just found out myself." Cass glanced at him but let the lie slide. Ben didn't need to know.

Ben shook his head. "Hell if I know if this old ship will handle a red, but let's give it a go. Not even sure I know how to hook this up. What did the connections look like in the other ship?"

Cass described them to him and Zack. "I didn't have

a lot of time, but after I got the clamps loose, the whole mechanism came out of some sort of plug. There's a port on the back of the casing. Maybe you can adapt our port to fit?"

With a lot of swearing and switching out of components on everyone's part, they shortly had the crystal embedded in the power unit. As soon as they did, lights came up, air moved, and Cass felt the artificial gravity kick in. Ben closed the door to the power unit before signaling her to remove her helmet. The temperature was still cold enough for Cass to see her breath. Warmth would come later. She didn't look at Ben as she headed back to the bridge, unfastening her suit as she went. She dropped the suit off in the decontamination unit, as did the men.

"I'll stay in the engine room and make sure what we did stays secure," Zack said.

"What about the red?" Cass asked. They'd sealed the crystal in multiple layers of shielding, but nobody really knew what a red could do.

"We're good. My scans showed no radiation," Zack assured her.

"Okay. Just be careful, please?" She wasn't sure how she felt about him working in there, but, again, they didn't have a lot of choices. Cass nodded and headed for the bridge.

"Timmons? You back?"

"Yes, ma'am."

"What the hell happened?"

"Unknown. But I felt like someone kicked me in the head, and I went dark."

"Ben figures we got hit with some kind of a pulse. But unknown from where or by whom."

"That is logical. I see you landed us on an asteroid."

"Best I could do with manual thrusters. What else can you tell me?"

"First, what is powering me? Feels like super energy. I like it!"

Cass snorted. "Red crystal."

"What?" Delta's voice yelled at her. "Boss! Where's Ben? Where's Zack? Are you all right? Do you need medical? Not that they would help much. Why aren't you dead?"

"Because we were careful. I'm happy to hear your voice, Delta. Now, give me a status report, please." She slid into her seat at one of the lower monitor stations, leaving the captain's seat for Ben. After all, the *Raider* was his ship.

"All systems are functioning at beyond peak performance with the exception of main thrusters," Timmons said. "I have maneuvering ones only. We can leave any time you want. Just give the word."

"First, check for unfriendlies out there. I don't want to take off only to be stuck again. One piece of red is all I have." Ben joined her as Cass waited for Timmons to scan the area.

"I can't tell for sure because there are so many asteroids, but I don't see any telltales or get any ship markers. However…"

Cass hated *howevers*. "What?"

Timmons brought a picture up on the front view screen. Cass saw an odd-looking lump attached to the rear hull. The device looked like a large metallic spider, but its feet were firmly embedded in the ship.

"Any idea what that object is?" Cass asked.

"No," Timmons answered.

"Are you getting any kind of readings from that contraption?" Cass asked as both she and Ben stared at the device.

"An electronic signal of some sort that keeps repeating but in no known language or code."

Cass glanced at Ben who just shrugged, eyes wide.

"Any idea where the signal is coming from?" Cass asked.

"No. But hypothesis would be that ship we discovered as there are no other similar objects in the area."

"I agree. Is the bug doing any damage to you or your systems?"

"No, ma'am. Though the device does seem to be draining some power from the crystal you installed."

That was disturbing. "Draining our power? How? And by how much?"

"The how appears to be through the connections to my hull. How much is a mere trickle. Not enough to affect us."

"Hypothesize. Are conditions safe for us to leave?"

"I believe so," Timmons answered. "The device does not seem to have affected any systems other than the power drain. Though I cannot state with complete accuracy, I believe you can even go to jump drive with a significant degree of safety."

"Hey, Zack," Cass called.

"Yeah?"

"Are you noticing a slight power drain?"

"Yes. I was just going to check the problem out."

"No need. We picked up some sort of bug attached to the hull. That's what's pulling energy."

"Just a sec. I'll be right up. Don't go anywhere yet."

"Understood." She waited until he showed up.

He stared at their uninvited passenger. "Any idea what the device is or where it came from?"

"No. Do you think we're safe to get moving?"

"Should be, but I'll monitor from down there while you watch up here. Let me know if there are any changes." He glanced back at Ben who was ignoring them both and gave Cass a questioning look.

She shrugged.

"All right. I'll go back down. But slow and easy, okay? Some of that craziness we did down there isn't any too secure. I'd hold off going to FTL for now."

"Okay, let's get out of here. I'd like to get home before anything else happens."

"You want me to drive, ma'am?" Timmons asked.

"No. I want you to run a full diagnostic of all systems, inside and out. You too, Delta. And do a full sensor sweep of the ship as well."

"Aye, ma'am."

Timmons almost sounded as if he were pouting. Computers. Hah. Some of them had as much emotion as a living being. Or at least sounded like they did.

Zack laughed as he headed out.

Cass set manual controls, and the ship rose. She maneuvered carefully through the rest of the field. Ben still hadn't said a word to her, just kept monitoring systems.

Chapter Five

Ian McClaren glanced up from his work as the com system pinged him with a communication. Strange. He wasn't expecting a message from his contact.

"Why did you go after Cass again?"

The anger in the man's voice amused Ian. He snorted. The man was far too emotionally involved. "Because I could. Because she needed to be taught a lesson. She needs to learn that I will control her and this area of space."

"She'll never come to you. If you keep pushing her, she'll just get more stubborn."

"So what do you suggest?" Curiosity pushed Ian to ask.

"Leave her alone. Let me work. Give me time."

"I've given you time, and you haven't done enough. My patience grows short." Ian tapped his fingers on the arm of his chair. Couldn't Cassie see how much more powerful they would be working together? Even when he was trying to outdo her and jump her claims, she proved to be a mighty opponent. Together, they'd be unstoppable. They could combine their skills and rule this entire area of space. Why did she keep denying him? Nobody said no to a McClaren.

"Just a little more time. We've come this far. Don't get all spaced out on me now. I'll be on station soon and can take care of any problems there."

"Fine, but soon," Ian demanded.

"Fine."

Ian clicked off the com unit. Yes, he'd give his contact a bit more time, but his patience wasn't infinite. Cassandra Brennan and all her claims would be his. She was like an itch that needed constant scratching. Her luck in finding good claims was almost legendary. How she did what she did, he'd never know. According to her, her talent was research. Hah. Ian had the best researcher money could buy, and the man was almost worthless compared to Cassie. He needed a big score and soon. The family was getting impatient for him to finish taking over this territory. He'd put a lot on the line with the family for this chance. But he had to produce. If he didn't get this sector in hand soon, they'd come in and kick him back to some hole in space. He didn't enjoy the other businesses the family engaged in. Buying and selling slaves, kidnapping, drugs… If an activity was illegal or illicit, you could be sure the family was involved. Claim jumping was Ian's specialty. But he needed Cassandra Brennan's expertise for his plans to work.

He sent off a message to his contact. *Get me the command codes for her ship.*

Once he had those, he could do whatever he wanted with Cassie, and there wasn't a thing she could do. He settled back into the comfortable seat, his cabin—in fact, the entire ship—a stark contrast to Cassie's little piece of junk. He had whatever a person could want and more. Six ships in his fleet. People who followed his every command. More weapons than anyone could possibly use. Power and money. Those were what mattered. And he had those.

So why didn't he have Cassandra Brennan? He had

or could get her whatever she could possibly want. She would live in luxury. What woman wouldn't want that?

He clicked on his com unit. "Bridge."

"Yes, sir?"

"Do we have full power yet?"

"We have all the main systems back online, but the engine is only at half-power."

"When full, set course for Pointe Noir. But don't let them see us. The rest of the fleet can go home."

"Aye, sir."

He tapped his lip and grinned. He could take a small shuttle from the ship over to the station. People were always coming and going there. He'd slip in and make sure all his strings were in place for pulling his plans together even without his inside contact. Maybe he needed to add some more pressure. Blackmail only got you so far. There had to be some scheme he could come up with to make sure his contact got the message that he worked for Ian McClaren.

Chapter Six

Cass thought about what had happened while they got ready to make the jump. She turned the ship around and headed away from the field at a slow pace to make sure all systems were working with the red. "An EM pulse doesn't occur naturally, so there had to be someone out there who sent the bug, but who? And why? And why didn't they come after us once we'd been hit?" No answers from Ben. "Okay. I guess the pulse could have been from that bug on the outside. But for what? There were no other derelicts around besides the one we found and there were no warning buoys out. Nobody claiming the area. So what hit us?"

Ben sat in the pilot's seat behind her but remained silent, and she sighed. Okay, so he was mad at her. But if she hadn't had the red, they'd be stuck. Maybe for good because even *Seeker's* systems had been affected.

As she watched, a second bug zoomed toward them and attached.

"Is the first one still taking a trickle of power?" Cass asked.

"Yes," Timmons answered. "And now the second one is putting out readings and also taking power. And there are more on the way."

"How many more?"

"At least two."

"I suggest you put a force field around the sections

of the hull where the attached ones are to keep them from damaging you further," Zack said from the engine room. "I believe we have enough power for you to do that."

"Done."

Cass figured if Ben wasn't going to come out of his snit, she'd talk with the ship. Besides, what did he have to be miffed about? Just because she had hidden a red crystal? Guilt hit her. Ben had saved her butt, and the *Seeker* needed repairs, as did the *Raider,* and still she'd held back. She couldn't change that now beyond apologies.

"Timmons, speculation. Where did these machines come from? And why hit us as we're leaving?"

"Unknown. Speculation is currently unwarranted as there is not enough data to provide a theory. I will say that the components of the items do not match any objects in either Delta's or my databases, though their makeup is similar to the derelict we left. And according to our data, they didn't show up until after we'd been stranded. Conclusion, they did not cause the problem unless they hit us before they attached."

That was troubling since Delta had one of the most extensive databases money could buy. Types of ships, stations, languages, missing ships, and more went into the lists. Current information was a necessary part of Cass's research.

They felt light thuds as two more bugs attached to the ship.

"Timmons?" Cass said.

"Shielding them as well. But I suggest we get out of here before more come."

"Agreed," Zack said. "But use standard speed, no jumping. We don't know how those bugs have affected our weight and drag or what the red will do in jump space."

"Will do." Cass studied all four bugs now attached to the ship. Ben still hadn't said more than a couple words even though this was technically his ship.

"That will get us to the station in approximately two days," Timmons said.

"Okay, notify station security and the bay chief about our bugs and our current status. And have Delta send a ping to our cargo buyers about the even later arrival."

"Done."

"Oh, and scramble our path. I don't want anyone tracing our track back here. This find is mine."

"Yes, ma'am. But that will add more time."

"Understood. Let the buyers know."

"Ben, you have a call from Pointe Noir."

Ben looked up. "Who from?"

"Advocate Jordan Li."

Cass watched as he did a double take. "Ben?"

"No clue. Timmons, give me a minute to get to my cabin and send the call there."

"Yes, sir."

Cass took the captain's seat and continued to monitor their systems, checking with Zack when necessary. She looked up when Ben rejoined her, a stunned look on his face.

"Ben? Is everything okay?"

"Depends on your definition of okay. My old man finally bought it. In the arms of an escort on Denova II." He chuckled. "At least he went out happy. Left me a bunch of crap, including a prime berth on Noir."

"I'm sorry?" Cass noted Ben didn't seem

particularly upset.

"Nah. Ain't seen him in years. Honestly didn't even know he was still kicking."

He went quiet, and she left him alone with his thoughts. A prime berth would be worth thousands of credits. That along with their find and Ben would be sitting pretty for quite a while.

They reached Pointe Noir with no further incidents and only a few hours behind schedule. Once there, Cass flew the *Seeker* out of the *Raider's* bay and parked in her usual slot. She noted that Ben parked the *Raider* two slots down at the end of the bay. There were times when docking was at a premium and only those with permanent status could get in. Cass was one of those. The one Ben took was a temporary but isolated one that could be put under high security. The rental on a permanent slot was high but worth the cost to her when she could come in when she wanted and unload on her time schedule. Plus, there was an actual security guard on this level as well as electronic security.

They'd notified their contacts about being a little late, and everyone was understanding. Accidents happened in deep space. And they had a good reputation with these particular vendors, plus, they'd give them a discount for being late, so everyone was happy.

"Ben, did you hear from the Throquins about the statue?"

"Yep. Got a meeting set up." He glanced at her, his face red. "Guess you were right about that moon base."

Cass just nodded. They both had some actions to apologize for.

Pointe Noir was inherently eclectic in the beings who came there. Not only humans, but Abooleans,

Orilians, Rujaz, Surians, hybrids of all sorts, and even the occasional Throquin—though security always kept a watch on them. Especially if any Rujaz were around. Unfortunately, fights still broke out on a regular basis. A little caution was in order as she and Ben brought in their find. Actually, a lot of caution. Especially if there were any McClarens around.

Cass grabbed several anti-grav units, and with Ben and Zack's help as well as the bay crew, they unloaded their merchant cargo, notified the buyers that their goods were available for pickup, and secured them in a locked cage. Cass also asked for high-security storage for the statuette, with an extra guard. She and Ben carefully stowed the figurine there, locked the unit, and nodded at the guard who took a stance outside the spot.

By the time they finished, the hour was late—or early, depending on your point of view—and Cass was dead on her feet, but first she went to one of the mysterious bugs still clinging to the *Raider's* hull. All four had attached near the engine area. When she touched the unit, she got a shock that knocked her on her ass.

"What the hell?" The night bay chief ran over to her along with Ben and Zack.

"Cass? Girlie, are you all right? What happened?" Ben asked, as Zack helped her up and checked her over.

"Yeah." Though she felt like she'd had a jolt with a taser, she seemed to be in one piece. Cass shook her head, her senses whirling and her nerves tingling. "That machine! You ever seen anything like that, Chief? Whatever you do, don't touch it!"

Chief Simon went over to the device and studied the contraption with his hands behind his back. He shook his head. "Nope. Are those the bugs your AI told me about? Where'd you pick them up?"

"In an asteroid field a half day away. They knocked my systems out of whack and me on my ass just now. Timmons has the particulars. I was kind of surprised you were okay with us coming in with them."

"I wanted to see 'em for myself. Timmons sent me what he had but assured me they didn't appear to be dangerous. Sure looks dangerous to me now." He held up a scanner. "I'll see what I can find out about them for you. However, since they are alien and unknown and possibly dangerous, I'm putting you under a level-ten security isolation."

Cass groused a bit but honestly wasn't surprised. The chief was doing what he should to protect the station and personnel. She was surprised he hadn't ordered Ben to move the ship off to a safe distance. "You sure you don't want us to move?"

"Not at this point. I think everyone wants to study the bugs, just taking safety precautions. Are you heading to your quarters?"

"Yeah."

"I'll let you know what we find."

"Thanks. Oh. Our suits need a complete cleaning and refitting, more than what the ship can do. Can you put them on the schedule? They're on that last grav lift."

"I'll see to them. How long are you going to be in station?"

She glanced at Ben, who shrugged. "I don't know. A couple of days at least. I'll let you know my schedule as soon as I figure one out."

"Understood."

Cass turned to Zack and Ben. "See you both later?"

Ben took off without a word, and Zack snorted. "Guess he's still pissed at us."

"His problem, not mine. That red got us home. You heading to your place?"

He yawned and stretched. "Yeah. I'm beat. You have to be too."

"I am. But I want to see if Katie's in the bar first. I'll see you later?"

He cocked his head to the side. "I'll go with you. I need to check with Omar about when he needs me."

"How do you do what you do and find time to work at the bar too?" she asked as they strode through the station. There weren't many people about at this hour. Cass loved this time of the night. When the station was quiet and calm compared to regular working hours. Oh, there were still people around. Just not as many as at other times.

"I'm super organized," Zack said. "Besides, working the bar is actually a break. Tending doesn't take any thought. You just pour, mix, and serve. I find the job kind of relaxing."

They stopped at Omar's bar. The place was little more than a hole in the wall with dim lighting and deep inside the central area of Level 1. Tourists didn't come there, and even locals didn't come in often, but the bar was a good place for spacers like Cass. They served decent food and drinks at costs spacers could afford. If anyone else did happen to wander in, they would probably wander right back out. Prices they would be quoted were exorbitant and the servers gruff. Only those who were *known* got a warm welcome.

Cass had been coming in for years and knew everyone, and they knew her. As she and Zack arrived,

Omar, the owner, was locking up. His wife, Katie, was Cass's best friend.

"Hi, Om. I thought Katie might be around."

"She left early. You want some food or a drink, Cass? Zack?" Omar asked. "I can open back up."

"Nah. I'm good. I'll get a meal from catering."

"I just need a minute," Zack said.

"I'll let you two talk. See you later, Zack," Cass said.

"Sure. Get some rest."

"You too."

She strode off. When she got to her apartment, she started shedding clothes as soon as the door shut. The tan-cream-green colors of her décor soothed her tired mind. One wall had a living hologram of the seven waterfalls at Baron Point on Jovani and a soundscape to go with the scene. She almost wished she were there now, feeling the warm spray on her face. Maybe even jumping into one of the hot pools at the base.

"Jovani beer." She didn't elaborate, as the unit knew her preferences.

The catering unit pinged, and Cass grabbed the glass from the slot, taking a gulp of the blue liquid and carrying the rest into the bedroom. She didn't usually indulge, but she'd had a rough day. Stripped down, she went into the refresher. "Sonics. Deep clean."

Cass leaned her head against the shower wall as the sonics did their cleaning, and she rubbed at the ache in her temples. She'd really like to not to have to worry about anything for a while. Not the McClarens. Not her credit account—though hopefully, that worry would soon be a little less. Not a ship that desperately needed repairs. She snorted. Make that two ships. Neither one of which was in long-term flying condition at the moment. And she would certainly not worry about lying, deceitful, bastard pirates no matter how doggedly they chased her. She jerked upright. She would not dissolve into self-pity. Never.

Exhaustion was starting to set in as her communications speaker beeped. Cass wrapped a robe around her and went out to her bedroom. "Answer."

"Hey, Cass, Omar told me you just got back." Her best friend's beautiful face and bright gold eyes smiled at her from the wall. Almost as tall as her husband, Omar, Katie was reed slender with waist-length white hair and gold eyes and was a member of the Aboolean Warrior Caste. Nobody messed with Katie. Or Omar.

"Hey, Katie. Yeah. Just got in."

"You look tired."

"I am. I had a rough ride."

"Okay. You can tell me about your trip later. Meet you for breakfast?"

Cass glanced at the chronometer. "How 'bout lunch? I need some serious sleep."

Her friend grinned. "Okay. I'll have your chips ready. See you then."

Cass didn't even bother checking her messages, just set her alarm and collapsed on her bed. But no matter how much her body needed rest, sleep was the last thing her mind wanted. All she could think about was that derelict, the bugs on the ship that had knocked her off her feet or on her ass, and what the two had to do with each other, because she was sure they did.

After tossing and turning until her bed looked like the aftereffects of an out-of-control ship's spin, Cass rose, donned a light shirt and shorts, and went to her office in the second bedroom. Unlike the rest of her apartment, this space was littered with equipment, pieces from various salvage jobs, and other parts of her life. The room might look like a mess to someone else, but she knew exactly what she had and could tell you where each bit was to the nearest millimeter. The pieces changed regularly depending on what she had brought in and what was going out or going down to the planet where she and Ben had a warehouse.

The front of the building on planet was an antique shop, but the rear of the building was where the real business happened. Backed up against a hill, the rear of the shop was a dug-out and reinforced cave where they stored the expensive stuff from her salvage runs.

"Lights, quarter power."

The dim lights came up, and she sat at her desk. Before she brought up any of her files, she reached under the desk, pulled a panel off the wall, and checked that her security measures were still in place. She had an alarm system of sorts that Zack had installed for her. The setup alerted her if anyone other than she came in. Or even tried to enter. She could access the system from anywhere but liked to make sure the main power pack was still in place and working when she was home. She smiled as she thought about the day Zack had installed the workings. Zack had done the work, then she made dinner for him. Okay, the catering unit did the actual work, but still, she'd programmed in his favorite foods and served them. They'd talked and laughed late into the night, and for the first time in a long time, she'd felt comfortable with a man. And in her private space where she'd never invited anyone before. Well, except Ben, but he didn't count.

Unfortunately, after that evening, she'd been gone on a three-month salvage run. And then Zack had been away for another month on a job. They rarely got to see each other, though they did talk almost every day. But she always seemed to back off when the relationship got heated. She needed to focus on her work. On finding her family. She couldn't afford to be distracted.

Cass shook her head at her foolish thoughts and checked her listings. Her possessions might not be of a lot of value to anyone else, but her files—especially the locations of her claims—were. Only she and the claims judiciary knew their exact locations. She'd been robbed once—and that was one too many times for her. She knew better than to trust Ian McClaren, but somehow, he'd found her claim listing, and she'd lost a lot of credits to him. Plus, he wouldn't stop coming after her personally. No matter how many times she said no, he kept up his pursuit.

Sure, he was nice-looking and charming when he wanted to be, but to her, he was just…someone who turned her stomach. Now Zack…with his dark good looks and the fact that he was an honest businessman, that was all that was important to her. Especially his honesty. And he was a wiz with all systems ship related.

Since the first theft, she'd upped her security and rarely trusted anyone, including Ben, with all her sites. Salvage was a competitive business, and the locations of her finds meant credits in the bank. No matter how many credits a salvager had, the locations were where the real money lay. Plus, each spot she found and searched was another tick on the map of where her parents might have gone.

Cass rolled her shoulders, cracked her fingers, and

brought up her files. "Okay, let's see what we've got."

She logged in the inventory Delta had loaded from the salvage job she had done earlier. Once that was done, Ben could run a list of what she'd brought back and see what was worth credits and to whom. She always had a fairly good idea of what she had and the value, but when she didn't, she had Ben and Delta for backup. Ben had worked the business with her father and knew the best contacts and who they could sell what to. He would get the best prices.

She glanced at the time and rubbed her eyes before shutting down the files. Then she brought up her credit accounts. The sale of the statuette would bring in enough to almost fund the entire operation she had in mind for the new derelict, and the red crystal and bugs might garner her a lot of favors from various entities interested in studying them. Still, there wasn't a lot of leeway in what was left. She shuffled some credits from one account to another, paid outstanding bills, and made sure the rent on her apartment and her landing berth were paid up and set to automatically renew. She had no idea how long this operation would take and didn't want to risk her berth being gone.

Before she could file the claim, her com unit pinged again. "Hi, Ben."

He grinned at her. "Figured you wouldn't be asleep. We need to talk."

At least he was speaking to her now. "I know. Come on up."

Cass went to the catering unit. "Double order. Eggs, scrambled. Bacon. Plain bagels, lightly toasted, buttered. Sliced rainbow fruit. Coffee—one black, one sweet and light."

A few minutes later, the door to her apartment pinged at the same time the catering unit did. "Enter. Breakfast is ready." She set the plates on the table and motioned for Ben to join her. "Eat first, then talk."

He was still wearing his ship-suit. Had he even been to his room yet? Knowing him, she doubted he'd left the landing bay. He'd probably spent the last hour with the chief looking over their bugs.

Silently, they dug into their meals. Cass was sipping at her black coffee and finishing her bagel as Ben sat back in his chair. Talk time had come. "So…"

"So…you had a red and didn't let me know?"

"Yeah, well…I don't know why I didn't tell you. I was just…" She shrugged. "I don't know."

"Okay. I get that. Kind of. But we could have used that earlier in the trip when we started to have trouble."

"Except I didn't have the crystal then. I got the red from that last ship. The big one."

Ben blew out a sigh. "Okay. Okay, but still."

"I understand. I do. But think about the timing. Even if I'd had the red, if we'd used it earlier, we'd really be stuck on that asteroid because that damned pulse would have fried the red like all the rest, and I do not have a second one hidden anywhere."

He snorted. "Okay. I'll give you that. But damn, girlie, you could have let me know. That hurts."

"I know. And I'm sorry, Ben. I really am."

"Hells, Cass. I've known you since you were a bump in your mom's tummy and been partners with you for almost seven years. If you don't trust me by now…"

"I do! Honest, Ben. I do. And I'm sorry. I really am. Can you forgive me?"

He snorted. "You know I do, girlie. Now, about

those bugs on the *Raider*…and that last derelict…"

She grinned, excitement fluttering in her stomach as she cleaned up their dirty dishes, dumping them in the recycle chute where they'd be broken down, sterilized, and reformed. "I know! Do you think the first bug is what knocked out the systems?"

"Possibly. Though the bug didn't show up until after we got fried. But them being there is too much of a coincidence. We sure gave the chief a puzzler. They've scanned them with everything they've got so far and are no closer to figuring them out than we are."

"I think our bug is somehow connected with that ship."

"Yeah, but how? If that's a warning, it's effective. Makes me wonder if there are more of them. And how the hell did whatever hit us move us away from the ship and deeper into the field?"

"Good questions. With no answers. Yet. Have you had a chance to talk to Zack? Maybe he knows more than we do."

"I couldn't get him. He's probably sacked out at his place."

"About our haul…"

"The statuette?"

Cass nodded. "And their derelict."

"The Throquin historians are grateful for the coordinates of the original ship but say the derelict is of no worth to them. All they wanted was the statue. So the ship is ours." He shook his head with a smile. "That one's almost worth the problems we had. And add a red on top of that. Damn, girlie, this was a good one. What else you got?"

Cass ignored his question and called on Delta. She

paid to have access to her ship's systems from here, a premium perk she paid a high price for. Ben already knew that, so she didn't hesitate. "Delta, you on?"

"Yes, boss."

"How are you doing?"

"Not great, but Chief Simon has a crew already at work."

"Any bidders we might want to reach out and touch with what we brought back?"

Delta brought up a list of bidders who might be interested in what Cass had brought back. Cass and Ben broke into smiles as this trip looked like they'd have a good payday for a change. Several museums were looking for pieces like she'd picked up, and nobody was clamoring about illegal grabs. That was always a danger in doing salvage. The ships, stations, and other places where she picked up relics might not be of any use to anyone, but sometimes what they contained was often when salvagers lost a good haul to a planet or family who claimed the pieces as stolen. The process could take years to prove, though, which meant years of storage and costs until the dispute was settled.

"Ben?"

Ben usually took care of their buyers. She was the *find it* person while he was the *sell it* person and why he didn't go on her flights with her. Often, he was off selling what they found, checking inventory, or schmoozing clients.

"I'm on it," he said. "Delta, forward those names to me. I'll send notices to the bidders along with a list of what they might be interested in. And send the inventory to Kevin at the warehouse. He was supposed to be meeting up with some people this week. Might be some interest there. I'll talk to him later."

"Done."

"And go ahead and file the claim," Cass said. "But make the claim a high priority private one with nonspecific coordinates, just the description." She figured that might keep the claim jumpers guessing for a while.

"Done," Delta answered.

"Ben, there's one more detail." She chewed her lip. "Or rather, three more. That aren't in inventory."

He gave her a narrow-eyed look. "What? You said you didn't have any more reds."

"I don't. But…um…how 'bout a white, a blue, and a yellow? Each oval about five centimeters long and half that wide." Those three alone would buy her and Ben each a year or more on station. And still leave a tidy sum in their pockets. The crystals were hard to find, making them valuable, and the scientists were still figuring out what all they could do. So far, they'd been found of use in communications, weapons, and more. Of all the colors, thankfully only the red was dangerous.

"What the hell? Cass!"

"I found them with the statue along with several others. I was only able to pry out those three before Ian showed up. Getting them nearly got me caught, but I have them stored in the *Seeker*."

Ben shook his head and sighed. "You got any other secrets I should know about?" He held up a hand. "Wait. Don't tell me. I don't know if I can handle the excitement. Keep them hidden while I make some discreet inquiries."

"Okay."

Ben yawned. "I'm going to head out and catch some

sleep. I suggest you do the same."

Cass grinned. "Yeah. I'll talk to you later."

He just snorted and shook his head. "Please, girlie. At least a nap."

"I will. I promise. Get out of here, old man, so I can get my beauty sleep."

"Hah. Delta? Don't let her work too long."

"Yes, sir."

Cass showed him to the door and went back to her computer. She brought up a scan of their newest find—and the bug that had taken them down. She peered at the image, enlarging and turning the view every way she could to make out any markings or any feature that would identify the devices—and who had set them. But there was nothing. Okay, not nothing, exactly, but the few markings she saw weren't like any writing she'd ever seen.

"Delta, do you recognize any of these markings?"

"Not in any of my databases. Do you want me to search further?"

"Yes. Let me know what you find."

"Will do. By the way, the crew chief left a message for you and Ben."

"What did he say?"

"That he hasn't been able to get any of his scanners to penetrate the bugs, but he'll keep working. And that the emissions they give off are comparable to the anomaly off station. Also, the station security chief wants to talk to you asap at the ship."

"Any idea about what?" The emissions were similar to the anomaly? Interesting.

"Besides the bugs on the *Raider*, your cargo in secure storage might be causing a problem. Seems there might be a previous claim on the statue."

Fardles. "Okay. Thanks. Send her a note that I'll talk with her after lunch."

"Will do."

Cass shut down her monitor and moved out to her living room. "Delta, give me a holo-image of the new ship we found, but reduce the size to fit in here."

A moment later, a perfect rendition of the ship appeared in front of Cass. The holo took up the entire space, blocking out her furniture. "Delta, reduce size by one half."

The image grew smaller to the point where Cass could walk around the ship. She noted the pockmarks left by space debris hitting the outer hull, as well as the hole in the side. Cass peered into the interior. The hole showed several levels inside, and she thought she could see a large boulder sitting on the middle one. So the ship had been hit by an asteroid. "Delta, slice and enlarge the area of the damage."

The rest of the ship disappeared except for the area around the hole and the hole itself. Cass walked into the space. Unfortunately, she couldn't see any more than what had been visible to Delta from outside, but there was enough to let Cass know at least five levels had been decimated by the damage and, going by size, that many more above and below. There were also scorch marks on the edges of the hole. From the rock? Or something else?

The wall opposite where she stood had some kind of writing, and she tried to get a closer look, but the scan hadn't captured the entire phrase. Looking through even just the scans would take months, if not years, but what a find! Her mind racing, she stepped back out of the ship. "Delta, restore previous size."

Once again, she was looking at the entire ship. Cass stepped around the craft, studying each centimeter as closely as she could, having Delta enlarge or reduce sections as she looked at each. She would need a large crew to handle this one. At least a dozen. Even she recognized that fact. She rubbed her eyes when the image blurred, then yawned, her lack of rest catching up to her.

"Delta, close holo."

The ship disappeared, and Cass reluctantly headed to bed.

****

Cass's com unit buzzed, waking her, and she groggily answered. "Who the hell is this, and what the hell do you want?"

"Cass?"

Cass shook her head, trying desperately to wake up. "Chief Simon?"

"Yeah. I'm sorry I woke you, but I have some news for you."

That woke Cass up. "The bugs? You know what the devices are? You know how to get rid of them?"

"Yes. No. Maybe."

"Okay. Do you need me down there?"

"If you wouldn't mind."

"Give me ten minutes."

"See you then." He signed off.

"Catering. Coffee. Hot. Heavy caffeine. To go."

Chapter Seven

Ben whistled as he strolled through the corridors to his new apartment. His dear old dad had left all his possessions, including a prime berth, to him. He would finally have the recognition he deserved. He got to the apartment and punched in the security code.

The door swished open, and he stopped and stared.

The prime berth was not like he imagined a first-rate place would be. Lurid was the best word he could think of with red-and-black furnishings and decorations that left nothing to the imagination what they were for. He stepped in and let the door close behind him, still not sure how far into the room he wanted to go.

Then he heard a noise coming from an open door to his right. To his surprise, Ian McClaren strolled out, a nearly naked woman on each side of him. Ian wasn't wearing much more.

"Bennie! It's about time you got here." He patted the women on their rumps. "Party's over, girls. Credits in your accounts. See you the next time I'm in."

They pouted for a few moments, then grabbed filmy robes and sashayed out.

"What are you doing here, Ian?"

"Taking care of business." He sauntered over to a low divan and dropped into the plush seat.

"So I see."

Ian snorted. "Them? They're just recreation."

"How did you get in here?"

Ian let out a loud laugh. "Bennie, you think your old man could afford a place like this? Yeah, this berth is in his name, and now is in yours, but who do you think footed the bill for this? I like to have my fun, and this is where I come."

Ben had had about as much from Ian as he could take. "Not anymore. Find somewhere else to have your fun. This is my place now, and I'm claiming what's mine."

Ian rose from his seat, his face dark with anger. "Watch your tone with me, Ben. I own you. And I own these rooms. You will do what I say when I say so. Or your sweet Cassie will find out what you've been doing all these years."

"You don't scare me. You need me. But I won't be needing you much longer. We got a job that will pay off all my debts. I'm done with you, Ian." Too late, Ben realized what he'd let slip as Ian's brows rose and he narrowed his eyes at Ben.

"A big job, huh? Anything to do with that red crystal you came back with?" He strode over to Ben and wrapped his arm around Ben's shoulders. "Tell me."

"No."

The arms tightened, and Ben felt a twinge of pain. "Ben."

"I can't."

One arm slid up to wrap around Ben's throat. "You will."

"Can't. Breathe," Ben gasped out. The arm loosened but only slightly.

"Where is the claim?"

"Don't know the exact coordinates. But I can give

you the general area."

"You can and will give me more."

"Not until we're there. Then I can give you what you need. Cass knows the details. Not me. But the ship is big. Bigger than any one you've ever seen."

Ian let Ben loose and grinned at him. "Get me that information, and we'll see what we can do." He tapped Ben on the head. "I'll get dressed and leave you to explore *your* new place. We are going to clean up, Bennie. This sector will be ours. Heck, I may even buy the station!"

Ben remained standing where he was as Ian dressed and strutted out, looking like he did own the station. When he was gone, Ben slumped against the wall. "Computer, change security code on this door."

"Enter new security code."

Ben did and then went to look through his new rooms. What he found made him sick. He'd known Ian was depraved, but some of the equipment Ben saw went beyond the imagination. "Computer, are there any decorators on station?"

"Yes, sir. Would like to contact them?"

"Start at the top of the list."

Chapter Eight

Zack slept better than he had in a long time. The bed in his room was not only comfortable, but the room was quiet, unlike when he'd lived with his family and had two younger brothers always after him, like little brothers did. Here, there was only darkness and soft warmth. Definitely not as spacious as his room on the farm, but not bad. Though he missed his family.

But he could definitely get used to the quiet—at least until someone banged on his door.

He stumbled over to press a release button. "What?"

Ben strolled in. "Sorry I woke you."

Zack shook his head, trying to wake up. Ben? What the heck was he doing here? Had Zack let a hint of his investigation slip, and he was here because of that? "Is something wrong? Is Cass okay?"

"She's fine. Sleeping, I hope. But I wanted to talk to you."

Zack sighed and went over to the catering unit, trying to cover his nerves with busyness. "Coffee. Hot. Sweet. Extra caffeine." He glanced at Ben who shook his head. A minute later, the unit pinged, and he took his drink from the cubby hole. He inhaled deeply, then took a sip. Zack motioned Ben to one of the two chairs in his room.

"So talk."

"The red. You knew she had a red?"

Zack blew out a breath of relief. Okay, not about the farm. His secret was still safe. He'd been expecting this but still winced. "Cass showed the crystal to me when she got back from the ship but asked me not to tell you." He held his hand up before Ben could say a word. "Before you ask, I don't know why. But she found the red, so I had to honor her request."

Ben blew out a long breath. "Okay. I get that, but keeping me out hurt."

"I know, and I'm sorry. But we did manage to get the red to work!" He had to keep his conversation normal. Keep up the ruse. Zack sipped at his drink as Ben chuckled.

"That we did."

The com unit pinged, and both men looked up.

"Now what?" Zack asked, then saw Cass on the screen. "Cass? You're supposed to be sleeping."

"So are you. And you too, Ben. Chief Simon says he might be able to get our bugs off. He's working on them now. Thought you might want to know. I'm heading down there."

"Damn straight we do," Ben said. "We'll be right down."

Cass signed off with a laugh as Ben turned to Zack. "I gotta be there. You coming?"

"Definitely. Just let me get dressed."

Zack grabbed his clothes and went into the fresher. A glance in the mirror showed his hair standing every which way. He quickly combed through the strands, splashed some water on his face, and tugged on his clothes. When he emerged, Ben handed him his coffee, now capped.

"Thanks."

As they strolled through the mostly empty corridors, Zack noted how tired Ben looked. He had dark circles under his eyes, and his shoulders drooped like he was carrying the weight of the entire station on his back. "Hey, you doing okay?"

"Yeah. Sure."

Zack believed that about as much as he did in a rainstorm in space.

They got to the landing bay and found the area crowded with techs, security, onlookers, and more.

"Let us pass," Ben ordered as he elbowed his way through the crowd with Zack close behind.

They finally reached the ship, and Zack saw Cass standing there arguing with the head of security. He'd never met the woman but had heard she could be a real hard-ass as far as station security went. His heart sped up a little as he saw Cass looking like an avenging angel. Several other people stood nearby like they were waiting for the argument to get over with.

Cass looked up as Zack and Ben arrived. She glanced at Zack, smiled at him, then looked at Ben.

"What's goin' on, girlie?" Ben asked.

"This idio—" She blew out a long breath. "The security chief says we are being charged with carrying illegal materials. In addition, she's claiming our bugs are a danger to the entire station and is charging us with the same endangerment. And if that's not enough, she found out about the red and is charging us with illegal use of controlled power substances. She wants to impound both our ships and fine us the equivalent of our entire salvage take and more."

"What the hell?" Ben turned to the woman. "Jalee?"

"That's Captain Kulanie to you."

Ben glared at her. "All right. Fine. *Captain* Kulanie, what the hell?"

Zack held back a snort. Ben was in a fine dander, his face red and his fists clenched.

"You and your partner"—the captain sneered at Cass, making Zack wonder if there was a problematical connection of some sort between them—"brought in a questionable object and stored same questionable object in a highly secure bay without proper notification or protocols. My guards aren't in your employ. Plus, there is a previous claim on the object, which means you are holding that relic illegally."

"If you check closely, you'll see that the guard standing there, looking after my merchandise, doesn't work for you. He works for Chief Simon and is on temporary merchant assignment as per my legal rights," Ben said.

"That may be, but the object he's guarding is of questionable ownership."

"In what way?" Cass asked.

All those times they'd talked and gone out together and Zack had never seen Cass mad like she was now. Zack hoped he was never on the front end of that anger. From the dark circles under her eyes, Zack knew she was tired, yet she stood straight and tall and didn't give an inch. She was beautiful.

"I have legal right to that claim, as filed by my AI. The artifact is ours by way of that claim," Cass stated.

The security chief snorted. "I have records stating that one Ian McClaren filed for that derelict. Therefore, the artifact is his."

Zack watched a muscle in Cass's cheek work as she gritted her teeth. Emotions were running high, that was obvious, but to him, the security chief wasn't happy with Cass and Ben bringing in their load and the bugs attached to the ship. Maybe he could figure out how to help her and Ben. He continued to listen as he formulated what to say to tone the situation down. Working in a bar often meant breaking up fights, preferably before they got physical.

"If you look at the time stamps on the claim, you'll see that mine takes precedence. We beat him there. I already told you all this." Cass's fists clenched and unclenched at her sides, and Zack wished he could help her more.

"What about the other two charges?" Ben demanded. "We were attacked. Those bugs attached themselves to my ship without provocation. We did not bring them here willingly, but nobody can get the damned bugs off."

"Then you shouldn't have parked in the bay. You should have alerted security and stayed off station."

The woman simply would not let go. She reminded Zack of a canine he'd once seen with a chew toy. The animal had refused to give up its prize.

"We did alert security," Cass said. "And the bay chief. Both of you knew what we were bringing in. Check your fardling logs."

Jalee frowned at both of them, then reached her hand back, and a man slapped a pad into her palm. She scrolled through the screen, her face turning darker before she all but threw the pad back at her aide. "Fine. I'll give you a pass on that one. But what about the red crystal? You have a red! Who did you steal that from? Because I know damned well neither of you can afford one."

"I already told you, Captain," Cass said. "I picked

the crystal up with salvage. I just haven't registered my inventory yet."

Zack stepped slightly in front of Ben. "Captain Kulanie, if I may, I believe you have three issues here. The first is the cargo. They have a valid contract and claim." He didn't know whether they had or not but assumed as much. "They have a buyer lined up who should be here later today. If the buyer doesn't show within five days, the item will be considered their property, correct?"

"Who are you?"

"I'm Zack Anderson, a friend of Ben and Cassie, and am advising them on these issues. So…property. They can lay claim in five days?"

"Yes." She gritted the word out. "Are you some kind of law advocate or something?"

"Something. Your bay chief has the right to assign his personnel as guards on some cargo if the carrier requests and pays for such services, correct?"

The woman sighed. "Yes."

"So if the buyer doesn't show, they can declare the cargo theirs and dispose of said item or items however is necessary, correct?"

Another sigh. "Yes."

"So…five days. That's not too long a wait, is it?"

"But they shouldn't have brought an object like that on station. A rare artifact such as that one could bring all sorts of trouble to us. And in fact, already has with the disputed ownership."

"But you've seen the claim. This McClaren has no real right to the item, correct?"

A third sigh. "No."

Ben moved to push forward, but Zack held him back

with an arm. As for Cass, she just stared, mouth gaped open, at him. "Now, as for the endangerment…both security and the crew chief were advised of the problem, and Ben was given the go ahead to park on station, correct?"

"Yes, but that shouldn't have been allowed."

"Even with a level-ten security isolation?"

"Level…" She gave him a narrow-eyed glare. "Did you say level ten?"

"Yes. Really, Captain, your people should do a better job about informing you of these situations. But we'll let that go for now. The ship has the highest level of security isolation that there is, so technically, there is no real danger."

"But the chief admits that they have no clue about those bugs. What if one, or more, explodes? They could take the entire bay out. Or even the station. We don't know how powerful they are."

"I agree. But again, level-ten isolation. That's strong enough to contain even the largest blast known. So the danger is minimal at best, agreed?"

A disgusted sigh. "Agreed." He watched as her shoulders dropped.

"Finally, the red crystal. Cass and Ben just came in with their salvage. They've barely had time to get any sleep let alone catalogue every single item they have in their bays. They couldn't en route because of the damage they sustained." He turned to Cass. "Do you have any more crystals you found with the red?"

She gave him a narrow-eyed grin. "No. I can emphatically state that I do not have any more crystals that I found with the red."

Zack gave her a side-eye, knowing she was holding

back, but he returned his attention to the security chief. "So she had only the one piece of red and used the crystal according to known guidelines in order to return here to the station where she could deliver the remaining cargo to her customers and let the proper authorities know that there may be a risk out there in a nearby asteroid field that others need to be aware of. So, in effect, Cass and Ben were doing the station a favor by alerting you and the crew chief to the problem."

This time, Jalee did snort at him but with a smile.

"So are we good here, Captain Kulanie?"

"Name's Jalee. And yes, we're good." She turned a narrow eye on Cass. "But no more. Understood?"

"Yes, ma'am. Thank you, Captain," Cass and Ben muttered together. Jalee and her people turned away.

"Everyone who doesn't have business here, out! Now!" Jalee barked to the crowd who quickly dispersed.

Ben just stared at Zack. "Where'd you learn to advocate like that?"

"Picked up a few skills as a bartender."

"Thanks," Cass said with a grin. "You can advocate for me any time."

Zack shrugged and grinned back. "Just helping out where I can."

Cass studied him with narrowed eyes and pursed lips before glancing at Ben, who nodded at her. He wondered what was up.

"About that helping…how would you like a job? One that pays better than checking systems for someone else."

Interesting. He was sure he knew what she was talking about but wanted specifics. "Where? For how long? Doing what? What's the pay?"

78

"Be at Omar's in two hours, and you'll find out." She turned and headed out as Zack chewed his lip. Then Cass turned back. "I really hope you'll be there, Zack." She gave him a smile that would melt tritanium and strode off.

"Ben?"

Ben shook his head. "She's the boss. I'm not saying a word until she says so. But if you're interested, be there."

Zack went back to his room and paced. Well, as much as he could in the small quarters. He was sure Cass was putting together a team to go after the giant derelict. So did he want to go? Going along would give him a chance to keep a tighter eye on Ben. And maybe find out more about Cass and her ties to Ben. He knew the basics, but more was always better. He really hoped she wasn't involved—and honestly didn't think she was—but her close ties to Ben were a problem. First, he had some calls to make.

"Computer, place a station-to-planet call."

"Number please."

Zack rattled off a string of numbers. The call went through, and he saw his younger brother's damaged face looking at him. The scarring was a lot better than the last time he'd seen him just a month ago.

"Hi, Danny. How are you doing?"

"I…I…I…I'm   g…g…g…good." His brother grinned back at him.

"Hey, your speech is improving. That's good." The fire that had killed their parents had severely damaged Dan's face and throat. The surgeons had managed to return his face almost to normal, but therapy on his vocal cords took a lot longer. "How's Jimmy?"

Dan's eyes grew sad, and he shook his head.

"Is he still having nightmares?" Their youngest brother had been only eleven when the raiders hit the farm. He hadn't been too badly hurt in the fire, but the damage to him mentally was worse.

Dan nodded.

"Have the meds helped any?"

Dan shrugged one shoulder.

"Okay. I'm not going to keep you. I may be out of touch for a couple of weeks on a job. I've put more credits in your accounts, so you should be good for a while. Is there anything you need?"

Dan pointed at Zack.

"I know, buddy, but I need to work. I'll come as soon as I can, okay?"

Dan nodded and crossed his arms over his chest, his hands on opposite shoulders.

"I love you too." Zack closed the link and bowed his head. He wanted to be with his brothers, but he needed to track down the men who had done this, and Ben was his only lead. Plus, specialists weren't cheap. He needed Cass's job to boost his credit base.

Zack took a quick shower and headed for the bar. Time to find out what she wanted from him.

Chapter Nine

Two hours later, Cass sat across from her friend Katie at a back table in the bar. A plate of her favorite spicy chips drowning in gooey cheese and topped with loads of veggies sat on the table between them, half of them already gone. Cass took a sip of her beer and settled back against the chair. "Amazing as always. Thanks."

Katie laughed, her voice deep and husky from years of singing, talking, and yelling orders. Close to the same age as Cass and married to Omar, Katie had a tough exterior but was as soft as a cloud on the inside. She didn't take crap from anybody and could spot a scammer from a parsec away, but if you were true and needed help, she was the first one there. Katie was as tiny as Omar was big, with the white hair and gold eyes of an Aboolean—and had the fighting skills for which they were famous. Nobody messed with Katie. Cass met Katie when she moved to the station six years ago, and they'd become fast friends.

"One of these days, I'm going to get you to try something else here. You know, I do cook other food," Katie said as she sipped at her iced tea. That was one issue Cass never understood. Katie—and Omar—owned a successful bar, but Katie never touched a drop of alcohol herself. Synthetic or real.

Cass shrugged as she scooped up another chip, cheese dripping off and the topping falling. "Why should

I eat anything else? This is all I need, and this is sooo good." She took a bite, closing her eyes as the spices and melting cheese atop the crunch of the chip filled her mouth with Heaven.

Katie just snorted and shook her head. "Any good finds this time around?"

Cass grinned, nodded once, then glanced around to see who might be nearby. She and Katie were isolated at the back of the bar, but that didn't mean what they said was private. "Is the privacy room available?"

Katie's eyes widened, and she rose. "Right this way."

Cass picked up her plate of chips, then glanced up as Ben and Zack entered the bar. Zack didn't look happy, and she wondered what that was about. She indicated for them to follow her as Katie led them to a doorway in the back, then down a short hall to another door that she opened with her palm print. She stepped aside for the three to enter, then turned to leave.

"Katie, if you're interested in joining a crew, I'm putting one together."

"I might be interested. Depends. What's the find?"

Katie had worked with Cass on a few longer salvages. Cass trusted her like no one else, but even so, she wouldn't reveal where the site was or what she had found. "Trust me, you are interested."

One perfectly sculpted eyebrow rose. "Now I am intrigued."

"Bring lunch for the guys, on my tab. Steaks and all the trimmings."

Katie stared at her. Rarely did people order steaks. They were the most expensive item on the menu and were kept in a specialty container that could keep them fresh for years. When one was ordered, they unwrapped the meat and flash grilled the steak, taking less than five minutes from stasis to delicious. "That good, huh?"

"Yep. And bring Omar."

Katie sauntered off as Cass sat down with Zack and Ben, and the door closed.

"Okay, what's up?" Ben demanded.

Cass watched his face, knowing he was keeping something back, but hoping he would tell them.

"What do you mean?" Zack asked.

"You look like…you got problems. So…what's wrong? This job is big, and we don't need no problems," Ben said.

Zack blew out a long breath. "Just a family issue. And no, there aren't any concerns that will affect the job or me doing what I need to do."

He shook his head, looking so dejected Cass went to him and hugged him. She knew the basics about his brothers, but not the whole story. "We all have family issues."

"You got that right," Ben muttered.

Cass sat back down. "If you need some help, let me know."

"Thanks, Cass. I appreciate that."

Cass looked up as Katie and Omar joined them. Omar set two plates with sizzling steaks and tubers on the table in front of Zack and Ben.

"I have a proposition for you three. Could be worth a lot. More than any of us have ever seen."

Omar's eyebrows rose, but he sat down. "What's the job? Who do you need? And for how long?"

"I'll need a big crew. Supply, cook, general workers. We have two ships, both of which are in for repairs right now. A couple smaller ones for back-and-forthing, but… Once we're at our location, I'd like to keep that to a minimum. No daily trips. And no communications beyond what's absolutely necessary. Omar, you'd have to either sub the bar out or shut down for at least a month, I figure."

Now everyone except Ben was looking at her, questions in their faces. She sighed. "Katie, open up the com unit in here and let Delta in, please."

Katie went to the wall and tapped a few buttons on the panel. "We're still private, but Delta has access."

"Delta, you on?"

"Yes, boss."

"Show the scans of our latest find in here."

"On the wall or holo?"

"Holo. But reduce size to fit on the table and show a scale map with the *Seeker* as reference."

The mystery ship appeared in the middle of the table, and everyone leaned forward. The *Seeker* showed as a tiny spot next to the bigger derelict.

"How big is that ship?" Katie asked.

"Massive. You know how big my ship is." She pointed at the smaller ship. "I'd say the salvage one is a quarter to half the size of this station."

"Claims?" Omar asked as he peered at the holo.

"None that we've found so far. And even Delta can't decipher the markings. I was inside for just a few minutes. I discovered the red that got us back here in what appeared to be their engine room. Whoever was flying the ship used crystals to power the engine."

Omar chewed his lower lip, head cocked to one side. "You'll need a big crew for that. At least another six or seven along with us. Maybe more."

Cass nodded. "Yep. Got any suggestions?"

"Paul and Donnie are in port. They could use the work. Their last one was pretty much a bust. And Annie and June are in as well. What are you looking for?"

"We probably ought to have a couple with linguistic abilities with us as well as someone who can keep an eye on security and help with general work." She glanced at Zack. "Zack will work as engineer, but I'll want one more."

"I can take care of security for us," Ben said. "I know a couple—husband and wife team—who are good. I think you know them too. Tom and Meri Baron."

"I do. Both of them are Aboolean so have the fighting and security skills we need, and Tom's an advocate, so that takes care of the legalities. Delta, close scan." Cass nodded at Ben as the image faded and thought about the people Omar had mentioned. Paul and Donnie were a father/son team with almost as much experience as she had and were honest. Plus, Donnie had a degree in historical artifacts that made him a valuable resource on any recovery. They were both talented and loved what they did as much as she did. And they were from a heavy-gravity planet, which made them stronger than most spacers.

Annie and June weren't as experienced, but they were successful to the point where they could not only afford to go out when they wanted, but could also help with funding for a larger slice of the pie. They were a solid couple, shrewd as they came, and worked well with others—as long as you didn't ask them where they came from. Plus, Annie was a fully certified medic—a good asset on any salvage operation. Cass didn't know June's background—and wouldn't ask—but she knew a lot about a lot of stuff. She was smart, skilled, and knew how to keep her mouth shut, as did the others.

"How long to get everyone and everything together?" Cass asked.

Omar glanced at Katie, who was making notes on a pad. "We can have supplies in four or five days."

"Okay, let's say a week," Cass said. "That will give us time to get the teams together and get the ships repaired. I also want Hopper," Cass said. The others stared at her.

"Why?" Ben groused. "We already found the ship. We don't need him."

Cass knew Ben and Hopper didn't get along, but Hopper was important to her, and she liked him. "I think we do. Omar, can you get him?"

Omar shook his head. "I haven't seen him for a few days. Put out a general call."

"Who's Hopper? I mean, I've heard of him, but who is he?" Zack asked as Cass went to the com unit.

"A bum," Ben gritted out. "I don't know why Cass likes him. He's a thorn in my side."

She glared at him as she punched buttons on the com. "This is Cass calling Hopper. I need you at Omar's Bar." She repeated the request twice more. "I guess we need to get back out there."

They all trooped out to the bar, and Omar nodded at his day manager. The place wasn't packed but full enough for an afternoon. There was a large open booth near the back, and they all sat there.

"Zack, Hopper is a bit unusual. He's had a rough life, but he's a genius in some ways. I'm just asking you to give him a chance." She ignored Ben's *humpf*. "Look, I know you both don't get along, but Hopper is good with almost everyone else. Just…give him a chance, please?" Zack cocked his head at her, then shrugged. "I've got no issues."

"Um, when Hopper gets here, don't move around. Stay still and stay quiet, please." She frowned at Ben. "Hopper is unique. He's not smart, but he is a genius. If you want something moved or done, Hopper can do the work. He can also find anything. But make sure you want whatever you're looking for found. Once he starts, he won't stop until he's found whatever he's after. Plus, he's effing brilliant when you're talking about fixing ships. You'll probably be working with him a good bit, so let me know right away if you can't handle that."

Cass turned as a person came into the bar. He wasn't much taller than she was and wiry thin with wisps of hair sticking out from under a knitted cap. Myriad scars crisscrossed his face and hands. He wore patched pants held up with a rope and rainbow suspenders, a boot on one foot, a shoe on another, and fingerless gloves. Under an oversized coat that had more pockets than any coat should have, he wore a faded T-shirt and a ragged, long-sleeved shirt.

Zack looked at him and immediately felt a certain kinship with the man. He was injured, like Zack's brothers, but he was still a person and needed to be acknowledged and accepted.

"Cass called. Hopper came. What does Cass need?"

"I am going on a treasure hunt, Hopper. Do you want to come?"

He smiled with more gaps than teeth in his mouth. "Is the treasure big?"

"Awesome big."

Hopper's grin grew. "Then Hopper will come.

Hopper needs the funds. Omar has been supporting Hopper, and that's not good. Hopper needs to support Hopper."

Cass glanced at Omar, whose eyes had gotten wide. He shrugged and nodded.

Hopper looked at the floor. "Hopper knows. Hopper not smart, but Hopper knows."

"This treasure hunt will bring Hopper funds," Cass said. She glanced at Zack.

"Hopper, this is Zack. He is a good person. Omar knows Zack. He says Zack is good."

Hopper stared at the floor but gave Zack a quick glance. "Cass knows Zack. Cass says Zack is good. Omar knows Zack. Omar says Zack is good. Hopper accepts Zack as good."

She watched as Zack stuck his hand out, and the soft look on his face when Hopper engulfed him in a strong hug. Then Hopper stepped back, his gaze once more on the floor. "When does the treasure hunt begin?"

Cass glanced at her watch. "Seven days, two hours, sixteen minutes. Landing bay four. Tell no one."

"Hopper will be silent. And will be there." And with that, he scurried to the bar.

"What was that?" Zack asked.

"That…was Hopper," Cass said. "Like I told you, he's unique. But he is a genius. Just don't ever ask him to back you in a fight and don't ever approach him. Let him come to you. We're not sure exactly what happened, but he limped into the station on a ship I wouldn't even use for salvage, barely alive, several years ago. Nobody knows where he came from or who he is. They ran all sorts of ID tests and got no matches. The medics did what they could to save his life, but as you can see, there was a lot of damage, some years old. Once he was released, he settled in and is what you see. He's never been the life of the party, but almost everyone likes him. I'm not sure what the deal is with him and Ben. If you need an item fixed that nobody else can, he's your man, but he's skittish and withdrawn and will only interact with certain people. He does mostly odd jobs around the station now. Omar is his advocate and handles his affairs. The rest of us look out for him."

She stopped when Hopper rejoined them with a bowl of soup. He sat next to her, avoiding Ben as he ate. Cass glanced at Ben, not sure what his issue with Hopper was, but he'd need to get over whatever the problem was because she wanted Hopper along.

"Okay, Ben, I need you to get ahold of your contacts and see if they can join us. I'll take care of talking with Paul and Donnie and Annie and June. Katie, Omar, you get supplies together and get what you need settled with the bar. Omar, I'll add credits to the same fund we used before. I'll give you the new code."

He nodded.

"Hopper, you'll be with me on the *Seeker*. Everyone else will be on the *Crimson Raider*."

"*Seeker* is good. Hopper likes Delta and *Seeker*. Hopper likes Timmons. But Hopper doesn't like *Raider*. *Crimson Raider* is bad."

Cass turned to him, not knowing what he meant. "Hopper, how is the *Raider* bad? Because of whom used to own the ship? We don't have to worry about them. Ben bought the *Raider*."

Hopper shook his head. "*Crimson Raider* has red. Red is not good."

Cass was beginning to understand, but she wasn't

completely sure. After all, *crimson* meant red. Did he want them to rename the ship? "Hopper, what are you saying?"

"Red crystal brings bad bugs. Red crystal sends out signal. Bad bugs come. Bugs like red crystal."

"Damn. So that's what happened," Zack said. "Can Hopper remove bad bugs?"

"Bad bugs go away when red crystal goes away. Hopper can fix, or Zack can fix." He looked directly at Zack, then back at the ground. "Hopper and Zack can fix together. Zack understands."

Wow. That was a new one for Cass…and everyone else. They stared at Hopper, then at Zack, who shrugged with wide-eyed confusion.

"Bad bugs go away…" Zack muttered, then turned to Cass. "I think I know what he means. You have a red crystal drive on Ben's ship that you need to get rid of. Unhook the drive and send the crystal out into…somewhere far away. Then the bugs will detach and follow."

"But what will we power the ship with? That red is all we have," Ben said.

Cass was sure he was thinking more about the prestige having the red brought him than the actual power from the crystal.

"Hopper and Zack will fix," Hopper said. "Ben will have new drive. Hopper will fix *Seeker* and *Raider*."

"Hopper, I appreciate the offer, but I don't have enough funds for a new drive." Yes, she had money and could sell some stuff to get more, but she needed funds for this expedition, more than what that statuette would bring in. People would expect to be paid. But if the red attracted those bugs, she sure didn't want one on the ship.

90

But what choice did she have?

"Cass does not need funds. Hopper will fix."

Cass shook her head. "Hopper—"

Hopper held up his hand and stared directly at her. "When Hopper says Hopper will fix, Hopper will fix. Zack will be at ship in one hour, twenty-two minutes." He turned and walked away, leaving Cass and the others to stare after him.

"Well. I guess that settles that. Zack, if you want, you can work with Hopper."

He gave her a side-eye stare. "What's your opinion? I have no problem with him, but I just met him."

"Hopper isn't always willing to work with others. That he chose you is huge. I can't tell you what to do, but you'd do well to work with him."

Zack pursed his lips, then nodded. "Okay, I'll do it."

"Thanks. But please, be gentle with Hopper."

"Uh, sure. I have some experience with people who've been injured."

Cass glanced at him, wondering if he meant his brothers, but he had his head down and didn't look like he wanted to chat. She'd let him alone for now and maybe talk to him at another time. "All right, folks, we have a lot to get done and not a lot of time. Let's get moving." Cass followed Ben and Zack out into the main area. "Got a minute to talk?"

Ben nodded. "Let's go up to the new digs. I can give you the grand tour."

Cass chuckled but went with him to the new apartment. When she entered, she let out a low whistle, then started laughing. When she could, she caught her breath, then started laughing again. Finally, Ben and Zack joined her.

"Oh, Ben, your old man must have been interesting." She eyed the deep-red carpeting, red-and-black textured walls, and mirrored ceiling. The furniture consisted of lounge chairs, sofa, low tables, lots of pillows, and little else. And the pictures on the walls left absolutely nothing to the imagination as to what the participants were doing. "And this is just the living room?"

Ben chortled. "Yeah. The bedrooms are worse."

"I'm not sure I want to know!" Cass could barely believe what she was seeing. The pictures alone were enough to get anyone's blood heating. She refused to glance at Zack.

"Looks like your father had…proclivities," Zack said around a chuckle.

"At least the apartment is paid up for the next six months," Ben said.

"Now I really don't want to know." She started laughing again. "I guess you're going to have the place redone?"

"I'm going to meet with a decorator this evening," Ben said.

"I think you need an 'un-decorator' before you do anything else," Cass said around another laugh.

"Yeah. Not sure I want to move in here just yet."

Cass glanced at Ben. "You didn't know your dad had a place here?"

He shook his head. "Not at all. If he was ever here, I never saw him."

"Well, Noir is a big station, and you're on planet at the warehouse or off meeting buyers more than you're here."

"Maybe."

Zack leaned against one wall, the picture above his head giving Cass ideas that she really didn't need at the moment. She turned away and ran her hand over one of the lounge chairs.

"What can you tell me about Hopper?" Zack asked.

"What you saw pretty much says all you need to know. He's got issues but is a good person at heart and great at fixing whatever you give him. We were all blown away when he asked for you to help him. Hopper never does that. You must have some kind of special vibe for him to do that. Just…be gentle with him."

Zack snorted. "Me? Special? I'm not special. But I'll take care. Thanks."

"Ben, you'll get the team you know and outfit your ship." Cass chewed her lip as she studied Zack. "Zack, since Hopper will be riding with me, maybe you should too. He seems to like you, and having you with us might make the trip and working together easier. I can convert my workroom back into a berth without too much trouble."

"Why don't you let me do that since I'm the one staying there? I don't need much room."

"Good. Because there won't be a lot. *Seeker's* a great cargo ship, but not much room for passengers."

"Understood. Is there anything in there I shouldn't touch?"

Cass cocked her head. "Yeah. I'll take care of them. Ben, what about our buyers for the statuette?"

Ben startled. "Damn. I gotta get goin', or I'll be late. Talk to you both later. Lock up when you leave." He dashed out, leaving Cass and Zack staring.

It bothered her that Ben was so tight-lipped over who was buying the statuette. There were a lot of beings on the station and flitting around outside Pointe Noir, but why wouldn't he tell her who beyond a Throquin? Okay, he didn't always tell her everything, but he usually did when she asked. So why not now? What was he hiding?

Then there was Zack. He was an engineer and a bartender—and a good one according to Omar—but he was hiding something too—something beyond lying about who and what he was. The two men had secrets—and so did she—she just hoped their secrets didn't come back to bite them in the ass, especially with this upcoming trip.

"I still can't believe this place," Cass said.

"Me neither. Wow." He turned to her with a wicked grin and pulled her into a hug. "But those pictures do give one ideas."

She felt her face heat. And then he kissed her. She melted into his arms. Yeah, the room gave one a lot of ideas. Reluctantly, she drew back. "Put those ideas back in your brain. Come on, let's get out of here."

Zack raised an eyebrow, giving him a rakish look, and her heart fluttered. She had definitely fallen for him. He was good-looking, a good person—as evidenced by Hopper liking him—and he was someone she'd grown to like. A lot. She hadn't been seriously interested in anyone in a long time. Zack hit all the other buttons on her list. So he'd kept some secrets. So had she. She brought her head back to what they'd been talking about.

"Spoilsport."

Cass grinned. "Yep. Besides, I have some people to see." She glanced around the room again. "And you…I'm glad you're meeting Hopper and getting out of here!"

"Cass?"

She stopped at the open door and looked back at him. "Yeah?"

"I might need to go down to Jovani for a day to take care of some stuff. Will that be a problem?"

"No. Just let Hopper know how long you'll be. You need any credits or anything?"

"Nah. I'm good. Thanks." He thought about his accounts. With what he needed for the trip and paying off Jimmy and Dan's bills and lodging and their private nurse, there wouldn't be much left. He might need to give up his room and bunk on one of the ships until they left. "Cass, I won't let you down."

She smiled at him. "I know, Zack. Otherwise, you wouldn't be here."

Chapter Ten

The *Seeker's* proximity alarm erupted through the bay, the harsh wail turning everyone's heads and sending several people scurrying either toward or away from the noise. Zack jumped, knocking his head on the panel above him. "Dammit! Hopper, can you shut that blasted noise off?"

Seconds later, the noise did stop, and Zack crawled out from the hole he was in. He ran his hands over his head and blew out a frustrated sigh. He and Hopper had been working together for several days, and he was no closer to understanding how Hopper did what he did than he'd been on the first day. Zack was a damned good engineer, but Hopper took what they did to a new level—almost as if he were part of the ship. "Okay, what did I do this time?"

"Zack tied red to green, not red to blue."

"In this light, I can't tell green from blue."

"Feel, not look. Blue is thicker, and there is something else."

Zack ran his fingers over the offending wires. If there was a difference, he could barely detect one.

"Close eyes," Hopper said as he leaned over Zack. "Use feelings, not sight. Other senses important."

Zack blew out a sigh but did as Hopper directed. He'd discovered not only was doing what Hopper said easier, but Cass had been right. Hopper might not be smart, but he was certainly a genius in some areas. Zack thought he knew a lot about electronics and systems, but he was an amateur compared to Hopper.

He closed his eyes and fingered the wires. There! He could feel the distinction. The blue *was* slightly thicker, but there was something else too. Not a shock, but…more like a buzz. He felt the green. The buzz was there too, but different. Like notes in music. A variation on the tone.

"Zack feels the energy. Hopper knows."

Zack grinned at him. "I could feel…I don't know…"

"Zack feels the energy. Come. Zack and Hopper need to eat."

As soon as Hopper said that, Zack's stomach rumbled. "Shall we go to the bar?"

Hopper shook his head. "Test catering unit. Make sure Zack and Hopper and Cass eat good on treasure hunt."

"Works for me." He followed Hopper to the small galley where they both cleaned up before accessing the catering unit. Unlike higher-end restaurants on the station and even Omar's bar—which made him unique— that served actual food grown on the planet or hydroponically, catering units used pastes that contained all the nutrients needed by various beings. All you had to do was ask for what you wanted, and the food or drink appeared—eventually. And tasted sometimes better than the original, plus whatever you got was healthier for you. All the good without the bad.

"Let's see," Zack said. "What shall I have? I think I'll have a bowl of beef stew with freshly baked bread and butter." Five minutes later, the unit delivered his order. He sniffed at the steaming bowl, inhaling the tantalizing aromas, and looked at the thick broth brimming with what appeared to be carrots, potatoes, and chunks of meat. "Looks good to me."

"Hopper will have macaroni and cheese."

Zack laughed. Ever since he'd introduced Hopper to the gooey meal, that had been almost all he'd eaten. "You know, you can get other food."

"Hopper likes this, so Hopper will get this."

As they dug in to their meals, Cass entered the room. "I thought I smelled food. You got the catering unit working again?"

"Not only working, but we also restocked the supply units and programmed in some new foods," Zack said. "Join us?"

"Don't mind if I do. Grilled beef burger with all my trimmings, fries, and cabbage slaw." She grinned a few minutes later as she got her meal and took a bite of the roll piled high with caramelized onions and mushrooms and topped with light cheese. "Stars, that's good. I don't know what you did, but you are both geniuses. Last time I had this, I got a burger smaller than half my palm and thinner than one of Katie's chips. And the trimmings consisted of a limp piece of lettuce. Period."

"Hopper and Zack programmed what Cass likes. Program knows now."

She smiled at him. "Thank you, Hopper. So how are we coming on other repairs? Will we be ready to go in time?"

Hopper stared directly at her. "Cass set time. We leave in one day, two hours, thirty-six minutes."

"Good enough for me." She turned to Zack. "You got all you needed to do taken care of on planet?"

"Yeah. No problems there."

"What about your berth here? You good to go?"

"Yes. Hopper helped me fix the cabin up." He frowned as Hopper took care of his dish and left. "Cass, Hopper said something funny about the room when we were working there. He said there was strange energy in there before but not now. You know what he meant?"

Cass startled. She'd taken the crystals out of her hidey-hole shortly after they returned to the station. How could Hopper have known? "I have no idea. I mean, that's where I take some artifacts so I can study them or encase them when I'm on a job. But that's all."

"Interesting. But then, so is Hopper."

She studied his face, but he gave nothing away. "You getting along okay with him?"

Zack gave her a small smile. "Yes. He's definitely unique, but you were right about him. His skill set is amazing."

"I know he said we'll be ready to go, but I'd like your assessment."

"We got the *Raider* all ready. *Seeker* may take a little more tweaking, but we can do that on the way. If necessary, you can put her in the *Raider*'s bay, and we can finish her there."

"Any major issues I need to know about?"

Zack shook his head. "No. Just some minor stuff."

"Delta?" Cass glanced at the ceiling even though she knew Delta was pretty much everywhere.

"Yes, boss?"

"You're good?" Cass asked.

"Boss, I'm better than good. If I were a person, I'd be dancing a jig. Give those guys a hug for me."

Cass laughed. "That's good enough for me." She turned back to Zack. "I understand Chief Simon and the

99

scientists who came in are having a field day with the red crystal and those bugs."

"Yeah. When Hopper told them the bugs were attracted to the reds, the chief got that crystal unhooked and on a drone. As soon as he did, the bugs detached and went after the red. Got an entire crew of techs and scientists out there working on them. They were most grateful to you. Chief Simon told Hopper to do whatever repairs we wanted, and they'd comp us on the equipment. Even gave us some extra crew to help."

"Yeah, I saw my credit account. We sure don't have to worry about financing this trip."

Zack grinned at her. "A red that size? You probably don't have to work for the rest of your life!"

Cass sobered. "Maybe not, but I won't stop looking."

Zack reached out and laid his hand on her arm, and she felt the warmth all the way through her. The touch went beyond comfort. Almost as if he really did understand her feelings. "Your folks? I know you told me they disappeared some time ago, but you didn't say how or what happened."

"Seven years ago. You ever heard of the *Phoenix*?" She tamped down the feelings that threatened to overwhelm her. The sadness. The frustration in not being able to find them. The hope that refused to die. Zack reached out to draw her into a gentle hug, and she felt his warmth flow through her.

"Who hasn't? That's the ship the head of Ki Enterprises was on, right?"

"Yes. Along with almost a hundred others, my folks included." Her voice hitched, and she swallowed hard. She hadn't talked to anyone about them in a long while.

"I thought the searchers stopped looking a couple of years ago."

"They did. I didn't." She pulled away from Zack and turned to leave, then turned back. "Thank you."

"For what?"

"For this." She waved her hand at the ship. "The *Seeker* means a lot to me, as does Hopper. Thank you for taking care of both of them." And she hugged him then. A brief one, but enough that he hugged her back. Cass felt a sensation she hadn't felt in a long time—comfort. Not a feeling she was used to. She'd have stayed longer, but she had her own tasks to take care of. Reluctantly, she drew away. "I'll see you later."

She strode for the exit, trying not to look like she was running, but maybe she was. She hadn't had a relationship with anyone in a long time. One-night stands to scratch an itch, yes. But someone she cared for? No. And she could care for Zack easily. Too easily. But she had a job to do. That had to be her focus now.

She checked in with her team members on Ben's ship. Everyone was busy stowing their belongings in their berths. Paul and Donnie were sharing one, Annie and June another, Omar and Katie had a third, Ben the captain's rooms, and the one she'd had when she was aboard went to the other team of Meri and Tom. A dozen people.

Not a bad-sized crew. And Zack was right. With the bonus she'd earned for bringing in a red crystal the size of her fist, she could settle down somewhere and be secure for the rest of her life. But she couldn't do that. Not yet. Not when the *Phoenix* was still out there somewhere. And she knew the ship and crew was. That was one belief Cass wouldn't—couldn't—give up. She just needed to keep looking. Each derelict she found was one more she could cross off her list. She dreaded the day she would find a wrecked ship that was the *Phoenix*, but that day hadn't happened yet, and she'd keep looking until she found either of them or answers.

Cass went back to her rooms and packed what she'd need for the next few weeks. She figured at least a month on site. Maybe more. "Delta, did you finish those checks I asked you for?" She settled into her chair. Ben had urged her to investigate everyone on the crew, even though they'd known some of them for years. But he'd especially pushed her to look into Zack.

"Yes."

"Show me."

The file opened in the air in front of her, and she scanned the pages, checking the information Delta had dug up on Zack. She trusted him…up to a point.

"Delta, did you see any incriminating data in this file?"

"Possibly. Do you remember the White Mountain disaster a couple years ago?"

Cass sat straight up. "Yes. Some farmer burned out by raiders. Husband and wife killed, two of the three sons seriously injured. Why?" The tragedy had been in all the news reports for weeks as authorities tried to track down the people responsible, but they'd never been found, and the media dropped the story.

"I believe Zack is the older son. The one who wasn't there when the raiders hit the farm. The authorities even investigated him at one point, but his alibi was solid. He was on a job out here on Noir and had a half dozen witnesses. Speculation was he might have hired out the raid."

"Oh. My. Word. That must be what he's been hiding. But why? And I can't believe he'd do that to his own family."

"He didn't. The only reason for the investigation was that he came into a large settlement, including the farm with the crystal, which he sold off. The inquiries cleared him completely. Though records show most of his credits go to the Jovani health and rehab center where his two brothers live. One was badly scarred by the fire, and the other, a younger one, has had to go into reconditioning therapy for severe PTSD. Zack only keeps enough credits for basic living expenses."

Cass had known he had two younger brothers, but not that they'd been injured or lived in a therapy center.

"Wow. No wonder he gets along so well with Hopper. He's lived with those kinds of issues." She understood him a lot better now. They'd both lost their parents. They'd both suffered at the hands of raiders. They'd both survived, but not without damage. She admired him even more now for what he'd gone through.

Cass sat back in her chair. "Okay, next file."

That one was much smaller, with only a couple pages.

"Sorry, boss, but this was all I could find. And believe me, I tried."

"I do believe you, Delta. Thank you." She stared at the little information there was on Hopper. Nobody knew where he came from or what had happened to him. He'd been in several medical facilities but left them all after just a few days—some he'd escaped from, according to the information, and she shuddered to think of what had happened there. No wonder he didn't trust anyone.

Finally, she checked on everyone else on her crew.

She knew them all, but she wasn't going to go into a job this big on friendship alone.

Her com unit pinged. "Who is this?"

"Hi! Is this the Cass Brennan who's putting together a crew? I'd like—"

"Stop. My crew is full. I don't need anyone else."

"But—"

"End transmission."

Cass sighed. She'd been getting at least a dozen of those calls a day. So were the others. Nobody on her team had told anyone, but word had gotten out not only about the expedition, but about her finding the red. The only person who hadn't bugged her was Ian. She was just waiting for *that* one.

"Boss, Zack is at the door."

Cass looked up when Zack came in. He leaned over and gave her a quick kiss.

"Hey, Cass. What's up?" He frowned at her. "You look like you just lost the claim. You didn't, did you?"

Cass shook her head. "No. The claim is safe." She brought up the file for him to see.

"You investigated me?" He frowned at her, the hurt in his eyes obvious to her, and she bit back a wince.

"I had to. I checked out everyone on this trip. So yes. I investigated you." Well, almost everyone. She didn't bother with Ben. After all, he was her godfather, and she knew him better than she knew anyone. But that wasn't what was important right now.

He glared at her. "If you wanted to know all this, you could have just asked."

"And would you have told me everything I found out here?"

He snorted. "Maybe. But we'll never know, will

we?"

"Your brothers—"

"Are my responsibility. I make sure they're safe and taken care of."

"So why are you up here instead of down planet with them?"

"Credits. Pay's better up here."

"You got a pretty good settlement from your parents plus the sale of the land." She watched as Zack winced. He certainly seemed to be telling the truth. Or was he feeling guilty about getting caught?

"And all my credits are in reserve accounts for my brothers. That's what I was taking care of a few days ago. I was setting accounts up so if I'm gone for a while, they'll be okay."

Cass nodded and held out her hand, hurt when he backed away, but not surprised. After all, she'd forced him to admit secrets. Why had Ben pushed so hard to have him investigated? And why had she listened? "I'm sorry. But I had to know."

Zack gave her a sad look. "Are we done?" Without waiting for an answer, he turned and left.

"Yeah, I guess we are," she whispered.

Cass swiveled back around to glance at the files one more time, then shut them down and headed out. She had work to do and not much time to get everything done.

Chapter Eleven

"Pointe Noir station, this is the *Seeker*. We are ready to disengage."

"Locks are disengaged. Have a good trip, *Seeker*. And Cass? Good luck."

"Thanks, Chief."

Cass glanced over at Zack in the copilot's seat and grinned. "Ready?"

"Yes."

They were at least on speaking terms if not back where they were. And that bothered her more than she thought. She really cared about him and knew she'd hurt him but felt she had to do what she did.

But did she really? She'd found issues about the other members of the teams that she hadn't known but hadn't called them on the carpet. So why him?

Cass forced her thoughts back to the here and now. They had to go.

"Hopper?" she called over the com. "You ready?"

"Hopper is ready."

"Let's go." Cass engaged the engines and slowly backed away from the station. Ben, in the *Raider*, was already out and waiting for her. As agreed upon, they set course in the opposite direction from where they wanted to go. And as expected, at least four ships followed them—that they could see. Cass was certain there were others tracking them as well. She'd filed the claim as ultra-secure, which meant no one could look up the specifics, but there were always ways. Heck, even Zack had the skills to break the security on the claim.

"Zack, were you and Hopper able to engage those anti-trackers I got?"

"Yep. Anyone tries to tail us that way will get an earful of static. Can't do much about the visual ones."

"I got that taken care of. Hold onto your stomachs. Delta? Are you ready?"

"Ready when you are, boss."

"Let's go!" They did a slingshot around a small moon back toward the station and zoomed out faster than Cass had ever gone without being in FTL. "FTL now!"

The ship shot forward. "How long in FTL?" Zack asked.

"One day. Then a half day on a different vector. Once we're sure no one's tracking us, we head back."

"You're serious about this. Would someone really try to jump you?"

Cass snorted. "You saw those ships trailing us? Those are the little blips. The bigger blips are what I'm worried about. The ones you don't see. Not only will they try to overtake us, jump the claim, and steal everything worth stealing, we'd be lucky to get away alive. Especially since everyone knows about the red I found. This is serious business. Do not let your guard down for even a microsecond out here."

He frowned, and she hoped he understood the problems they could face. "Zack, you've never been on a salvage operation this big before, have you?"

"No. Not really. Well, a couple times I went out with different crews. Picked up a couple small, abandoned ships."

"Those barely count. This is so far different than those as to be entirely new. Here's what to expect. In addition to working with Hopper, you'll be hauling stuff. Manual labor. Helping whoever needs help. Ben and I and one of the others will figure out what is valuable and what's scrap. The other two teams can help with that to an extent since they're experienced. Ben's ship will be our main base of operations, and we work pretty much around the clock, catching naps when we can. Since this is a breached ship, all the work will be in E.V. suits. One of your jobs will be taking care of the suits, making sure everyone has air, and that they don't spend more than the allotted time in a suit with regular breaks in between."

"Understood. Katie and Omar filled me in on that. I'll also be helping with supply runs."

"Yes. Though we shouldn't need any with what Omar and Katie put in. A supply run shouldn't be necessary unless we run over time. If you do have to do one, your path will have to be as convoluted as this. You'll be using *Seeker* for them, so Delta can help you with that. She's a good AI."

"Aww, thanks, boss."

"Right now, I suggest you get as much rest as you can for the next two days. Once we get on site, you won't have time for anything but work."

"Understood. What about you?"

His concern touched her, but Cass chuckled to shuffle the emotions off. She had to be about the upcoming job, not her personal feelings. "Yeah, I need to rest as well. Delta, keep to the planned course. No communications unless there's an emergency."

"Got you."

Cass rose and followed Zack off the bridge and back

to their berths. She got to her cabin and settled at the desk. "Delta, show me the scans."

"You're supposed to be resting, boss."

"Uh-huh. Show me the blasted scans."

"Yes, boss."

Cass spent the next hour going over the scans, then had an idea. "Delta, set up a holo in cargo bay one."

"Size?"

"Fill the space but leave me enough room to walk around. I want to study the outside."

"Done."

Cass headed down to the cargo bay. Once there, she studied the exterior of the relic closely, looking up when Zack joined her.

"Couldn't sleep either?" he asked with a smile.

Cass grinned back at him. "I never can when I'm doing a new job. Especially one like this. Look at this." She pointed to some symbols at the front of the ship. "Have you ever seen markings like that?"

He peered at them, frowning. "Delta, can you enlarge this section?"

The symbols grew. "Look at that," Zack said. "Each one is not just a single mark, but marks within marks."

"Huh! I didn't see that before. Delta, enlarge just the first one." The image grew to almost the same size as Cass was. What she saw settled into her stomach. "Zack…do you see what I'm seeing?"

"That looks like a star chart and drawings of bipeds with feline heads."

"Delta, get me the *Raider*."

"*Raider* here," Ben said.

"Ben, have Timmons do a hologram of the ship in one of your bays and enlarge the symbols on the nose

109

multiple times. There are symbols within the symbols. Have the rest of the crew look at the scan. Tell me what you all see."

"Will do. You want to give me a clue?"

"No. I want your fresh opinion."

"Okay. Will get back to you."

"Delta, is this star chart on any of your maps?"

"No. Though the one underneath might be."

"Underneath?"

"Yes, boss. I took the magnification down as far as I could. There are layers upon layers here. At least twenty-seven that I counted."

"Delta, make files of each symbol down to the lowest layers and upload them here and to Timmons."

"Yes, boss. Might take a minute or two."

Cass laughed. "Fine. You may take as much as five minutes, if needed."

"Boss! That's an insult."

"Sorry, Delta." She turned back to Zack. "Opinions?"

"If this is just one small section, we have a lot of work ahead of us."

"You think? Let's look at the rest. Delta, can you continue to record files if we shrink the holo?"

"Yes."

"Return to original size."

The ship shrank to where they could walk around the image just as Hopper joined them.

"Hopper and Delta talked. Hopper can see ship?"

"Yes. Come on. We don't have a lot of the interior. I didn't have time. We got the entire exterior, though, and the interior around the breach."

"Hopper will look at *Amaya* inside."

"What's *Amaya*?" Cass asked.

"Ship's name."

"How do you know that?" Her heart pounded. How could Hopper know an answer even her AI didn't know? Maybe from his past? Nobody knew where he came from. Could he…? She stopped that line of thought, or she'd drive herself nuts.

Hopper touched the first symbol. "This."

Cass glanced at Zack who shrugged. "Delta, do you know what he's talking about?"

"Possibly. Some of the symbols resemble an ancient language that we only have snippets of. Though not Throquin or Rujaz, the language does come from the era of their last war. Do you want me to analyze?"

"Yes. And let Ben know."

"Done."

"Hopper, can you decipher any of the other symbols?"

He cocked his head to the side and frowned. "Maybe. Hopper will work on them."

"Get some food and rest."

"Macaroni and cheese." He gave her a grin.

Cass chuckled. "Yes, Hopper, macaroni and cheese. Go on. And rest too."

He rushed out, but Cass knew he wouldn't quit working on the puzzle they'd given him.

"He can decipher ancient languages?" Zack asked.

Cass shrugged. "Nobody really knows exactly what Hopper can and can't do. The medics have done all sorts of tests and remedies, and none of what they did seemed to work. Whatever he went through, this is the way he is."

"What if he was always that way? You said nobody

knew who he was when he came in and he didn't show up on any data scans. So maybe there wasn't an accident that made him this way. Maybe he was born this way."

Cass cocked her head at him, thinking. "I guess it's possible. We all just assumed whatever had hurt his ship had done this to him. Whatever the reason, he is who and what he is, and we'll take care of him no matter what."

"Like my brothers," he said quietly.

"Yes. Only instead of actual family, Omar and I and several others watch out for him like family."

"You make your own family," Zack said. "And sometimes that's better than actual ones."

"Sometimes," Cass agreed. "But I'd give up all I have to have mine back again."

"I know what you mean."

Maybe they could get past their issues, Cass thought. She hoped so.

They spent the rest of the day going over the ship, chatting with the rest of the crew, and formulating a plan for the work while Delta and Timmons worked on deciphering the symbols. With all the detours and false paths they were taking, they had two days travel time ahead of them. Cass and crew put the time to good use planning and preparing.

****

By the time they reached the *Amaya*, each person on the crew knew exactly what they were to do and how and when. They would scan the interior first, working in pairs and in shifts. Then figure out a plan of attack for salvage. Ben would work as a floater, loading inventory and helping where needed.

"Okay, folks, let's get to work."

Cass, Zack, and Hopper suited up, climbed into a

small shuttle they'd use for going back and forth, and headed out.

"Wow," Zack said as he got his first glimpse at the huge ship up close and personal. "That is some ship. You're only planning on spending a month here?"

"A month on scanning, prepping, planning. I'd really like to tow the ship in, but not until we know what we're dealing with. Remember what happened to us the last time."

"Yeah, but that was when you had a red to deal with. No red crystals on you this time."

"Darn right. And we won't pick any up, either."

She aimed for the highest landing bay as other shuttles from the *Raider* landed on lower levels. Timmons and Delta would continue to scan the exterior, keeping a lookout for pirates and other non-friendlies as well as scanning the workers.

"You'll need magnetics on if you don't want to float. Stay with your partners and be careful," Cass warned everyone. "This is unknown territory, and I don't want any accidents."

"Yes, Mother," Ben said with a laugh.

She gave him a raspberry as Hopper took off. Cass knew there was no way they could get him to work with a partner the whole time, so she had extra tracking on his suit for Delta to watch. Cass would know where he was at all times with the readout. She could bring up anyone's tracking if she wanted, but she was most concerned about Hopper.

"Let's see what we can find," she said to Zack. Less than ten minutes after they exited the bay, to her surprise, dim lighting came up in the corridor. "Hey, anyone else have lights?"

"Yeah," came from multiple people.

"How does this ship still have power?" Donnie asked.

"Hopper found the engine room," Hopper said. "Hopper turned on lights. Will have gravity in five minutes."

Cass looked at Zack, seeing the surprise and concern in his face that she felt. "Set rovers and drones to record this level. Let's find Hopper and the engine room."

"Engineering can't be too far," Zack said. "Or he wouldn't have had time to get there and fiddle with the controls."

"Possibly. I wouldn't put anything past Hopper."

"Where were you when you found that red?"

Cass grinned. "Oh! I forgot about that. This way."

They headed out through a doorway into a long corridor that branched off left and right at regular intervals. "We need to get to where the rock came through the hull, then just beyond that, on the left. Pretty much the center of the ship."

"Makes sense."

Cass really wanted to take her time and check out the markings on the walls, but she didn't want Hopper doing anything that might cause problems for all of them. When they entered the engine room where Cass had removed the red from, they found him sitting on the floor in front of what she assumed was the power unit, since that's where the red had been. Only now, there was a large yellow crystal in the space. Hopper glanced up at them, his hands full of tools.

"Hopper got lights on and one more minute for gravity. Hopper can give you air on undamaged levels. Close blast doors and have air on all levels except where big hole is."

"Hopper, where did you get that crystal? And how did you know what to do?"

He tilted his head toward the left. "Room there. Many crystals and tools. Hopper can adapt. Hopper knows *Amaya*. *Amaya* knows Hopper. Hopper can help *Amaya*." He frowned, cocked his head, and stared at the floor. "Hopper cannot remember why, but Hopper knows this."

Cass glanced at Zack, who shrugged, then she headed for the door Hopper had indicated. Inside, there were indeed many crystals. Hundreds of them of all sizes. Sorted by color. Even two more large red ones in what she assumed were specially shielded clear containers, since none of her warnings went off.

"Oh. My. Stars. Zack, do you see this? This room alone…" She chinned on the mic in her suit for everyone to hear. "I'm going to send you all what I'm seeing. Take a look. And Timmons and Delta, you'd better be recording this."

Cass scanned the room with her headlamp at maximum. The comments she got back were as colorful as the crystals.

"Suggestion," Zack said. "If Hopper can actually get us air on most of the levels as well as other power, we should conserve ours and park both ships in the bays. *Seeker* up here on the second level, *Raider* down lower in the larger one, probably four or five from what I saw on the outside. That way we won't have to keep using our suits, and the work will go faster if we don't have to keep going back to the other ships."

"Agreed," Cass said. "Delta, move into the bay on the second level. Timmons, move the *Raider* into the fifth level. Ben, make sure your shuttles are out of the way."

"Will do."

"Meanwhile…" Cass looked at all the crystals and sighed. "Let's go see what else we can find. Though honestly, this is enough to make this expedition worthwhile."

They went back out to the engine room. "Hopper, do you need Zack to help you?"

He shook his head as he kept working. "Hopper will fix *Amaya*. Zack needs to be with Cass. Zack and Cass will find more."

Cass just shrugged. "Okay, come on, Zack. Let's go see what we can find."

They took a ladder tube up to the first level. "This looks like the main living level," Cass said as they found room after room of what appeared to be living quarters. Some of the rooms were singles, some doubles, and some with multiple bunks.

"Comparable to ours, so bipedal and with a classification system," Cass said.

"How do you know that?"

"Look at the rooms. The singles are more luxurious. Nice beds, sitting areas, privacy screens. Probably for upper officers or valued guests. Then less luxury in the doubles, but still nice. Those would be for lower officers. The bunk rooms would be for the regular folks. Bipedal because what we've seen and walked through so far has been easy for us. The furniture is like ours. If the areas had been built for quadrupeds or other shapes, what we found would have been different. I also think whoever ran this ship was about the same size as us. Maybe a little taller, but not huge."

"Makes sense." Zack forced open a door near the end of the corridor.

They entered, Zack in the lead, but at the entrance to what would be a bedroom, he stopped and blocked Cass. "Cass, let's go."

"Why? What's wrong?"

"We need to put a lock on this door so no one enters." He stepped away so she could see what he saw. The remains of a being lying on the bed. The captain, maybe? That would make sense. A captain would have stayed with the ship.

"Oh. Yeah."

"Delta, scan the remains and construct a possible image. Then see if the image matches anything in your databases."

"Will do."

They both left and shut the door.

"Zack, do you have any of those red tags I gave you?"

He took them from a pocket. "Yeah. What are these for?"

Cass took one of the hand-sized triangles and slapped the warning sign on the door. "This is a danger symbol that salvagers use meaning do not enter. I don't want anyone else going in here."

"Check the last door at the end of the corridor."

He opened the door, stepped in, then back out. "I think we found the bridge."

Cass joined him, and they entered the space. "Wow. This is amazing."

"I agree."

There were three levels to the bridge in a semi-circle with ramps leading from one to the other. At the lowest level were two stations, the middle level held three, and the top level held at least a half dozen.

"What do you think?" Cass asked as she strolled the area. "Navigation and pilot?"

"Probably. And this would be the captain's seat," Zack said, standing in front of the middle chair at the second level. "But not sure what the other two would be for."

"One is probably first mate. No clue on the other. And I guess the top level would be systems like weapons, communications, and so on."

They looked at each other as full lighting came on.

"Hopper has air and lights now," he said. "Hopper will soon have warmth."

Zack went to remove his helmet, but Cass stopped him with a hard shake of her head. "Wait, everyone, before you take your helmets off. This air is a couple thousand years old. Annie, can you test for safety?"

"Already doing so. Give me a couple."

While they waited, Cass ran her hands over the controls. The panels were flat with no external parts. She sat in one of the seats, but when the substance started to mold to her form, she jumped away.

"Cass, you okay?"

"Um, yeah. But watch the seats. They…um…conform? Not sure I want to find out how much or what happens when they do."

"Interesting." He stepped away from the seats, giving them the side-eye.

"Hey everyone," Annie said. "The air is good. A little oxy rich and stale but overall, safe."

Cass grinned at Zack as they both unhooked their helmets and pushed them to their backs. Cass took a deep breath and exhaled. "Just think. We're the first people to breathe this air in a couple thousand years."

"Does Cass want bridge control?" Hopper asked over the ship's com.

"You can give me bridge control?" Her eyes widened, then she shook her head. Hopper continuously surprised her. How did he know how to do all this stuff?

"Bridge control will take Hopper three hours, twenty-two minutes."

"Do we have life support on all levels?" Cass asked.

"All levels supported in sixteen minutes."

"All right, Hopper. Finish with life support, then yes, give me bridge control."

"Hopper will do."

Zack chuckled. "Now I understand why you brought him along."

"Oh, not just for what he can do, but Hopper's kind of like a good luck charm. With him around, you just feel like whatever you're doing will work out."

"Superstitious much?" He grinned at her and winked. Then he frowned. "So why don't he and Ben get along?"

"I honestly don't know. Ben won't tell me and Hopper…" She gave him a one-shoulder shrug. "As for superstitious, what spacer isn't? Let's take a look around. We'll come back here later."

"Yeah, in three hours and twenty-two minutes. Or thereabouts."

"There's no *thereabouts* with Hopper. If he says a job will be done at a specific time, then the job will be done then and not a minute more or a minute less. I don't know how he does what he does, but never doubt him."

"I don't. I learned that working with him over the

last week."

****

Several hours later, Cass had everyone meet on the *Raider* for a break and a meal. While they ate, they discussed what they'd all found. Everyone was beyond excited.

"Where's Hopper?" Cass asked as she looked around at the crew.

"Probably still in the engine room," Zack said. "I'll take him some food. If I know him, he won't come up to eat."

Cass nodded, and he took off. She smiled to herself. Zack had really taken to Hopper, which was good for both of them. His compassion touched her heart. He cared about Hopper and for him. Making sure he ate and rested, but not in a condescending manner. Kind of like Omar and Hopper. She knew she was losing her heart to Zack. But her feelings had to take a backseat to the job at hand. Though there was still some friction between them, he was slowly coming around. She hoped he'd forgive her soon.

"We found what I think is a med center on the third level," Annie said. "At least, the area looks like one. There are multiple diagnostic units, and all of the objects seem to be crystal based. I've never seen anything like what we found here. There's some kind of scanner in there that can diagnose all sorts of stuff. I think. I'm not sure how to decipher the readout, though."

"We found a dining area near there," Katie said. "As well as what appears to be a recreation area. We're not completely sure, but that's what we think."

"Okay, so the first level is bridge and officer's quarters. Level two seems to be lower crew quarters and

120

the first of the landing bays. Level three, life services," Cass said, ticking the levels off on her fingers.

"All the areas below level five seem to be cargo, landing bays, or some sort of storage units," Paul said. "We're not exactly sure what they are. They look a little like cold-sleep pods, but there are hundreds of them."

"Maybe this was some sort of colony ship," Omar said.

"That would make sense," Paul agreed. "Except the pods are all empty. None of us has found any sort of remains."

"Um…" Cass said, and everyone got quiet and stared at her. "Actually, we did. One. In what I believe is the captain's quarters. That room has been sealed off. Nobody is to disturb that space."

"Are the remains…humanoid?" Annie asked.

"Yes. But there are some differences. Annie, you can get together with Delta and check the scans she did, maybe determine what types of beings were on this ship."

"Will do."

"As for the rest, we still have a lot of ship to explore. Hopper gave Zack and me bridge access, but we haven't been able to figure out any of the controls. Paul, have you figured out any of the history of the ship yet?"

He shook his head. "Beyond the possibility of a colony ship, no. But like you said, we're just getting started."

They discussed their plan of attack for another hour, then went back to work. When Zack returned, Cass drew him aside before they headed out.

"Zack, I have a special job for you."

"Ooookaaay."

"I need you to build me some secret weapons I can use from the *Seeker* for when Ian McClaren shows up."

"When, not if?"

"Yes. He knows I took a big crew out and that we took two ships. That might as well be an invitation for him. He won't pass up the chance to raid us. He *will* be here, just not sure when, but I want to be ready."

"What do you want?"

She outlined what she wanted him to build. "They're like the ones Ben has on the *Raider*. Can you create them?"

Zack tilted his head and scrunched his eyebrows, then nodded. "I believe so. I think we have all the components on either *Seeker* or the *Raider* that I need. Or even here on this ship. I'll let you know. But are you sure about this? And what about your rule that nobody works alone? Where will you be?"

"After what happened to me the last time I was here, and what Hopper told us about the reds, I think those weapons might be the perfect solution. And I'll be heading back to the *Seeker*. I have a mountain of forms to fill and file."

Zack laughed. "The problems of being a boss."

She chuckled. If he only knew. Actually, she had Tom doing most of the filling and filing since he was the expert in that area, and Ben handling inventory. She had other duties to take care of. Duties that required a bit of secrecy. "Oh, if you get the chance, find out if this ship has some more of those bugs. I'm not sure where they are, or even what the system is that the weapon comes from, but we might need some."

"I'll make sure of that first. Maybe Hopper will know. He seems to understand more about this ship than any of us."

"Good idea." She reached out, but he ignored her hand, gave a quick shake of his head, and took off.

She watched as he headed out, her heart hurting, then turned to find Ben staring at her. "What?"

"You seem to be turning to him more and more, girlie. You sure you trust him?"

Cass wondered what Ben was getting at. Why wouldn't she trust Zack? Why didn't he? Ben was starting to concern her. He had changed since they'd found this ship. He'd become…harder. More secretive. "I do trust him, Ben. And so does Hopper."

"Hopper trusts a lot of people I wouldn't give the time of day to."

"And he's almost always right, you know that."

"Almost," Ben said.

"Look, we have your special weapons on the *Raider* that we can use too. Plus, the *Seeker* has some new deterrents. I just want a little extra security. Now, what do you think of our little find?"

He grinned at her, but she knew their discussion was far from over. "I think, girlie, that this may be the one that sets us all up for life. The drones and bots have already recorded two levels, and from what I'm seeing on the readouts, the finds are amazing. Almost this entire ship is crystal-based, and what isn't is based on technology I've never seen. Their science is so far ahead of us…"

"So why is this all still here? Why, if they were attacked, didn't the attackers strip her?"

He gave her a shrug. "Who knows? Maybe they assumed the ship was destroyed. Or that they'd come back later. Or…you know, a thousand and one other reasons. But their loss is our gain, that's for sure." He smiled wider. "Now, git out of here. I got work to do."

"Yes, sir!" She laughed and headed back out into the ship, passing Omar and Katie on the way.

"Hey! How're you doing?"

"We're going to team up with Annie and June and look closer at the third level. The scans are good, but we want to see what we can with our own eyes."

"Understood. See you all later."

A few minutes later, she heard Katie yelling and a bad-sounding grunt from Omar over her com system.

"Omar. Katie. What's going on?" Cass's heart sped up.

"Got some kind of nasty bots on our tail. Can't shake them."

"Where are you?"

"Level three. Dining area. Damn things came out of nowhere."

Cass took off at a run. "Zack? You got your ears on?"

"Yeah. What's up?"

"Meet me on level three. Omar and Katie are in trouble. Bring weapons. Everyone! Heads up! Might be bots coming for you. They're armed. Get back to the *Raider* for now."

Cass felt like she was taking forever to get to the third level. When she did, she skidded to a stop. Omar and Katie were in the dining area, ducked behind a counter with a half dozen small, squarish mechanicals facing them. Scorch marks on the counter showed where they'd fired on her friends. One of the bots swung around to face her, and she quickly sidestepped away from the door into the corridor just as Zack caught up to her.

He tossed her a weapon. "What's up?"

"Six bots holding Katie and Omar down. They're behind a counter to the right of the doorway. One of the bots saw me but hasn't come out yet. Suggestions?"

"Give me a sec." He tapped his com. "Hopper. This is Zack. We have six bots holding Omar and Katie hostage on level three. Can you stop them?"

"Hopper does not yet have access to those systems. Does Zack need help?"

"No. We'll figure something out. Thanks."

Zack glanced at Cass and shrugged. "Go in shooting? What kind of cover do we have?"

"Tables and chairs to our left, counter to the right. Don't know if the tables will be much help."

"I vote for the counter." Zack readied his weapon. "You go low, I'll go high."

Cass nodded and scrunched down. "Omar, Katie, get as far over behind the counter as you can. Zack and I are coming in fast. On three…"

They ran in, firing at the bots as they went, hitting several. And the bots fired back. One lucky shot caught Cass on the leg as she dove for the counter. "Fardles!"

"You hit?" Zack demanded, a worried look on his face. At least the remaining bots had stopped firing.

"Minor. I'm okay." She glanced at Katie and Omar. "What about you two?" Cass noticed a bloodied towel wrapped around Omar's side. She grabbed another one from a nearby shelf and tied the cloth around her calf.

"Omar got hit in his side. Grazed him. What are these darned things? We weren't even doing anything that would warrant this."

"We don't know what their programming is."

"What about the other teams?" Katie asked.

"I sent them to the *Raider* just in case," Cass said.

"Good call. How many are out there?"

"We took out two or three, but that still leaves a few. Around six total. I wasn't exactly counting. Zack, you think we can flank them from both ends of the counter?"

"Yeah."

Cass glanced at Katie and Omar and handed Katie her weapon. "You're closer to that end than I am and a better aim."

Katie took the weapon and grinned. "Nice of you to finally recognize that."

Cass chuckled. She and Katie often played against each other in the weapons gaming room, and Katie always won. "Just get them for me. And don't hit each other!"

Katie looked to Zack who nodded back at her. He held up three fingers...two...one... They both leaned out and fired at the remaining bots. Sparks flew, and bots went flying. A minute later, the fight was over.

"Cover me," Zack said to Katie.

She nodded and held her weapon at the ready as Zack stepped out. He checked each bot. "Looks like we're clear. But we should get moving to the *Raider* in case more show up."

Weapons at the ready, Katie took point, and Zack took up the rear as they moved out into the corridor. They made their way to the *Raider* with no more incidents, and Annie immediately took charge of both Cass and Omar.

"Take care of Omar first," Cass directed. "I need to talk to Hopper and see if we can't get these bots neutralized." She turned as Hopper entered the ship.

"Hopper?"

"Hopper is sorry Cass and Omar got hurt. Hopper

has stopped the bad bots but needs Zack to help reprogram them." From his quiet tone, Cass knew he was feeling guilty.

"Hopper, we're all right. This wasn't your fault. And we're not hurt badly. Both Omar and I will be okay." She lightly touched his arm. "Honest, Hopper. We'll be fine. Thank you for stopping more from coming."

Annie came up to her. "Your turn, Cass. Let me see your leg."

"I'm fine."

"Cass, you may be in charge of this expedition, but I am medical. You answer to me. Now come."

Everyone chuckled as Annie pointed to the first aid room. Cass raised an eyebrow at her but went into the room. Omar was sitting on one bed, white bandages attached to his right side. "You, okay?"

"Yeah. Grazed me. Nothing major hit."

"But you still need to take care. That sealant needs to do its work," Annie scolded, then turned to Cass. "Up you go. Let me see your leg."

Cass unwound the towel and tugged her pants leg up to her knee. Blood seeped from a dime-sized hole on both sides of her calf.

"Through and through," Annie said. "You're lucky the shot was in a fleshy part and didn't hit the bone." She sealed both holes and wrapped a clean bandage around Cass's leg. "Give the sealant fifteen minutes to work, then you can go. But I want a full fifteen minutes. Not a second less."

"Yes, ma'am." Cass saluted her and leaned against the back of the bed. "We got lucky."

"Yeah," Omar agreed from his bed. "Could have been a lot worse. Is everyone else okay?"

"Yes. Zack's going to help Hopper reprogram the bots so we don't get any more surprises. But I want to know where everyone was and what they were doing when those bots attacked."

"And why they didn't attack us earlier. After all, we've been here a while," Omar said.

"Exactly. I'll have Zack talk to Hopper. See if he knows where they came from."

"And if there are any more."

"Definitely."

"Good. Katie and I would really like to get a better look at that dining area. And I know Annie wants to look more closely at that med unit on the third level."

"As soon as we know the areas are safe. For now, everyone stays put here on the *Raider*, and we let our own bots and drones do the work."

****

Several hours later, after Zack and Hopper determined they were safe, Cass checked in with the other teams who had gotten back to work and then headed to the *Seeker*.

"Cass? You got your ears on?" Ben nearly yelled at her through her com.

Cass startled at the excitement in Ben's voice. "Yeah, Ben. What's up?"

"Girlie, you got to get down here! Now! You're not gonna believe this."

"What? More crystals?"

"Oh, girlie, this is so much better than crystals. You really need to get here. Level four, bow end, port side."

Cass closed the files. "Okay. I'll be there in a sec." What could be better than all those crystals they found?

She strode through the halls, shimmied down the

ladder to the fourth level, and headed toward the front of the ship. When she got there, she found the entire group crowded around the doorway. "What's going on? Do we have a problem?"

They broke away to give her entry. All she saw were wide-eyed smiles. Okay, not a problem.

Then she went into the room. And stopped.

Chapter Twelve

Cass stared at the star fields surrounding her. She moved into the center of the room and spun slowly. "What...?"

"What you're seeing is a star map, girlie. An incredible, moveable, detailed star map."

"I see that. But...where...?" She focused first on one area, then another, but couldn't find a familiar pattern.

Ben pointed to a tiny red spot blinking in the corner to Cass's right. "Near as I can figure, this is us." He swiped his hands over a board, and the red dot enlarged and moved to the center of the room. "And over here..." He pointed at a planet behind her. "That's where Pointe Noir is...or will be. Remember, these charts are a couple thousand years old."

"Your information is being inaccurate," a slightly feminine voice announced, and everyone jumped. "The charts updated are being as I speak."

Cass stared at Ben, who shrugged, wide-eyed. "May I ask who I'm talking to?" Cass spoke up.

"My apologies, madam. My name is being Amaya-an. I am being the partner ship of Mituna-an." That got a lot of "wows" from the group outside. An alien AI that was several thousand years old! Her Delta was barely five years old.

"Partner? Oh. You mean AI. You're the ship's AI."

"A. I?" There was a couple-seconds' pause. "Ah. You will be forgiving myself. I am still being learning your language. Your Delta and Timmons are being most helpful. But I am being sorry. You are being misunderstood. I am not a computational device. I apologize, but I cannot find a word in your language for myself. I am being the ship, and yet I am also being myself."

Cass frowned. If not an AI, what then? "Are you a living being?"

There was a pause. "Not as your language defines that designation. I am not existing outside the ship. I am the ship, and yet I am myself."

Cass wasn't sure what she felt besides surprised, awed, confused, excited, and more all rolled into one. "Okay. We'll let that definition go for now. So you control the ship?"

"Yes. And I apologize for attacking your ship and your people. The protections were automatic, though they were being slower to respond than they should have been. I have neutralized them."

Cass could barely breathe. Her heart sped up. She was talking to the ship. A three-thousand-year-old ship. But she was also wary. After all, this ship had attacked them multiple times. How did she know the AI wasn't damaged or telling lies to catch them unawares? Maybe she'd start with the basics?

"Thank you. Can you tell me what happened to you and your people?"

"Do you want a visual report or verbal?"

"Give me the short version." Cass paused. If this Amaya was still learning their language, she probably needed to be more specific. "Um, an abbreviated verbal version please. And thank you."

"You are most welcome. I am pleased to being speaking with others after being asleep. My sister ship and I and our people were on an extended colonization trip when we were caught between two warring factions. As we attempted to get away, one of the sides deployed a weapon that caused a moon we'd landed on to disintegrate, and we were hit with a sizeable rock, the remains of which I believe you have seen."

"We have."

"My sister ship, Kataya-an, was…changed. I believe she and her people are no longer of this plane. Do you know where Mituna-an is being? She was gravely injured. When I went to sleep, so did she."

"Who is Mituna-an?"

There was a slight pause. "I believe you would be calling her a captain? She is my…I cannot find the word. We are one, yet not one."

"Symbiotic?" Annie asked.

"As I understand that term, possibly. We exist together but can also exist separately."

"What happened to you?"

"I was severely damaged by the opposing factions. There was no time for repairs without endangering the lives of my people more. Those who survived the attack took to the colony shuttles with the protections of the security fliers. We did not know if they made their way to safety before I went to sleep. Complete shutdown was necessary until such time as being safe for them to return to me and do repairs. Is the war being over now?"

"Um, Amaya-an, you might want to sync your chronometer with ours. I'm afraid a long time has passed since you went to sleep."

There was another brief pause, then Amaya-an came back, her voice sounding dejected to Cass. "You were right. Mituna-an could not survive such a long sleep."

Cass glanced at Annie, who shook her head, sorrow on her face. "I'm sorry to tell you, but I believe we found the remains of your captain in her cabin."

"That is…not unexpected. She, too, was severely damaged in the fight." There was a longer pause. "May the Great Nine bless her."

Cass bowed her head in response to the ship's obvious grief. She wondered if Delta would feel the same if something ever happened to her. A quick glance at Zack and Ben and the others. Would anyone?

"We left Mituna-an in her quarters. Are there some sort of rites you would have us perform for her?"

"No. If you would transfer her remains to the morgue in the wellness center, I will tend to her. As I am without, please to be calling me Amaya."

"Is the *an* part of your name a designation?"

"When we are partnered with a physical captain, we both become *an*. There are other designations for others. But my people. Where are they being? I cannot find a record of them in your databases."

"I'm sorry, Amaya. We're not even sure who your people are. Can you show us?"

The star field disappeared, replaced by several figures. They were almost the same size as the people with Cass, and bipedal as she had said, and had arms, hands, and fingers, but that was where the similarities ended. Their features were feline in appearance. And they had tails.

Cass turned to the others. "Have any of you ever seen beings like these? Or read about them?"

133

There was a collective shaking of heads. With one exception.

"Hopper knows. Hopper has seen."

Cass—and everyone else—turned to see Hopper at the back of the group. A space opened up for him to walk through, and he shuffled up to Cass.

"Hopper, you know who Amaya is talking about?" She studied him. He seemed different, but she couldn't quite figure out why. He looked the same…and yet not. Almost as if he stood straighter.

"Hopper has seen. Long time ago. Far away. Bad memories. Good beings, but held as slaves. Bad man hurt Hopper. Beings helped Hopper. Bird ship gone."

Bird ship? Could he be talking about the *Phoenix*? For the first time in seven years, Cass felt a tiny spark of hope and excitement. Had the answer to her dreams been with her the entire time in Hopper? "Hopper, do you remember where you met these beings?"

Hopper tilted his head to look up at her, a frown of fear on his face. "Hopper does not want to remember. Bad times. Bad people. Good beings saved Hopper from bad people." He ran from the room.

Cass moved to go after him, but Zack held her back. "Let me."

"But…"

"You're too intense right now, and you know it. I'll go."

"But…"

Ben laid his hand on her arm. "He's right, girlie. Let him do this."

Cass really didn't want to admit that either one of them was right, but they were. She gave Zack a curt nod and turned back to Amaya.

"Amaya, can you bring up the star charts for where we are right now?"

The starscape appeared once more. "I have updated my records with the information from your Delta and Timmons. What you see now is current."

"Can you trace your route from here back to where you originated?"

"I can."

A red line appeared just as all sorts of alarms started sounding.

"Proximity alert. Proximity alert. All hands to stations," sounded over the ship.

Cass looked at her people. "You heard her. Get to your ship. Now. And lock down. I'll take *Seeker* out. Go!"

Chapter Thirteen

Cass dashed for the landing bay. "Delta! Report!"

"There's nothing showing on my sensors, boss, but that could be because I'm inside Amaya. Though I have been chatting with Amaya. Her sensors are the ones going off."

"Are hers stronger than yours?"

"Significantly."

"Which means whoever is out there might be pretty far away." Cass reached the bay and the ship. "Be prepared for takeoff."

"Will do."

Cass ran in, sealed the door, and headed for the bridge. "Delta? You ready?"

"Powered up and ready."

"Let's go." She buckled into the pilot's seat and waited for the *Seeker* to take off. "Ben? You got everyone in?"

"All but Zack and Hopper. We're good."

"Stay where you are for now but keep security up. Let me see what we're up against first."

"Will do. But it's probably nothing. A glitch in the system. Timmons isn't detecting anything."

Cass studied the readouts on her panel as the *Seeker* took off, but there was nothing. "Delta, can you connect with Amaya and see what we're dealing with?" Though she was pretty sure she knew.

A moment later, a blip came up on the extreme edge of her screen. "Delta, can you enlarge?"

"That *is* enlarged, boss. They're at least ten days out standard speed."

"Can you tell how many?"

"Amaya's sensors say six ships deployed in a standard search pattern."

Six? Wow. Ian wasn't fardling around. "Okay, we have a little breathing space. They'll be slow since they're searching. Ian knew I was in this sector earlier so he's looking here but doesn't know exactly where we are. Maybe."

"Boss, do you want me to contact station security?"

Cass snorted. "You can, but they're too far away to be of any use and probably won't come anyway. Too many of them are on Ian's payroll. Ben? You all can relax a little. The blip is Ian, but we have some time before they get here. So…everyone, work as fast as you can. I want as much recorded and inventoried as we can before they get here. Or, Zack, if you and Hopper can get the ship mobile, we can fly her into Pointe Noir. That would be even better."

"Will do what we can, Cass," Zack said. "What about setting out buoys as perimeter alarms?"

"Not a bad idea," Cass said. "I'll take care of them. You have your assignments."

Cass took the *Seeker* around Amaya so she could take a closer look at the hole in the side and the rock that made it. As she did, she sent out buoys that would act as a kind of security blanket. Once they were all set and connected, they would signal if anything came into the area.

"Delta, could we put a tow line on that rock and get

it out of there?"

"Possibly. That would depend on whether you want to loop the line around—in which case we'd need someone on the inside—or I can try a harpoon."

"That sounds like a better idea. Talk logistics over with the other two ships and get a consensus before we do anything."

"Both ships agree with my assessment. We are ready to commence when you give the word."

"The word is given. Get into position and proceed."

She watched as Delta moved the *Seeker* into position and the harpoon anchors shot out, spearing the giant rock. Slowly and surely, the *Seeker* hauled the boulder from the wreckage. Cass thanked the stars that lack of gravity made the task easier. Once clear of the ship, they towed the load toward the asteroid field, stopping well clear of the other flying debris. "Delta, put on some speed to match the larger rocks, then release ours."

"Understood."

As soon as the tow lines released, Delta flew the *Seeker* up and away from the rock, and their rock moved into orbit with the others.

"Okay, take us back to the landing bay," Cass said. She took those few minutes to look over the files Delta had for her once again, then toggled on her mic.

"Ben? You busy?"

"Yep, but I have time for you. What's up? Please don't tell me you found another derelict." He laughed, and Cass bit back a chuckle.

"No. But can you meet me in the landing bay? We should be there in a couple minutes. We need to talk."

"Sounds serious."

"Might be."

"Okay. I'll see you there."

Cass sat back and studied Amaya. The edges of the hole from where they'd towed the rock from sparkled in the darkness, and Cass could swear the gap was smaller than earlier. "Delta, is Amaya repairing the hole in her side?"

"Yes. She said the damage should be completely fixed in five hours, twenty-three minutes. She is also repairing other systems with the help of Zack and Hopper. According to her, she should be flight-worthy in approximately one week."

"Approximately?" Cass had noted that Amaya seemed as precise as Hopper usually was.

"Do you want the exact timing as Amaya stated?" Delta asked.

Cass laughed. "No. The approximation is fine. Thanks. That should be just in time for our friends out there to become an issue." There was a slight bump as the *Seeker* settled into the bay, and Cass unstrapped her belt.

She exited the ship to find Ben waiting for her.

"What's up?"

"Ian. He's on his way."

He shrugged. "Figured as much. How soon?"

He seemed a little too blasé about the fact that Ian was coming. But then, she'd known Ian would eventually find them, so Ben had probably figured on that as well. "A week, more or less."

"What do you want to do?"

"Work harder. I set out proximity buoys, but see if you, Zack, and Hopper can talk with Amaya about defenses. I want to be ready."

He nodded. "We'll figure out what we need to do."

****

The teams spent the next week cataloging whatever they could on Amaya, mostly with her help as they couldn't identify all that they found. Cass made use of the time learning Amaya's systems and how to work them but became increasingly frustrated when she discovered she couldn't command the ship without giving up *Seeker,* joining with Amaya, and becoming an *an*.

"I am sorry, Cassandra. But you cannot be a captain of two ships," Amaya said. "Nor can Benjamin. And the others are either tied to their own ships or do not have the necessary skills."

"Amaya, can you fly yourself?"

"I can, but I still need a captain to be at my full capacity. This was a stipulation when we ships were created."

"There were more than you and your sister-ship?" From the corner of her eye, Cass saw Ben shooing the others off, back to work. He motioned to his ear, and she understood their conversation was being transmitted through their com system.

"No. After Kataya was created, there was a…civil disturbance, and the creators were killed in an uprising. After the disturbance was quelled, those who disagreed with the new order were placed on Kataya and me and were sent away."

"So you had a war of your own to get away from. What was the war about?"

"There were two factions. One side believed going out into the stars was wrong. That our people should be…isolated."

"Was there a reason for this?"

"Yes. A few years before we left, our world was visited by…others. They were unlike us in many ways but still bipedal and air-breathers. Unfortunately, they were intent not on contact, but on conquest. They brought illnesses we had no defenses against and killed many of the Masaaki looking for our crystals. Though my people were able to overcome them, eventually, the damage was done. The Isolationists wished for no contact with the outer worlds. The other faction was more of the belief that one group does not represent the whole. They built the sister ships in secret but were found out. Their punishment was to send them out into the stars."

"Sounds like they got exactly what they wanted."

"Yes and no. Unfortunately, we found more warring factions than peaceful ones."

Cass sighed. "Yeah, that seems to be the way of most beings. But you…"

"I am as I was created. I was grown from seed crystals and implanted with what you would term a brain. Unlike your Delta, though, I am the ship and cannot be removed. Though I look different, I am essentially a living being. But I cannot fully function without a biped."

"Understood. I'm just not sure what to do. There are many of my people who will wish to study you. To talk with you. Will you allow us to take you back to our home?" Zack rejoined her. "Hopper?" she mouthed.

"He's okay," Zack whispered, and Cass nodded, drawing her attention back to Amaya.

"I am not comfortable with that idea. My preference would be to return to my home. There may still be others of my people there. You seem nice, but you are not my people. There are many beings on your Pointe Noir, but none are Masaaki. I would really like to go home."

Cass blew out a long breath she didn't know she'd been holding. "I understand, Amaya." And she did. How could she not? Alone, in a strange place—and time—surrounded by strangers. She'd want something familiar too. What she found even more interesting was Amaya saying no. Delta would never say no to her. She would obey every order, no matter how odd, as long as the order didn't involve mortal danger—like flying into the sun type of idiocy. But Amaya was reluctant to the point of refusal. Because she didn't have a captain directing her?

"But can you get to your home without a captain?" Zack asked.

There was a minute pause. "I do not believe so."

"Can you take on a temporary captain?" Cass asked.

"I do not know. A temporary one has never been done. When I join with a captain, the joining is supposed to be permanent until the ninth level of life has occurred, as with Mituna."

"Ninth level? Oh. You mean until the captain dies."

"Yes."

"What about you, Amaya? Can you die? I mean, you've been here for three-thousand years. Can you reach the ninth level?" Zack asked as he moved closer to Cass. Not quite touching her, but definitely close enough for her to feel the heat from his body. A heat that she welcomed.

"Yes, and no. The ninth level for me is only achieved through complete change, as what happened to Kataya."

"So a catastrophic incident is the only way you

can...achieve the ninth level?" Cass found that interesting. After all, ships deteriorated over time. Even in space, vessels broke down after being hit by space dust or junk, through deteriorating orbits leading them to burn up or crash. Many incidents could—and did—happen to destroy a ship. But, Cass had to keep reminding herself, Amaya was a living being with the capability of getting out of trouble—most of the time.

"But a temporary captain might be possible? What about someone like Zack?" Zack startled and stared at her, a slight frown on his face. Cass was trying to figure out how to get Amaya home. If not Zack, who? Her? But could she give up Delta and *Seeker*? If she was understanding this right, she'd have to in order to be one with Amaya. And did she want to be joined? What exactly did that mean?

"Zack is an engineer. An excellent one, but—"

"But I am not a captain," Zack said. "Have others who were not captains taken over?"

"I do not know. We never tried as we were the first ships and Mituna was my captain from the beginning. And I would still want to return to my home. Would any of you wish that?"

Go to an unknown area of space with a sentient ship to a world no one had ever heard of? That wasn't a trip Cass was comfortable with. Just like Amaya wasn't comfortable staying here. "Amaya, would you consider staying so my people could look you over and learn from you?"

A longer pause. "That would be a possibility. But can you guarantee my safety? I do not wish to be...dissected."

Cass snorted, though she thought hard about what

Amaya said. Could she guarantee her safety? Probably not, but she'd darned well try. "You will not be. I have placed a claim on you, which means that technically, I own you, but no one, not even my own people, will do anything to you without my permission. And I would not allow them to do so without yours. But this would give you time to look for a suitable captain. When you have found one, you would be free to go."

"That is an acceptable compromise. Though I do not like this *ownership* you speak of."

"Neither do I now that I know who and what you are. But unfortunately, your autonomy may not be recognized by others without that."

"Understood."

"But that doesn't get us any closer to figuring out how to get you back," Zack said. "Hopper and I have done pretty much all we could. Amaya has taken over most of the repairs, and even the hole in her side is much reduced."

"I believe if Delta and Timmons have the ships place tow lines on me, they can guide me under my own power. My systems are already nearly back to normal, thanks to the efforts of Hopper and Zack."

"Then that's what we'll plan on."

"What about this small fleet of ships coming?" Amaya asked. "They grow closer every day, and I understand you are in conflict with them."

"Oh. Yeah. Ian." Cass sighed. "The man in charge of that fleet is…not a good person. If he has his way, he will take over ownership of you, and trust me, he will have no problems dissecting you."

"Then we must do what we can to discourage him."

"We're going to try. Thank you, Amaya, for talking

with us."

"Our discussion was my pleasure. You and your teams are acceptable to me. I will teach you what I can."

"That would be amazing." Cass felt better now that she and Amaya had reached at least some sort of an accord. "Zack, I'm heading for the bridge. Are you sure Hopper is okay?"

Zack gave her a puzzled frown. "He is, but there's something odd going on with him. Almost as if…" He shrugged. "I don't know. I can't put my finger on what, exactly, but he's different somehow."

"I noticed that too. We'll keep an eye on him. Where are you heading?"

"Back to the engine room. Hopper said he wants to show me something." He took her hand and smoothed his thumb over the back, sending tingles through her. "I know we need to talk, but we haven't had a lot of time."

"We do, but first, tell me what you think about this *an* stuff."

"You're wondering if you should give up *Seeker* and become captain of Amaya."

"I am. I mean, look at this place! This ship is amazing. And to be captain of a vessel this…powerful." She shook her head. "But look at what I'd have to give up. I'd probably have to stop searching for my parents."

"Probably."

"And you." Cass wasn't happy with that possibility.

"Most likely." He drew her into a hug. "How would you feel about that?"

He seemed to be anxious to hear her answer, his grip a little stronger than usual. Was there still an *us*? Even after what she did?

"I don't want to lose you. But I need to find my

parents. Can you understand that?"

He sighed and dropped his arms. "I can. But we really need to talk. About a lot of things."

"We will. For what it's worth, I am sorry."

"I know. But what you did hurt, Cass. I thought we had more trust between us."

"We do. I don't know why that file bothered me so much. Ben told me I needed to look at your background more closely, so I did."

"Ben told you?"

"Yeah. But it's done. Are we okay?"

Zack sighed. "Yes? Maybe? We'll talk. Later." He gave her a quick peck on the cheek and took off. Cass touched her cheek where he'd kissed her. Maybe they could get past this issue.

Cass headed for Amaya's bridge, the lack of sleep starting to catch up with her, but they had to get a lot done before Ian showed up. She settled into the pilot's seat. At least this one didn't try to envelop her. She glanced back at the captain's seat. There was no way she'd ever sit in that one, but a part of her wished she could.

Cass turned back to the console and tried to remember what Amaya had been teaching her about the controls. The smooth surface was so different from her own, and instructions were in the Masaaki language—which she was not learning as well as some of the others. If they could just get the ship completely repaired and headed back toward Pointe Noir, that would solve a whole lot of problems. She stared at the controls, her eyes going bleary…her head dropping…

****

Cass jumped upright, twisted around, and slammed

into something hard and unyielding. Strong hands caught her as she aimed a fist at whatever was there.

"Whoa! Cass! It's me! Zack!"

Cass slumped down onto the chair she'd been dozing in. "Don't creep up on me like that!"

"I wasn't aware I was creeping. Hey, are you okay?" Zack asked as he massaged her shoulders.

Cass rubbed a hand over her face. "Yeah. Just…exhausted. Frustrated. Jumpy."

"Yeah, I got that." He sat down across from her. "I'm sorry I startled you. I didn't realize you were dozing."

"It's okay. I'm just…"

"Tired. Like all the rest of us."

"Yeah. We all could use a break."

"I was hoping you'd say that. Annie suggests a few hours off." He held up his hand to forestall her arguments. "A couple hours aren't going to hurt us and may help us. We're all beyond tired. Even Hopper is showing signs."

"Oh. Well, if Hopper is, then we definitely need rest." She gave him a tired grin.

"Good. I'm glad you agree. By the way, have you looked at Hopper lately?"

"Not really. Why?"

"He is definitely different. Almost as if he's changing."

"Changing how?" Cass remembered she had thought he seemed different the last time she'd seen him.

Zack shrugged. "Nothing specific. He's just…been looking me in the eye when he talks to me. And he's not always talking in third person anymore."

"Do you think he's okay?"

147

"Yeah. Maybe he just needed this treasure hunt to come into himself." He shook his head. "Anyway, Omar and Katie are setting up a special meal for us all in Amaya's mess hall."

She pushed against his chest…his incredibly broad, solid chest. "You can let me go now."

"Sorry." He shook his head as if surprised he was still holding her. "Actually, no, I'm not. Cass, you hurt me, a lot, but you have to know how much I care for you."

"I know. And I do. Zack, all I can say is I'm sorry. Again. I'll keep saying so until you believe me."

He leaned down and pressed his lips to hers until she opened to him. The kiss seared her from head to toe and back up again. When he pulled away, the loss went beyond physical, though he still held her in his arms.

"I believe you. And I forgive you."

She laid her head against his chest, listening to his steady heartbeat. "Thank you."

Then she pulled back. "I could use a drink. You said something about a meal?"

He chuckled. "Yeah. Katie and Omar are putting one together. In an hour. Mess hall." He nodded at her rumpled clothes. "You might want to put on some fresh clothes."

She chuckled. "I think I need a shower too."

"I wasn't going to say anything."

He laughed as she aimed a weak punch at him. "Fine. Go. I'll be there in an hour."

Chapter Fourteen

An hour later, refreshed from a quick sonic shower and a lot of caffeine, Cass headed for the mess hall, the same place where the bots had attacked them. When she got to the cavernous room, all the damage had been cleaned up.

"Hey, Cass, we're down here," Omar called as he poked his head out of a door at the end of the room. "We're using the captain's mess. The room is much smaller. Nicer."

Cass headed that way through the aisle formed by sets of tables set up for nine persons on either side. There were six rows of tables, three on each side of the aisle, and she counted fifty-four tables in all. That meant this room could seat almost five hundred beings. Wow. She couldn't even imagine.

The captain's mess was smaller but still large enough to accommodate all of them with room left over and decorated in shades of cream, tan, and green, with three tables that seated nine each. Omar and Katie had done an impressive job fixing the room up, though in the cold vacuum of space, not much would have deteriorated on the inside, even after all this time.

"They have an obsession about the number nine, don't they?" Cass asked no one in particular.

"Nine is our holy number," Amaya said. "The Masaaki believe that we are each given nine lives, each life a different level, with the ninth being the highest and holiest."

"Thank you, Amaya." Cass took her seat at one table. Zack, Hopper, Ben, Katie, and Omar joined her. The other six sat at another table but still close enough to chat. Cass noted everyone was looking clean and wearing nicer clothing than what they'd been working in over the last few days. Katie and Omar had laid out the food on large platters so everyone could serve themselves. She nodded as Omar poured a drink for each person.

Cass stood, and everyone looked at her. "Before we start, I'd like to propose a toast."

Everyone pushed back their chairs and rose as Cass raised her glass. "To all of you for joining me on this adventure, and here's to a successful outcome."

"Hear! Hear!" they all echoed.

Then Omar raised his glass. "And to Cass for inviting us along!"

"To Cass!" they all yelled, and she felt her face heat.

"Enough! Let's eat!" Cass said to cheers and the scraping of chairs as they all sat back down.

They spent a couple of hours eating, chatting, and laughing but always with the undercurrent of urgency, knowing what was coming. Nobody really wanted to talk about the pirates, but everyone knew they were out there.

****

"How close are those raider ships?" Cass asked Amaya.

"They are two days out."

"They got here faster than we thought. Will we be ready in time?"

"Possibly. Though my repairs are nearly complete,

without a captain, I cannot reach optimum function."

"Okay. We'll just have to figure out what we can do. Thank you, Amaya."

Cass checked in with the teams. Everyone was tired but still excited about the finds. Amaya had been teaching Annie how to work the med units, and Katie and Omar were learning about crystal-based food prep. There was a lot of new technology to absorb and a new culture. Zack and Hopper were learning about new engineering techniques. Everyone was getting more than just credits out of this trip. Even she was studying new star charts and routes. Cass had never heard of beings like Amaya and her people. She was certain historians and scientists from all over would want to study this amazing find.

She went to check on Zack and Hopper. Or maybe just Zack. Though Hopper was important too. She'd made so many trips to the engine room she was surprised there wasn't a rut in the floor.

"You here again?" Zack smiled at her from his position at the engine controls.

"Yep. What're you working on now?" She peered over his shoulder but couldn't read the panel.

"This symbol shows me that all systems are working at optimum capacity. This one tells me how the crystal is faring. And so on. But I told you that the last time you were here. And the time before that." He grinned at her as he took her hand.

"Maybe I'm a slow learner?" She smiled back at him, a tiny flutter in her heart from the warmth of his grip.

"Not a chance." He took both her hands and clasped them to his chest. "But I love seeing you, so I'll explain as many times as you want me to."

She closed her eyes and let his words flow over her, then sighed. "Where's Hopper?"

"Down in weapons control. He's showing Omar and Tom the ins and outs. Katie and Paul already had their lessons. We don't do more than two at a time so Hopper doesn't get leery." He frowned. "But he really is changing, Cass. The others are noticing the differences in him too."

"I'll check on him." She grasped his shoulder. "I'll let you get back to work. Thanks." A quick peck on the cheek and she was gone.

****

Everything was going well. Too well. Especially with Ian on the way. Still, that didn't keep Cass from spending as much time as she could in the star-charting room. Amaya showed her the route she and her people had taken, updated to include as much current information as they could. Unfortunately, there wasn't much since most of what Amaya had was uncharted territory as far as Cass's data went.

"Amaya, take us back to where Pointe Noir is." The stars and planets shifted around until Cass was standing almost on top of Pointe Noir. She stepped one step to the left, away from Noir, but still not close to the Jovani planet. "You see this point here?"

"Yes."

"Do you have any idea what the object is? We've been trying to figure this anomaly out for a long time."

"There is a large gap between when my records end and yours begin. But the anomaly was not there when I arrived in this area, or the point would be on my charts."

"But it is there now. And ancient records on Jovani show the phenomenon to have appeared during the dynasty of Donali II, about the time his successor was born."

There was a pause, then, Amaya continued, "That would be concurrent with when we came to this area. Wait a moment, please. I wonder…"

Could a ship wonder? Cass had never thought about that. But then, she'd never met a sentient ship before. In less than a minute, Amaya was back.

"I believe the anomaly may be the remains of Kataya and her crew. Matter can neither be created nor destroyed but can only be changed. When Kataya and her people ceased to exist, this is what they became. I saw such an occurrence on a much smaller scale back on our home world, when the scientists were learning to create us. Before I was fully formed, there was another, but he did not develop correctly, and the scientists were forced to end him. When they did, I remember seeing a cloud like this."

"Wow. That's amazing. But how does this anomaly send ships somewhere else? Like you did when I first came here?"

"The deterrent is a part of our security that we developed as we flew. We did not wish to harm anyone, so we established a way to repel a possible intrusion without firing weapons. I am sorry my methods harmed you."

"No, you did what you had to." Cass smiled. "In fact, that gives me an idea. Can you show Zack or Hopper how to create these methods, and can they work with *Seeker*?"

"I believe with some modifications they can work with your *Seeker*. And I believe Zack and Hopper have the ability to facilitate the necessary changes. I shall initiate the work. However, I will tell you that the upgrades will not be finished in time to turn away what is coming. And even though the repellents used on you were automatically engaged, since I am now awake, those systems will no longer work. This is why I need a captain."

"Oh. Okay. Thank you. Now, back to your world." She turned back to the star charts. "Show me the path of the *Phoenix* from the records we have."

****

A few hours later, tired from work and following flight paths, Cass knew she needed a break. "Hey, everyone, I'm going to take the *Seeker* out for a bit, just to check on our perimeter."

"Be careful," Zack said. "I know Ian's still a couple days away, but he could have scouters searching. Do you want company?"

Cass thought for a moment. Did she want company? Part of her did, but a bigger part didn't. She needed to think. "No. I'm good. You keep working with Hopper and Amaya. I'll just take a look around and be right back. See you all later."

She took off and did a quick perimeter check, all the while thinking about Zack and her growing feelings for him. "Delta, are all our perimeter alarms still functioning?"

"At optimal levels. Nothing's getting through without us knowing."

"Okay. Thanks."

"Boss, are you all right?"

Cass sighed. Sometimes her AI was just a little too human. Maybe there was some Amaya in her. "Yeah. Just tired. We all are." Plus, there was something she was missing. She knew it in her gut. Something…was wrong about how fast Ian was coming. He was no longer searching. More like he knew where they were. She yawned. She was so tired. Her brain just couldn't catch the answer.

"Get some sleep, boss. I'll keep a lookout."

Cass grinned tiredly. "That sounds like an amazing idea. Let me know if anything happens. I'll be in my bunk."

****

The *Seeker's* proximity alarms blared through the ship. Cass tumbled out of her bunk, landing hard on the deck. She jammed on her boots and dashed for the corridor. "Delta! Report!"

Cass reached the bridge just as a flash streaked across the nose, and they stopped.

"Delta!" She strapped into her seat.

"Six ships surrounding us. Already boarding Amaya. The other teams have gone silent, but Amaya says they are safe, except for Zack."

Zack? Where was he? And why wasn't he safe? And what had happened to the fardling perimeter alarms? Had someone done something? Amaya had neutralized her defenses for them, and they'd never turned them back on. How stupid could she be? She should have had Amaya turn all their defenses back on. Only she didn't have a captain. Cass should have just given up *Seeker* and taken Amaya on. But that was too late now.

"Zack! Where are you?"

"He can't hear you right now, my darlin'."

Her breath caught in her throat.

"Ian! What the…? Never mind. Are my people okay? What do you want, as if I didn't know?" Cass checked her screens. Using Amaya's scanners, she panned three-sixty around the area. Six ships. All nosed toward her. The one closest to Amaya had shuttles and personnel zipping out and over to the ship. Great. Just great. How was she going to get out of this one?

"People?" Ian asked.

She could hear him swearing at someone as her fingers danced over the board. Lights strobed and flashed through the bridge as Cass tried to get an idea of what was happening. Where was everyone? "Yes. Zack is people. Is he all right?"

Why had they taken Zack and not anyone else? She hated the tiny bit of distrust seeping in. But Zack needed credits for his brothers. Though his cut with what they found with Amaya should alleviate that problem. But he hadn't known about Amaya until a few weeks ago. Her thoughts formed a maelstrom in her brain that she couldn't shut down.

"Your concern is touching," Ian said. "He's fine. For now. I assume you checked your screens and see that I have you boxed in. There's nowhere for you to go, love. Sign the claim over to me, and I'll let you and...Zack go."

"Delta," Cass spoke on her ship channel. "Did Zack get that little side project done?"

"Mostly, boss."

"How many?"

"Four."

Cass weighed her options. Four weapons against six ships. Six big, bad ships. "Ian, send Zack over, and we'll talk."

"Cass?" She heard Omar's whisper over the com, and she breathed a tiny breath of relief.

She toggled over to him and hoped she kept the channels straight. "Omar? Where are you? Are you all okay?"

"We're good. We're all on the *Raider* in the fifth landing bay. Ben and Hopper are out in the Amaya somewhere."

At least the majority of her teams were safe. But Zack? And Ben? And Hopper? Fardles. "Okay. Stay where you are. Engage security shields and don't let Ian or any of his people on board the *Raider*. If they come into the bay, take care of them. But stay safe. Please."

"Will do. What about you?"

"I'll figure something out." She toggled Ian back on.

"That's not how this works, darlin'. I get what I want first, then maybe you do."

"I need time, Ian. I'm not the only one on the claim. My partners have to sign off as well."

"Then you'd better be gettin' them to sign. I am not a patient man. You have one hour."

She toggled Ian off. "Delta, prepare to deploy weapons, then go to plan Alpha One."

"Aye, boss."

She flipped to another channel. "Zack. You have your ears on?" She should have settled her issues with him before this. What if he died? What if she died? What if— She cut those thoughts off before they went out of control. But still…if the worst happened and she didn't survive this encounter, would she be happy with her life as it was? Maybe? Could she give up everything, including a relationship with Zack, to keep searching for her parents? Yes, her parents meant a lot to her, but they'd been gone seven years. Zack was here and now…and in the future? But first, there had to be a future. "Zack, are you okay?"

Please, let him be okay.

"Mm-hmm," he muttered.

He was barely audible, and she realized he was trying to stay silent. That had to mean he was a prisoner and not a cohort. Didn't it? "Okay, you can't talk, right?"

"Uhn-uhn."

"Are you on one of their ships?"

"Uhn-uhn."

"Okay. You're still on Amaya. Can you get away?"

"Mmmmm."

"Not sure what that means. I'll take it as a maybe. Okay, here's what I know. Ben and Hopper are somewhere on Amaya. The rest are on the *Raider* in the fifth bay. Can you let me know where you are? Landing bay?"

"Mm-hmm."

"One?"

"Uhn-uhn."

"Okay, not one, two, or five. Three or four?"

"Uhn-uhn."

"Okay. That means lower down. Let's assume they took the first one they came to. So…seven?"

"Mmm-hmmm."

"Okay. Good. You're in seven. That's the smallest of them all, so they can't get all their ships in there. And since I'm looking at six of their ships, I'll assume they just have either shuttles or even just people with jet packs. So…shuttles?"

"Mmm-hmmm."

"Are you on one?"

"Mmm-hmmm."

"Since you can't talk, I'll also assume with a guard."

"Mmm-hmmm."

"Hey! You! What's with all the muttering?" Cass heard a deep voice say.

"Um, my throat's dry. Got any water?" Zack said, adding a cough to his voice.

"Suffer."

"Thanks a lot." Cough. "So what'd you do to piss off your boss and get stuck with guarding me? I mean, you got what, a dozen men swarming this place, and you're here? No treasure for you, I guess."

"What'dya mean? What treasure? Where?"

Cass allowed a small grin as she listened to Zack work the guard. He was good. Her heart beat harder as she realized how much she really did care for him. That she loved him. And would do whatever was needed to have him safe.

"Couple rooms full, just there for the taking. Crystals as big as your head. All colors. Even saw a couple of reds in there. Shielded in a case, but they were there."

Cass could just imagine the guard's eyes bugging out at that. Maybe the lure of rooms of crystals would be enough to get the guard out.

"Where? Where are these rooms?"

"Suffer."

Cass heard a thud and hated to think what that meant, then a splash.

"Okay, there's your damned water. Now where're the rooms?"

"Two levels down, aft."

Cass checked her map of Amaya. Two levels down from the bottom landing bay, aft...and she started laughing. That was the lowest level in the aft section and consisted of the garbage dumps and other nasty stuff. The only *treasure* he'd find there was petrified…waste.

"Sit there." Cass heard the guard's voice command Zack. There was some shuffling, a grunt or two, and then the guard again. "No funny business. I'll be back, and you'd better be here. And just to make sure, I'm setting the static fields on high. You move, you die."

The next sound was the swish of shuttle bay doors opening and closing. Cass chewed her lip. Static fields? On a shuttle? Ian wasn't messing around. A low-level charge would jolt you a bit. Mid-level would knock you out, but a high? That would kill.

"Zack?"

"Yeah. I'm here."

"Are you okay?"

"Yeah. Nothing a little ice and TLC won't fix. But he tied me up pretty good. I might be able to get loose, but I have to be careful how I move. He's got high-level static fields surrounding me."

"Okay. I haven't heard from Ben or Hopper yet. The others are on the *Raider* and safe for now, but time is a factor for them being found."

"Can you patch me through to them? I might have an idea."

"Better be a quick one. We're running out of time."

Cass toggled on the coms between both ships and Zack. "*Raider*, you got your ears on?"

"*Raider* here," Tom said. "We heard. Zack, what do you want us to do?"

"Not sure you can get me out of here since I don't know if there are any guards outside, but you can do some damage and slow them down. The *Raider* has some secret weapons, but you'll need to get outside with the

Raider."

"Zack, if you mean what I think you mean, I'll get caught too," Cass said.

"I know. I'm sorry, but I can't think of any other way."

"Maybe I can. I have enough of our pulse weapons to take out four of their ships. Tom, do you think you can handle the other two?"

"Damn straight," Tom said. "Paul, Meri, and Omar are going outside. They're going to try to get to Zack and find Hopper and Ben. I'll help you take down those ships."

"Okay," Cass said. "Here's what we're going to do."

"Cass, if I may?" Amaya cut in on their conversation.

"Yes, Amaya?"

"I believe I can be of help to you."

"In what way?"

"Without a captain, I cannot fire lethal weapons, but Hopper has designed and implemented deterrents to my specifications. I can initialize them both internally and externally. Unfortunately, with the internal ones, I cannot distinguish between your people and the intruders."

"Folks, what do you think?"

"External," Omar said after a moment. "If you can stop people from coming in, we can take care of the rest."

"I don't want any of you taking risks," Cass said as she ran back through her ship. She got to the weapons room and loaded all four of their EMT bombs. Fortunately, they were neither large nor heavy but still took a lot out of her to get them loaded. "I don't want you hurt."

"Cass, they're trying to take Amaya from us. We will not let that happen," Annie said. "She is our friend."

"Yes, she is," Cass agreed. "Okay, folks, let's do this. Amaya, initialize deterrents, external only. Omar, you and Donnie head for the bay where Zack is being held and see if you can get him released. The rest of you, arm up and spread out. Take them down easy if you can, with force if you can't."

"Hopper can free Zack," Hopper said, breaking into the conversation.

"Hopper! Where are you? Are you safe?"

"I am hiding in the bay. They do not see Hopper, but Hopper sees them. I can get Zack free."

Cass noted his use of "I" as Zack had told her. He wasn't quite done with third person, but there was a definite change. But why? She shook her head. She didn't have time to wonder about that now. "Hopper...I don't want you to get hurt."

"I appreciate Cass's concern. I will be safe. Zack will be safe."

Cass sighed. She couldn't stop him from her position. "Okay. Just be careful. The rest of you, get those pirates who boarded Amaya."

"What about you?" Omar asked.

Cass blew out a breath as she raced back to the bridge, then grinned. "I've got a few tricks up my sleeves. Tom, you get the *Raider* outside. Take the two pirates closest to Amaya. I'll get the ones port, starboard, and aft of me. I'll wait until I see you."

"Got you."

"Okay, folks. In five...four..."

Cass hated waiting, but there wasn't anything she could do until Tom showed up with the *Raider*. What was only about three minutes sure seemed like a lifetime. But as soon as Tom left the bay, Ian would know something was going on.

"I'm ready, Cass," Tom said as the *Raider* emerged from Amaya.

"Delta! Deploy weapons!"

The little ship shuddered as all four weapons shot out. At the same time, she saw *Raider* come up behind the other two ships and fire.

"What the…?" Ian yelled over the com unit.

Chapter Fifteen

She could hear Ian swearing before he was cut off and all his ships went dark. "Take that, you fardling bastard. Tom, are you okay?"

"Yep. Took a couple hits, minor damage."

"Okay, let's get back on board Amaya and help out where we can. Amaya, let us back on."

"Done."

Cass landed back in her original bay, grabbed a laser weapon, and took off at a run. "Where is everyone?"

"Heading for Zack and Hopper," Omar said. "Met some…resistance." Cass could hear laser fire.

"Do what you can, Omar. I'm heading for the bridge."

"Cass, this is Zack. Hopper got me free. I'm heading out to help the others. There was only one other guard in the bay, and he's been taken care of."

"Okay. Meet me at the bridge. Is Hopper all right?"

"I guess so. He took off like he had red crystal in his system. Said he had something special to do. I don't know where he is."

"He is here with me," Amaya said. "I am now Amaya-an and in full control."

Cass skidded to a stop. "Amaya-an? Who? How?"

"Later, Cass. We are busy."

Cass heard Hopper's voice, but he didn't sound like Hopper. "Hopper?"

"He is now Hopper-an," Amaya-an said. "The way to the last landing bay is now clear for you. All others have been taken care of."

"Everyone, report!" Cass said.

"Tom here. I just landed in my original bay."

"Omar here with Donnie. We're good. The pirates all just went…down. Don't know why. They're still breathing, but…out cold."

"Same here," Annie said along with the other teams.

"Gather them all up and haul them to bay seven." There was one person who hadn't checked in. "Ben? Where are you?"

No answer.

"Has anyone seen Ben?"

A chorus of "no's" came back to her.

"Amaya-an, can you locate Ben?"

"He is not on board this ship."

"What? Where the… Ben? Ben! Amaya! Do you know where Ben is?"

"I do."

"Is he safe?"

"I believe so."

"Okay, we'll get him as soon as we can."

Cass reached the seventh bay where her teams were bringing in the pirates and dumping them into two shuttles. "Paul, Tom, disable those shuttles for now and engage mid-level static fields for them."

"Yes, ma'am."

Zack helped the others dump the unconscious pirates on the shuttles. She noted that he had multiple bruises on his face and a split lip and wasn't moving too fast. She ran to him and clasped him to her until he grunted and she let him go. "Are you all right?"

"I will be."

She stroked his undamaged cheek. "Wish we had time…"

He nodded. "Where's Ben?"

Cass shrugged and shook her head. "Amaya-an says he's safe for now."

Zack gripped her shoulder. "We'll find him and get him back."

Frustrated, Cass sighed and headed over to the shuttles. "You got them all yet?" There were at least a dozen pirates sealed up in the shuttles.

"We think so," Omar said. "Amaya-an pretty much let us know where each one was." He frowned at Cass. "Hopper?"

"I know. I'm going to go see what's going on. Make sure they're all secure and set a guard or two. Annie, do you need help with the injured?" Though when Cass glanced around, there weren't any serious injuries, just a few minor burns and bruises.

"No. We got this." She waved Cass off. "Go."

Cass turned when Zack joined her. "Go with Annie."

"I don't want to leave you."

Cass closed her eyes for a moment, then opened them again. "I know. But you're no good to me in your condition. Go with Annie. I'll be okay. And I'll see you soon."

He paused a long moment, but he nodded and joined Annie and the others.

Cass headed for the bridge. When she got there, she saw Hopper sitting easily in the captain's chair. But a vastly different Hopper than the one she knew. This one was wearing a clean black two-piece, high-necked suit with triangular insignias on the collar and sleeves and polished ankle boots. And he was looking directly at her.

"Hello, Cassandra."

"Hopper?"

He grinned at her. "Technically, I'm Hopper-an now."

"But…how?"

He sighed. "Full explanations will have to wait until later. We still have those pirates to take care of, and we need to get this ship home."

"But…?"

He shook his head, then looked directly at her. "My past is a long story, Cass. Short version, as soon as I boarded Amaya-an, I knew exactly what she was and what to do. I've been on a ship like her before. She and her sister ship were not the only ones built. There were at least two others that I know of. But my experience was a lifetime ago. If you can accept that I have changed, we can work to save us all from Ian."

Cass studied him closely. This was Hopper. Not the Hopper she knew, but still…Hopper. She had to trust him. The answers to the million-plus questions she had would have to wait. "Ideas?"

"We leave. Amaya-an is under full power now. Red crystal power, I might add, so we don't need to worry about the McClarens."

"Are…are you really all right, Hopper?"

This time he gave her the shy smile she knew. "I am better than all right. I'm…myself again. And more. By fixing Amaya-an and then blending with her, she in turn fixed me. The changes just took a few days to set in, but we're good now. Shall we prepare to go?"

"You're the captain," Cass pointed out. Which was

so strange. Hopper. No, Hopper-an was the captain of this amazing ship. She was sad about the loss of the old Hopper but also incredibly happy for him. For the first time since she'd known him, he looked…at ease.

"Yes, but you're still in charge of this operation. I would never think to take over."

Cass smiled at that. "Okay. Zack? Are you all done down there yet?"

A corner of the view screen at the front of the bridge changed to show the landing bay where Zack was climbing out of one of the shuttles. He grabbed the edge of the door and just stood there for a moment. "Zack? Are you all right?"

He looked up at the ceiling and nodded. "I'm fine. What do you want us to do?"

"Send the pirates out into space on two of the shuttles. Keep the rest for us. Then secure yourselves. We're about to take off."

"What about Ben?" Zack asked.

"No one knows where he is, and Amaya-an says he's not on board. Do you think Ian took him somehow?"

"Let me check. One of the pirates is coming around. Might be able to get him to talk."

Cass turned back to Hopper. "Hopper-an, do you have any idea where Ben is?"

He shook his head. "No. Though…" He closed his eyes for a moment, then opened them, sadness in his face. "There is a file you need to see and hear."

"What?"

Another corner of the screen changed, and Cass saw Ben sitting in one of Amaya-an's officer's cabins. He was talking to someone over a connection.

Then Cass heard Ian's voice.

"You sure you have the alarms turned off?"

"Yes. You have the coordinates, and I deactivated the alarms and security. You can come in any time. Use the lowest landing bay. I rigged that bay so nobody will see you coming in there. Be aware that the *Raider* is on level five. I have people in there, so stay away from there. I'll secure that bay."

Cass sat hard in the nearest chair, her heart pounding, her breath gone. "Ben? I… No."

Zack came onto the bridge. "What's going on? Cass? What's wrong? Is that Ben? Where is he? The guard wouldn't tell us anything."

"Watch," Hopper-an said.

The view switched back to the landing bay where they saw the first group of pirates come on board and watched as Ben took one of the personal flyers and left.

Zack sighed and turned sorrowful eyes to her. "I can't say I'm surprised. I've suspected him of being in with Ian for a while."

"He left us? He went over to Ian? But why? Why would he do that?" Cass asked the questions but didn't expect an answer. Her stomach roiled, and she felt as though someone had shot a laser straight through her heart. How could Ben do this to her? He was her godfather. Her friend. Her parents' friend. She'd trusted him like no one else. He was everything to her. How? Why?

"We will be arriving at Pointe Noir in six hours, fourteen minutes," Hopper-an said.

Cass snorted. At least that part of Hopper hadn't changed. She watched as two shuttles full of unconscious pirates went out. Beside the leftover shuttles they also kept the personal flyers. Cass figured they were adequate compensation for the hassles Ian had put her through.

She turned to Zack. "What do you know about Ben? Why would he do this?"

****

Zack shook his head. "I have no idea why. I know I'd never do something like this, and you've known Ben far longer than you have me. I couldn't betray you like that. Nor Amaya-an and Hopper-an. Or the teams."

"But...?"

"But I believe he was part of the group that took out my family's farm. I've been...investigating him for some time."

Shock froze her. "Why wouldn't you tell me? I've known Ben my whole life. I trusted him. He's..." She bent over, trying desperately to draw a breath, feeling sick.

A file came up on the screen. "Hopper-an?"

"This is coming from Delta. She says you need to see this."

Ben appeared on the screen. "Hey, girlie. If you're seeing this, then that means I'm on Ian's ship and...you're not. I'm sorry, girlie, but this had to be. That file you had on Zack? Well, what you saw wasn't exactly accurate. I knew you'd look into him. His family was taken out by the McClarens. The raid wasn't personal. Zack's family just had a piece of land they wanted. You see, girlie, I'm not exactly who you think I am. Seems like Pop had a penchant for McClaren women. When Ian moved out here, he looked me up. I kinda been working with him. But I'm watching out for you, like I always do. That was my one stipulation. I needed you to be safe. And you and the others will be as long as you turn the entire claim over to Ian. I might even be able to talk him into giving you a cut of the profits. That's the best I can do, girlie. I'm sorry."

The view shifted, and she saw Ben sitting in a com chair, Ian beside him, grinning at her. "Now, girlie, I know you're not going to give up Amaya easily, but you're gonna have to. I rigged a few surprises, and if you want everyone to be safe, you'll sign her over to me. As soon as this message appeared, I received a notice, so I know you're seeing my file. Sign the claim over to me, and we'll let you all go free. You have one hour. Oh, and your little bombs may have paused us, but we had taken precautions. We will be fully powered before you can get clear. One hour."

Cass shook her head, then rose and headed toward the door, stumbling. Zack caught up to her before she reached the exit. "Cass?"

"I…I need…" Tears streamed down her face, and Zack wasn't sure she knew where she was.

He looked back at Hopper-an who waved him off and nodded.

"You take care of her, and I'll take care of everything here," Hopper said.

"What do you mean?"

"I'll make sure everyone is safe and see what I can do about Ben's surprises. Amaya-an might be able to track where he's been lately and see what he did."

"I'll be back as soon as I can get her settled. I think she's in shock."

"Take her to the *Seeker*. She'll feel safer there."

Zack nodded and, grunting in pain, hauled Cass into his chest, hugging her tightly, shock at the truth of Ben's betrayal roiling his stomach even though he'd suspected. But the disloyalty had to be worse for Cass. Ben was her family. You don't betray family. "You need a good stiff drink. Or three. Come on."

She shook her head. "No. Can't. Too much going on. I need to... Um... I have to... Surprises. Ben rigged surprises. We have to find them. Save the crew. Save Amaya-an."

"You need to process. And you have to figure out what's next as far as Ben is concerned. Hopper-an and the others will take care of what's needed here. Amaya-an can direct them. Come on."

She fought him. Not hard, but she resisted. "No, Zack. They're my responsibility. The crew, the ship. Everything. I have to make this right. I need..." She looked up at him with red-rimmed eyes. "Why would he do this to me, Zack? Why?"

"I don't know, babe. I don't know. Come on. Give yourself a few minutes. That's all. Just a few."

"You're hurt."

"I'll be fine. Come on."

Keeping his arm around her shoulders, he led her to her ship. "Delta, seal the door, please."

"Done. And you'll find what you are looking for in the galley." Zack heard the voice in his earbud rather than over the com and blessed Delta's discretion.

"Thank you."

Zack guided her to the galley. Sitting in the catering unit were two blue beers. "Sit. Drink."

Cass moved like she was in a daze, and he figured she probably was, though tears swam in her eyes. She sat on the bench and held the drink like she wasn't sure what to do with the beer. Zack gently guided the glass to her mouth.

She gulped the drink down, then held the empty out.

Zack gave her the second one. "Delta?" he whispered.

"Yes?"

"Keep them coming."

"I can add a mild sedative if you think that would help, along with an analgesic and make the next drink nonintoxicating."

Zack thought about adding the meds to make her sleep, then shook his head. "No. She needs to deal with this. Putting her out will just make what's she's feeling worse. But I'll keep her here on *Seeker*. She probably feels safer here."

The catering unit pinged, and a third drink appeared. Zack took the glass out and handed it to Cass, taking the second empty one from her. She drank that one down as quickly as she had the other two. Zack was quite sure she hadn't tasted a drop.

"Cass? What do you want to do?"

"Kill Ian McClaren. And Ben. And forget I ever knew either one of them."

He understood that kind of rage and the need for vengeance. But he'd learned over the last few months that revenge was not the way to go. "Okay, but before that."

She took a deep breath, exhaled hard, raised her head, and straightened her shoulders. "I need to get to the bridge. Need to talk to Hopper-an and the others."

Zack helped her stand, and he held in a hiss of pain. Definitely some bruised ribs. He fought off the pain. Cass needed him. She was a little wobbly but not too bad. He figured the alcohol would hit her later when she rested. With his arm around her waist, helping her remain steady, they went to the *Seeker's* bridge where she sat in the captain's seat. He took the copilot's seat.

"Delta, patch me through to Hopper-an."

Calling Hopper an *an* still sounded strange to Zack. But even stranger was the new Hopper. He'd gotten used to the man's quirks, and this change—while good—was definitely different.

"Hopper-an here. How are you, Cass?"

"Pissed as hell. Are the others okay?"

"Yes. They are curious as to what happened, but all are well. Annie has tended to minor wounds. You should let Annie tend to Zack's injuries as well."

Zack shrugged, then winced and tried hard not to take a deep breath. "I'm okay."

Hopper-an snorted. "No, you are not. Amaya-an has detected multiple contusions, laser-fire burns, and two cracked ribs. I strongly suggest you get to Annie as soon as possible before she comes looking for you."

"But…" Now that he was resting, he could feel every one of the injuries Hopper-an listed, as well as a few more.

"Zack, Amaya-an has amazing medical facilities, and Annie can heal your wounds quite quickly." Cass glared at him. "Go. I need to discuss some details with Hopper-an. You need to get better. I'll be here when you get back."

Zack sighed. Looked like he wouldn't get any peace until he did as directed. "Okay. Okay. I'm going."

Zack got to the med unit just as Annie did. "Hopper-an told me I should see you."

Annie glanced over him and smiled. "Yep. Wait until you see what I can do. Have a seat."

Zack sat on the end of one of the diagnostic beds as Annie went to a cabinet and took out what looked like a laser gun but with a flat, wide end.

"What is that?"

"According to Amaya-an, this gadget is a diagnostic scanner and healer all in one. Hold still. This might sting a little, but you shouldn't feel any real pain."

She aimed the scanner at his face from just a couple inches away, and he felt a combination of heat and cold and a little discomfort. But nothing bad. And when she moved the instrument away, he licked his now-repaired lip and felt his face. "Wow. That's…amazing."

Annie grinned. "I know. Take off your shirt, and we'll tackle those ribs and other bruises."

With Annie helping him, he managed to get his shirt off, and Annie adjusted the settings on the scanner. A few minutes later, he sat up straighter and took a deep breath. No pain, no evidence of bruising, no nothing. In fact, he felt better than he had in days.

"That's… Wow." He stretched his shoulders. "Thank you!"

"Thank Amaya-an for teaching me about these gadgets. I can't wait to get back and show others. If we can figure out how they work and how to build them, this will change the medical field forever. Amaya-an has an amazing medical library that will take us years to go through." Her mouth turned from a smile to a frown. "We heard about Ben. I can't believe he'd do that to us. To Cass. Is she okay?"

"No. Not really. We need to figure out what to do about Ben and Ian. We don't have much time."

"What are we going to do?"

Zack shook his head. "I don't know. We all need to talk. Can you gather everyone in the captain's mess? I'll get Cass, and we'll put our collective heads together." He glanced at his watch. "We have about thirty minutes left until our deadline."

"We'll figure out some sort of plan. Ian is not getting Amaya-an. We've all agreed to that. The rest..." She shrugged. "Like I said, we'll figure something out."

"Meeting in the captain's mess," Hopper-an said over the com, and Zack knew he'd been listening.

"We're on our way," Zack said. He glanced at the dirty shirt in his hand, then grinned at Annie. "I'll be there as soon as I get Cass."

He headed back to the *Seeker* and Cass. She met him in the corridor outside the bridge.

"Hopper-an and I set up a meeting in the captain's mess. He told me some of the sabotage Ben did. We might not be able to undo them before the deadline, but we can try."

"I know. I was just coming back for you. Let me grab a clean shirt." But before he could, he felt the *Seeker's* engines powering up.

"Delta?" Cass called.

There was no answer.

Zack and Cass ran for the bridge, stumbling when the ship lifted away from the deck.

"Delta? What are you doing?" Cass yelled.

They reached the bridge and slid into their seats. Cass accessed the controls and hit every button, toggled every switch, and pulled every knob she could find. "Nothing! I can't get control!"

"I'll go to the engine room. Maybe I can do something there." Zack unstrapped and ran out, but he could hear Cass calling over the com unit.

"Hopper-an? Amaya-an? What's going on?"

Nobody answered her.

"Hello! Anyone! Can you hear me?"

The big bay doors opened, and the *Seeker* flew out. In minutes, Amaya-an was little more than a tiny dot in the distance.

"Amaya-an?" Zack called. He figured he might as well try too.

Nothing.

"Zack! Are you there?" Cass called.

"Yeah, but I can't get in! There's some sort of forcefield blocking me. Threw me back against the wall."

"Are you hurt?"

"No."

"This is Ben." Ben's voice boomed through the ship. "You should not have taken off. Because of that you have just activated one of my precautions. Please do not go any further, as the settings will increase with each try. I am sorry. But *Seeker* is now under my control. I will have her, as well as the other ships. This is the way it has to be."

"Sorry my ass. Ben, you will be sorry if I ever see your ugly face again." Zack rose from the floor and studied the field. He couldn't fix much from outside the engine room, but there were more ways than one to get in, and he knew them all. He'd bet Ben didn't.

He glanced up as Cass stumbled into the corridor. Her unsteadiness had nothing to do with the drinks she'd imbibed and everything to do with the pitching of the ship.

"Wanted to make sure you were okay. Is this Ben's work?" She pointed at the sparkling field blocking the engine room.

"Yep."

"Any way around that?"

"Don't know yet. I have a few ideas."

"You work from here. I'll go back to the bridge."

"Cass…"

She shook her head and straightened, determination in her face. "I'll deal with him later. Right now, I want my ship back."

"*We'll* deal with him. We both have issues with Mr. Ben Knoble."

"Yeah."

****

Cass got to the bridge and attempted to access her controls. Any controls. But every system was shut out to her. "Zack? Can you hear me?"

"Kind of."

"No good up here. How are you doing down there?"

"Not good so far. I'll let you know."

She heard him grunting and swearing as she focused again on her controls. "Okay, where the hell are you taking us, Ben? And why did you separate us from Amaya-an?"

"Cassandra?"

"Hopper? I mean… Hopper-an? Is that you?"

"Yes. I apologize for kicking you out. Ejecting you was the only way I could think of to save you. Ben has taken control of this ship, though I am working to thwart him. He took what Amaya-an taught us and is using those tactics against us. Unfortunately, I could not get the *Raider* free. Putting you out was not my first choice, but at least you and Zack are free."

"Not quite. Ben set traps for us too. We'll work around them eventually. You take care of Amaya-an and the others. Do not let Ian get you."

"Understood. Be safe, Cassandra."

"You too."

One system she could access was her navigation charts. She might not be able to change where they were going, but at least she could see where they were now. Which was right back at the coordinates where she'd been supposed to deliver the statuette from her last trip. The Dinarian system. The coordinates Ben had given her. The small moon loomed in her view screen, the dead planet below. Cass got out of her seat and crawled under the console. She'd owned the *Seeker* for almost five years and had worked on a lot of the systems. Maybe there was something she could do.

Cass undid the panels and looked at the wiring and plug-ins. "Zack? I'm going to try some modifications up here. How are you coming?"

"I have to give Ben credit. He knew more than I thought he did. I'm almost in, but I've hit some challenging roadblocks."

"That's because he's done all the repairs on *Seeker* since I got her." Cass tugged two plug-ins out and switched them with two others. "Besides, I thought you were the guy who could get around almost any system. Mr. Super-Engineer."

She heard him snort. "*Almost* being the operative word."

Cass plucked another relay and plugged that one into an empty slot. Sparks flew, singeing her in several spots as the ship bucked. "Damn."

She heard Zack swearing a blue streak. "What the hell are you doing up there? You nearly fried me!"

"Sorry!" She shook her hand where the sparks had hit her. "Whatever Ben did, I can't undo from up here."

"I finally got into the engine room, but our options

are not good. He's got some sort of field around the control panel. I can't even get close to the controls."

"Can you get out without getting hurt?"

"Yeah. I managed to disable the fields at the doors, but that's the best I can do."

Cass sighed. "Okay. Come on back. Maybe we can figure out a plan from up here."

"What have you tried?"

She told him.

"Okay. I can try one more idea. I have to get in from the aft bay…a sort of back door Hopper showed me, but we might have to go dark for a minute or two," Zack said.

"Just do what you can. We're blind, deaf, and hog-tied. We have to do whatever is necessary to get out of this."

And that's when events went from bad to abysmal.

A loud explosion thundered through the ship, throwing Cass forward by the force. Sparks flew, and acrid smoke filled the bridge. Cass coughed, and her eyes watered as she struggled for control of her ship. Pain brought her to the edge of blacking out, but she fought the feeling. One arm dangled uselessly at her side, and she refused to look to see what the damage was. She figured since the wound wasn't spurting blood, she didn't need to worry about that right then. Using her other hand, she punched at her console, but there wasn't much she could do. The moon was closer and growing closer by the second, and she had no control. She prayed to all the deities she could think of to help get them out of this one.

"Zack? Are you all right?"

No answer. She couldn't even go see if he was alive but hurt or…not.

The moon spun, filling her view screen. "Zack? If you can hear me, brace yourself!"

Clouds obscured her view, and all she could do was hang on.

The clouds cleared. Land. Water. Lots of water. Rocky mountains covered in snow and ice. Growing larger. And larger.

Chapter Sixteen

Ben paced the length of his cabin, trying to figure a way out of this mess. Using one of the personal transports, he'd snuck off Ian's ship and back on Amaya while Ian was shuttling his men over. This was going to be his ship, not Ian's. But Hopper—no, Hopper-an now—sat in the captain's seat. He hated the way that sounded. No matter how the man looked, he was Hopper. Not Hopper-an. Not normal. And the captain's seat was supposed to be Ben's. But the seat was wrapped around Hopper, and there was no way for Ben to extract him. All his plans were going to hell. He needed to be in charge of the ship. And where the hell were Cass and Zack and the *Seeker*?

He brought up the visual screen to talk to Ian. There was nothing Hopper could do. Nothing anyone could do without Ben's help, including Ian. Ben held all the cards.

If he just knew where Cass was.

"Ian, you got the rest of your ships moving yet?"

He needed to keep up appearances with Ian until he got this all figured out. Everything was going to hell. All his plans to keep Cassie safe, crumbling. But he still had all those lovely credits. Credits that would take him far away from the McClaren family. And with a ship like this, he could go anywhere.

But all his plans were collapsing. He needed to be the captain. Not stupid Hopper. Hopper-an. Hah. That title was his! Ben-an. No, maybe Benjamin-an. Yes. That sounded better.

"Five more minutes. Where are you?" Ian asked with a frown.

"I'm on the Amaya ship heading for the coordinates you gave me. We should reach them in five days."

Ian jumped from his seat and glared at Ben. "What the hell, Bennie? When did you get back on board? Okay. No matter. I'll be about an hour behind you. Is the ship secure?"

"Yes. I have all the other members of Cass's team secured in the *Raider* and our people stationed at the doors and all vital spots on the ship. I just wish Cass hadn't escaped."

"Ah, Bennie, you knew that was a possibility, especially with our girl. The only issue that surprises me is her leaving her people behind. That doesn't sound like her."

"Agreed. Makes me wonder…"

"Forget about her, Bennie. We have what we wanted. The ship is ours, and nobody—not even our Cassie—can take her away. You have any luck getting the captain's seat?"

"Looks like that's not going to happen. There's some sort of symbiotic link between the ship and Hopper. From what I understand, once the link is made, the bond is permanent."

"Unless something happens to the captain, right?"

Ben started. Ian wasn't suggesting Ben kill Hopper, was he? He didn't like the idiot, but he was no killer. "Ian, I did everything you asked for, but I will not kill anyone. That's not part of our agreement."

Ian snorted at him. "Fine. We'll do this your way.

But by the time I catch up to you, that ship had better be all ours."

"It will be," Ben assured him. Though he had no idea how that was going to happen without serious injuries. But one thing was certain—once he had that captain's seat, there was no way Ian McClaren was taking Amaya from him. The seat and the ship would be his. He just needed to hang on a little longer.

"On second thought," Ian said. "Why don't you turn around and come pick me up so I can be there with you?" Ian nodded with pursed lips. "Yeah, I like that better. Me, bringing in this prize. That would be something."

Ben didn't like the sound of that. "I'm not sure I can turn her around without compromising what I did."

"You'd better try, Bennie. That ship is mine. If nothing else, come to a stop, and I'll catch up."

Ian clicked off and Ben turned to Hopper, who stared straight back at him. The change in the man was unnerving. He looked…beyond normal. Even the color of his eyes, once pale blue, had taken on a greenish tinge, like they were changing color. Ben shook his head. His imagination was running away. If he wasn't careful, he'd imagine Hopper beating him and Ian. That was never going to happen. *Yeah. Right. Hopper.* "I'm going to check on a few details," Ben said to him. "We need to stop the ship."

"I cannot do that with the changes you made. Doing so would compromise too many systems. I may be able to slow down a bit, though," Hopper said.

Ben raised an eyebrow but nodded. That fit with his plans just fine. This ship wasn't Ian's. Amaya was his. "Fine, just keep to the same course."

"Understood."

Once Ben left the bridge, Hopper-an checked on the others as he slowed Amaya-an down. "Omar, can you hear me?"

Hopper waited a minute for Omar to answer. "Hopper-an? Yes. But you're really staticky. I thought they disabled communications."

Hopper-an smiled as he mentally flicked several switches on the *Raider*. Ben had absolutely no idea what Amaya-an and Hopper-an were capable of. And he planned to keep it that way. "Is that better?"

"Yes." Omar appeared on the small screen on the arm of Hopper-an's chair.

"Is everyone okay?"

"Yes. A few minor scrapes and bruises. No serious injuries. Annie's taking care of them. Are you all right? And where are Cass and Zack? Are they okay?"

"Cass and Zack escaped. I was able to eject the *Seeker* before Ian and Ben shut us down. I'm sorry I wasn't able to get you all off. They disabled *Raider* and the bay doors before I could stop them. Since that was Ben's and Ian's ship, I assume they had some backdoors on there that I didn't know about."

"That's okay, Hopper-an. But what are we going to do?"

"For now, sit tight. Ben is on his way to make sure you're secure. Once he's gone, we'll figure out a plan. From what I heard, our destination is five days away. Do you have enough supplies for that long?"

There was a pause. "Yes. We should be okay. Any idea what they plan to do with us?"

Hopper-an heard the tension in Omar's voice. "No. But I believe you are safe for now."

"Okay. Thanks."

Hopper-an clicked off the com unit in the *Raider* and changed to one that showed him the landing bay where the *Raider* was. One armed guard stood at the *Raider*, another at the door to the bay, just outside the office. As he watched, Ben strolled in, acting like he owned the world—and in a way, Hopper-an guessed he did. But not for long.

One part of Hopper-an's brain kept an eye on Ben and the guards while another part—along with Amaya-an—worked on rerouting systems. Ben had rigged his charges like one would a mechanical ship. But Amaya-an wasn't completely mechanical. Which meant she and Hopper could do what no other ship could. They moved switches and systems around subtly so no one would see any problems until it was too late. The changes might take him a few days, but they would regain control.

He set a warning alarm off in the engine room, which had Ben running for there. Hopper-an watched and listened as Ben yelled at the guards in the room.

"What the hell happened? What did you do?"

The wide-eyed guard stared at him. "Nothing, sir. We haven't touched anything. The alarm just went off by itself."

While Ben and the two guards there attempted to shut off the alarm, Hopper-an rerouted several other lines—ones Ben would have seen on the monitors had he been watching. As soon as that was done, Hopper-an cut off the alarm, laughing as Ben and the guards stared at one another with no idea what had happened. But the big question in Hopper-an's mind was why? Why was Ben doing this? He had never trusted Ben, but he knew Ben cared about Cass. So why would he do something to hurt her?

"Amaya-an, can you do a search on Ben? I want all the material you can find."

"With all the other actions we are taking, such a detailed search may take a few minutes."

"That's fine." Hopper-an turned his attention back to Ben and the guards.

"I'll be on the bridge," Ben announced.

"Yes, sir."

Hopper-an clicked off all com units so Ben wouldn't suspect he'd been spying. But in the background, he kept working, making some connections, severing others.

Ben stomped onto the bridge. "What was that alarm?"

"Just a glitch in a minor system," Hopper-an said. "I warned you that changing what you did, even just to slow down, might compromise some systems. The glitch has been taken care of."

"Taken care of? What did you do? You're not supposed to do anything without my permission."

"I'm sorry. Like I said, the glitch was in a minor system. Probably due to the damage Amaya-an sustained. She is still in repair mode."

"How much longer until everything is fixed?"

"Oh, a day or two," Hopper-an said with a smile.

Ben gave him a dubious stare. "Since when do you estimate?"

Hopper-an shrugged. "Must be because of the changes connecting with Amaya-an has done to me. Would you like me to be more specific?"

Ben ran his hands over his head. "No. Just get the repairs done. I want this entire ship fixed before we get to our base."

"The entire ship will be fixed by then," Hopper-an

repeated. Ben nodded and strode off the bridge.

"Omar, this is Hopper-an. We have two days to get our plans in place. There are two guards outside the *Raider*. Unfortunately, I cannot reroute my sticky fields without setting off alarms and other deterrents that Ben set up, or I would take care of them."

"Got it. We'll be ready. Where are the rest of the guards?"

Hopper-an showed the others where the guards were and the best routes to get to them.

"Do you have any weapons?" Hopper-an asked.

"No. Ben took them all. Don't worry. We'll come up with whatever we need and will have weapons once we take the guards out."

"You have forty-one hours, fifteen minutes to prepare."

"Understood."

Hopper-an clicked off the com-system and got back to work. The nanobots who'd been repairing the hole in Amaya-an's side had finished their repair tasks hours ago. She was once again a fully functioning ship and had been since before Ben took over, but there was no way he'd let Ben know that. He reprogrammed the nanobots and sent them off to do their new task—to finish removing what Ben had done. The job would take thirty-two hours, three minutes, but the ship would once again be in their control.

Hopper-an rose from the captain's seat, not needing to be encased to be in touch with Amaya-an. They were one now, and only his death would change that. But Hopper-an had been dead before and came back. He didn't plan on getting dead this time. He headed out, passing a guard stationed outside the bridge.

"Hey, where are you going?" the man growled.

Hopper-an turned to stare at the man. "I am a corporeal being like yourself and have needs. Food, water, to relieve myself. Is this allowed?"

The man sighed. "Yeah, go on. Guess there's nothing you can do. The boss has this place tied down nice and tight."

Hopper-an snorted, then strolled off. They had no clue what he could do, but they would soon learn.

Chapter Seventeen

When Cass woke, she took several minutes to figure out where she was. Okay, she couldn't figure that out at all. She knew what had happened. They'd crashed. But she seemed to be in some sort of—she tried to move to see where she was, then the pain hit her.

"What the effing…?"

"You're awake." Zack leaned over her. "Don't try to move. Not yet."

"Definitely not moving. So much not moving." She closed her eyes against the pain, then opened them again. "Zack?" He had a rough bandage on his forehead, a thicker one around his left wrist, bruises everywhere, and wasn't moving too fast, but he was alive. "What…? Where…?"

"Shh. Let me check you over. You've been out for almost a day and a half. Near as I can figure from this old medical scanner you had on board, you've got a concussion, a dislocated shoulder, more cuts and bruises than I can count, including a nasty gash on your right leg where a piece of the console speared you. I think you also have at least one broken rib."

He ran the scanner over her, shook the contraption, hit the gadget on his hand, and ran the scan again. Then he glanced at the screen, sighed, and tossed the instrument to the side. "What I wouldn't give for one of Amaya-an's scanners. So I'll go with what I saw earlier.

I bandaged you as well as I could, but you shouldn't move any more than necessary."

"You think?" Even taking a breath hurt, but at least she was breathing. "Where are we?"

"On the backside of nowhere. You managed to get us to a moon with breathable atmosphere, but I'm not sure I want to be out there. We landed on what looks like a big mountain from what I could see. Only low lichen-like vegetation on this side along with wind-scoured rock. And by wind scoured, I mean constant gale-force wind. No animal life that I could detect before the sensors went completely dead. Don't know what the surrounding land holds, but probably not much more unless we go over the top. I figure we're on the windward side. We have water from that small pool at the end of the cave. There's a crack in the rocks that the water comes through, so the stream seems constant. The water is drinkable but barely. I'll set up a filtration system of some sort when I can. I haven't taken a lot of time to explore. I found this cave close to where we landed. Looks like this place might have been the beginning of an old mine of some sort that never went any farther. But we're okay for now."

"Wasn't my choice where to go. Ben did this to us. He brought me here once before, so he knew this moon was livable. This whole mountain was probably part of the old mining system. Abandoned years ago. If I ever see him again…"

She struggled to sit, gasping in pain. Zack helped her, but any movement still hurt like hell. Cass tried to take a deep breath, then winced. He sat next to her and leaned his head against the rocks at their backs. She noted the dark circles under his eyes, ones not put there by the crash, and the haggard look on his face from exhaustion. She laid her good hand on his arm. "Okay. What about you?"

"Me? I'm just hunky dory."

"Uh-huh. Truth, please."

He sighed. They both seemed to be doing a lot of that lately. "Concussion. Not as bad as yours, but I've got one hell of a headache. Pretty good gash across my forehead that I managed to tape up. Multiple cuts and bruises. Possible broken wrist."

"I'm surprised you weren't hurt more." She frowned. "Not that I'm complaining, but how did you miss getting blown up? The blast sounded like the engine room took the brunt of the explosion."

"I was already on my way back to the bridge when the engine blew. I was in the corridor, so I was probably in the most protected space in the entire ship. Got tossed around a bit, but nothing really bad. If I'd been in there, I wouldn't be here."

"You hauled me and all this stuff..." She gestured at the camp he'd set up. Mattresses from the cabins. Blankets, pillows, a couple chairs, some small lights. To one side, she saw two containers with bright red crosses on them. Emergency supplies. Behind them, a curtained-off area she assumed was some sort of bathroom.

"How's the *Seeker*?"

Zack grimaced and looked everywhere but at her. "We only have enough supplies for about two weeks. A few days beyond that if we're careful. The catering unit was one of the systems destroyed, and the paste leaked everywhere, so even if I could scrape some up, the mess is unusable."

Cass closed her eyes and chewed at her lower lip as

she realized he hadn't answered her question. The drum concert in her head was keeping time with pain from her leg, shoulder, and ribs. She wasn't sure she wanted to hear the bad news, but she needed to know. "And? *Seeker*?"

"Not good, but we might be able to salvage her." He rubbed at the bandage on his wrist, as if trying to rub the pain away.

"Excuse me?" Cass jerked, then gasped as the pain threatened her consciousness again. "Salvage?"

Zack reached for her, but she waved him off as she clenched her jaws, willing the room to stop spinning and the pain to abate. "You said salvage?"

He shook his head, again, avoiding looking at her. "I'm sorry. Wrong choice of words. No. Not salvage. She's hurt pretty bad, but we might be able to bring her back."

Might? That didn't sound good to her. "So why are we here? And with all the supplies?"

"This seemed to be the best solution. Even though not ideal, this location is protected and safer than out there. *Seeker* might be fixable, but she's got a lot of holes. And the weather out there isn't nice. But first, you need some food and some rest."

"Food, I'll agree to. But rest? According to you, I've been asleep for a full day plus."

"Yes, but you are healing. If you'll let me, I'll look at your shoulder again, as well as your leg."

Just then, Cass realized she was wearing nothing more than her bra and panties, and heat suffused her face. "Um…"

Zack grinned at her. "I had to take care of you."

She snorted. "And I'll bet you hated every minute."

193

He got serious. "Another time, another place, I'd have enjoyed seeing your body. But here? Now?" He shook his head. "Your injuries were bad, Cass. Really bad."

She touched his arm. "Thank you. Okay, do your worst." She was excruciatingly aware of him as he helped her sit up straight, but the pain had her gasping and not from the sight of his muscles.

"I'm sorry. Let's look at your leg first." He struggled to take care of her one-handed. After he fumbled the bandages a third time, Cass gently grasped his good hand.

"Zack, let me look at your wrist."

"What? You're a medic now?"

She gave him a one-shoulder shrug. "About as much as you are. When you're out here alone, you learn skills you need to survive . Now, let me see."

He held out his arm, and she unwound the rough bandage. "Can you wiggle all your fingers?" He did, and she nodded. She probed his wrist, noting the bruising and swelling—and the way he winced. "Okay, I don't think your wrist is broken but badly sprained. However, I think we should immobilize the joint just to be safe. Can you get the first aid kit for me, please? Let's see what we can do."

When he returned, she made him sit down on the second mattress and face her. "Give me your hand."

With much wincing and swearing on both their parts, Cass managed to get Zack's wrist immobilized. He sat back, sweat beading on his forehead as Cass collapsed back against her pillow. "Blast it all."

"Yeah. Not sure I want to do anything else for a minute or two," Zack said.

"Me neither."

They looked at each other as the ground trembled.

"What was that?" Cass asked.

"Some sort of seismic tremor," Zack said. "That's the second one I've felt since we crashed."

"Let's just hope the tremors don't get any worse. I guess Delta's offline?"

"Yeah. I haven't been able to get her back."

"So what is working?"

"Not much. The bridge is a mess, and the engine room is worse. The bottom two cargo holds are pancaked. Our cabins and the galley are the best of the bunch."

"I thought you said *Seeker* was fixable. That doesn't sound fixable to me."

"Ah, but you haven't seen my magic hands at work yet." He held up his bandaged wrist. "Well, hand. As for Delta, I'm not sure. I don't see anything wrong with her components, but I might be missing something. I didn't work on that system much when Hopper and I were repairing *Seeker*." He handed her a nutrient bar and drink. "Eat, then rest. You need to heal." He bit off a portion of his own.

"How much do we have in E-rations?"

"Like I said earlier, enough for a couple weeks. More if we're careful."

"Okay." She finished her *meal* and blew out a short breath. "Guess we need to get this over with."

"First, take these."

Cass saw Zack holding out two white tablets. "I don't like to take meds."

"They're just analgesics for the pain, mixed with an antibiotic. And trust me, now that you're awake, you are going to hurt."

"Fine." She grabbed the pills and swallowed them.

Zack checked her shoulder and helped her into a sling. "I reset your shoulder while you were out, but you'll need to keep your arm immobilized for a few days." Then he unwrapped the bandages around her leg. The gash ran almost the entire length of her left calf.

"Wow."

"Yeah. Fortunately, you were unconscious when I took care of you. I cleaned the cut up and sprayed a sealant on your leg, but you should keep this bandaged. You'll probably have a scar." He wrapped more gauze around her leg.

Cass chuckled. "Not as if I don't have a few of those already."

"I noticed." Zack eyed her, one eyebrow lifted, a slight smile on his face, and his interest obvious in the heated way he studied her.

She tried not to notice, but it wasn't easy. Unfortunately, she was in no shape to follow where her heart and libido went. And neither was he. "Yeah, well, working salvage is a dangerous job. You get hurt on occasion."

"But not like this." He pointed at her leg and shoulder.

"No, not often, but accidents happen. And there are more than a few who lost their lives doing this job."

"So why take on a job that's so dangerous?" He picked up an elastic bandage and helped her shift so he could wrap the binding around her ribs.

She knew he was trying to distract her with his chatter, but his one-handed fumbling hurt more than her effing ribs did. "The pay's not bad if you find a good one, and being out here gives me a chance to keep looking for my folks. The next ship I find could be the *Phoenix* or give me a clue to what happened to them. Actually, Amaya-an's star charts gave me the first good hope I've had in a long time."

He finally finished, and she sat back in relief. "You need to rest," she told him.

"I will as soon as I finish—"

She shook her head, stopping immediately as the cave spun. "No. Now. I can't help you if something happens to you. We'll figure out what we need to do later. Rest now."

He closed his eyes, then opened them again. "I'm serious. I need to get a few more items from the ship. Once I have them, I promise, I'll rest."

"What about you?" She nodded toward the bottle of painkillers.

"I took a couple earlier." He didn't look at her as he said that.

Liar. Again. "Uh-huh." She gazed into his eyes. The pupils were almost as big as the irises, and the whites had a bluish tinge to them. "Along with at least one energy pill."

"Yeah, well, I needed to get you safe." He struggled to his feet. "I'll be back in about an hour. Get some sleep."

Cass watched him go, frustrated that she couldn't help him, but she could barely sit up, let alone walk or carry gear. She settled back against the wall, the pad at her back not much of a cushion against the unyielding rock. A few minutes later, she yawned and fought to keep her eyes open before she realized that the pills Zack had given her also contained a sedative.

"Damn you, Zack," she muttered as her eyes closed.

****

Zack peeked back into the cavern, nodding as Cass's body dropped into sleep. He hadn't told her the worst and wouldn't until she was better. He dry-swallowed a pill, but, unlike hers, his shot his system full of energy and numbed the pain so he could keep going. He had to get as much off the ship as he could before the winds pushed *Seeker* off the precarious landing ledge and into the roiling waters below. The cargo area was crumpled almost flat, and the rest of the ship had been smashed badly when they hit the mountain. He'd stripped what he could from the interior, but there were a few more items he could get.

Zack donned his EVA suit, pulled the helmet on, and checked that the anchoring line tying him to the cave was still secure. He'd didn't have more than a few hundred meters to walk, but in the driving wind, the short distance might as well have been a parsec. He struggled against the wind, leaning into the gale. By the time he reached the ship, he was breathing hard, and the meds he'd just taken were barely holding back the pain. What he wouldn't give for Annie and her magic wand right now.

The first task was to check the anchor lines he'd sunk into the hard black rock of the mountain the day before. They were all that was holding the *Seeker* onto the ledge. Fortunately, they were still stable, but he wondered for how much longer. He went inside and bundled up clothes and any other supplies he could into a couple of cargo containers, then loaded those onto the only sled he'd been able to salvage. He'd pretty much stripped the ship of any useful gear. This would most likely be his last run—at least until he could move without more pain.

Zack refused to think about Ben and what his betrayal had done to them. He'd stranded them on a hostile planet, and nobody knew where they were. All for what? Okay, the Amaya-an was worth more than what several people could spend in a lifetime. But Cass had been his partner for years and was his goddaughter. Didn't that count?

"Obviously not," Zack muttered as he tied the bins to the sled and then tied that to the guideline leading back to the cave. "Ben, if I ever see you again…"

Zack bowed his head, steadied his breathing, and headed out. At least in this direction, the wind was at his back, but that didn't make the trek over the rough ground any easier. By the time he got back, he was completely spent.

He stripped out of his E-suit, dropping the ensemble where he stood, and collapsed on the mattress next to Cass's. The drum band playing in his head was only a counterpoint to the rest of what he felt. He closed his eyes, fighting against the pain until exhaustion overtook him.

****

Cass slowly woke, this time more aware of her surroundings. She struggled to sit up, gasping as the pain in her ribs shot through her and dizziness threatened to help her lose whatever was left in her stomach. She gritted her teeth and managed to get to a sitting position and cautiously moved her head to see what was what.

She noted Zack lying on the mattress next to her, soundly asleep. She also saw that his clothes were damp—probably from sweat from the looks of him—and knew he had to be cold. As carefully as she could, she moved around until she could get his thermal blanket up over him. He'd be better off if he wasn't wearing damp clothes, but she didn't have that kind of energy. Just covering him up used almost all of hers.

She rested a few minutes, then got to her hands and knees—or rather, hand and knees—and, using the rock wall for stability, managed to stand. The room threatened to spin again, and dark spots appeared in her vision, but she made her way to one of the chairs and sat, breathing hard, swearing at her weakness. And at Ben for causing her and Zack's conditions and predicament. Cass wasn't used to being weak. She didn't do weak.

Gritting her teeth against the pain, she wrapped the thermal blanket around her shoulders like a cape, rose, and shuffled over to the emergency bins to find a nutrient bar. She downed that along with a drink and two analgesics—plain ones according to the container. Once that was done, Cass took stock of where they were.

Wind whistled from outside, and though she wanted to see where they were and what shape the *Seeker* was in, she had to let that go for the moment. Taking stock of their dilemma was more important. She looked around at the crates and piles of stuff Zack had brought back from the ship. "What'd you do? Strip the entire ship? Blast it, Zack. We're going to have to put all this stuff back." She refused to think about not being able to do that because that would mean *Seeker* was done.

They had beds, chairs like the one she was sitting in, crates of supplies, tools, and food—not a lot from what she saw, but as Zack had said, enough for maybe two weeks. He'd rigged up emergency lighting and a heater to keep them semi-warm. That's when she realized that even with the blanket, she was cold and shivered. To one side of the beds, she saw an open crate with clothes spilling out and shuffled over there to see what she could find.

She found warmer clothes, boots, and even toiletries and a hairbrush. As carefully as she could, she slid on a button-down shirt and jacket, swearing quietly as she tried to move her arm. By the time she was dressed, she was sweating and felt like she'd just run several kilometers. Up a mountain. In sand. Against a major headwind. She settled onto one of the chairs and studied their surroundings a little more closely.

The cave they were in was large—almost as large as the *Seeker* and made of some sort of shiny brown rock. She reached out and touched one of the rocks and realized what the substance was. Brown crystal. An entire mountain. And they were in the middle. So why had the miners left? Any crystal was worth credits. Though, when she really looked around, this didn't seem like a typical room for miners. More like a mine that was just getting started rather than one already established. Maybe just an outer station? Which meant there might be better accommodations deeper in the caves and tunnels.

"Nobody would leave a crystal cave. So why did they?"

She'd have to think about that later. For now, she was determined to see her ship. Giving herself a few minutes to rest, she gathered her strength and headed outside. Thanks to the bandages Zack had put around her ribs earlier, she was able to move a little better, as long as she didn't try to breathe too deeply.

The opening to the cave wasn't much more than a slot between two huge boulders and barely high enough to stand upright. How in the stars had Zack found the cave? At the edge, she noted the guideline anchored to one of the boulders. As she stepped around the rock, the wind hit her—hard. The force was like walking into a wall more solid than the rocks and stripped her of her breath. And the problem wasn't just wind. Water droplets and debris flew at her faster than she could dodge them, and the noise was deafening. So loud, she had to clap her hands over her ears.

She quickly stepped back and shook her head—which brought on another bout of dizziness and nausea. Swallowing hard against the bile, Cass leaned against the rock, amazement growing at what Zack had accomplished alone and injured. But that explained the E-suit she'd seen lying at his feet.

Cass went back and found her own suit and struggled into the ensemble, almost exhausting all of her strength, especially with the injured shoulder and ribs. But she had to see her ship. She had to.

Suited up, she went back to the opening and clipped her belt to the guideline. Leaning into the wind, she followed the line to the *Seeker*. What she saw almost brought her to her knees. No wonder Zack had stripped what he could. This didn't look repairable. His slip of "salvage" was closer to the truth. This time, *Seeker* was done. Cass knew that.

She stepped inside. The silence and end to the buffeting wind was almost as startling as being outside. Cass laid her palm against the wall. "I'm sorry I couldn't save you this time."

Tears threatened, and she blinked them back. Cass went to her cabin. Zack had stripped what he could down to bare bones. "But you don't know where I've stashed the most important stuff." Cass went to her bed and pushed a button. When that didn't work, she swore.

"Okay, we do this the hard way."

She struggled and swore, but she eventually had the frame lifted on hinges. Underneath, behind the storage lockers, she had a cubby hole. Cass sat on the edge of the locker closest to the outside wall and caught her breath before leaning over and opening a safe she had hidden there. Cass unhooked multiple wires and pulled out a data cube the size of a shot glass as well as several smaller ones. "Hello, Delta."

That made her think about Amaya-an. They couldn't just download her data, unhook some wires, and move her to another ship. She *was* the ship. Taking a data cube out like this wouldn't be possible. Cass appreciated Delta and all she could do, but she was still just a computer. Amaya-an was…a person. A vastly different kind of person, but still a living being.

She tucked the AI backup storage into a bag at her waist. Done with that task, Cass went through the ship and gathered a few items Zack had left behind. After all, she knew the ship better than he did, and knew where she had hidden stuff important to her. Some of them were lost as they were in parts of the ship she couldn't get to, but she got most of her stuff from their hidey-holes. She filled a small bin with trinkets from her childhood and other memories. Like the ID tag from her first solo salvage trip. Her dad's favorite coffee mug with the broken handle. A rose crystal pin her mom used to wear. All the little pieces of memories life was made of. They were worthless to anyone else, but they were priceless to her.

Finished with her task, she headed back to the cave.

With the wind at her back, the trip back wasn't as bad, but when she got to the cave, she collapsed in a chair, winded and tired from the trek, and made sure Zack was still alive. He didn't look like he'd moved, but his chest rose and fell in what she hoped was a comfortable rhythm.

Once she had her own breath back, she secured the belongings she'd brought back at the bottom of the bin with her clothes. She skinned out of her E-suit and settled down onto her bed, removing only her boots. Oddly enough, other than being tired, she really didn't feel that bad, but she knew that was a false sense from the meds. Right now, she needed rest.

Unfortunately, her mind wouldn't settle down. Cass leaned back against the rock and felt a tingle go through her, but from the contact with the rock or another reason, she wasn't sure. Either way, the sensation was a good feeling. Good enough for her eyes to close and allow her to drift off to sleep.

****

Cass woke to an amazing aroma, and her stomach grumbled. When she sat up, there was no dizziness, and she didn't have much trouble moving. Zack was standing a few feet away, stirring a pot suspended over red-hot rocks. "He sets up house, and he cooks. Wow. How did I get so lucky?"

He turned to her and grinned. "Good morning, sleepyhead."

She stretched and realized she wasn't hurting as badly as earlier. "It's morning?"

"Going by my pad, yes. At least on Pointe Noir. Here? Who knows? Morning, afternoon, night...the weather's all pretty much the same. Forecast for the day is high winds, cold temperatures, heavy overcast skies. Near as I can tell, that's the forecast pretty much the entire time. How do you feel?"

"Oddly enough, not bad. How 'bout you?"

"Same. Most of my cuts and bruises are healing already. And my head's not pounding. Wrist still hurts, but again, not as badly."

"Hmm. Let me see your head." Cass went over to him and carefully removed the bandage. The gash on his forehead was scabbed over and a healthy pink around the edges. "Your cut is almost healed."

"Your leg?"

She tugged up her pants leg and unwound the bandage. Her injury looked like Zack's gash—nearly healed. "I don't understand. How can this be?"

Zack shook his head. "I have a theory." He shifted the pot from the heated stones to cooler ones and divided the contents into two bowls. "Vegetable stew."

She startled as their lanterns flickered and went out, leaving just the red glow of the hot rocks.

"Damn. Give me a minute," Zack said.

Cass could hear him rummaging around, swearing, and then the lights came back on. She glanced at where he had wires strung from what looked like shards of crystals. "What in the seven layers of hell is that? Is that black crystal?"

Zack chuckled. "Yeah. The fragment was originally part of a figurine of a cat my little brother gave me before I left for a job. He made the piece himself and said the cat would bring me good luck. Ugliest object I ever saw but that ugliness held beauty at the heart. A piece of black crystal. Whatever he used to form around the crystal shielded the signature, or I'd never have gotten through security at Noir." His smile dimmed. "I guess he was right. I've been using the pieces of crystal to power our stuff. But they're really small pieces, not much more than large dust."

"Doesn't matter if the shards are small. Black has almost as much power as a red. I'd say the connections are important. Our stuff doesn't all handle crystal power well."

"I know. Took me most of a night to get this much working."

"Where in the Jovanian system did he get a piece of black crystal?"

Zack went quiet and still, and Cass could almost see waves of sadness coming off him. "Our farm. Seems my folks built the house and main farm on top of a series of crystal caves. When they bought the land, nobody knew about crystals. We boys used to play in the caves. They consisted of mostly blacks, but there was one spot where there were other colors. No reds, though. Whites and yellows with a few blues. Jimmy—he's my youngest brother—would often create sculptures using the crystals. He wasn't much of an artist, but he had a good eye and kept trying. He even sold a couple of his pieces."

"Which was what brought attention to your farm."

"Which is why he's almost catatonic now. He blames himself for what happened."

Cass rose and wrapped her arms around him. "Once we get out of here, we'll see about getting him the best help we can."

Zack turned in her arms and wrapped his around her. "Thanks. Now. Food. Hungry?"

"Starved." Cass took the bowl he'd dished out for her and sat in one of the chairs. "What's your theory on our healing?" She blew on the stew to cool the broth slightly.

"This." Zack indicated the rocks surrounding them. "Most scientists have been working on black, red, and white crystal. Not much has been done with brown, but what if brown has healing properties? When we were on Amaya-an, Annie used one of their scanners on me to heal my ribs and bruises. The scanner was crystal based. What if the scanner used brown crystal?"

Cass ate a bit of the stew as she pondered his theory. "Could be possible." She frowned. "But what if the brown has some bad properties like the red?"

Zack shrugged. "I'm not sure. Maybe this is like white or yellow—safe but not of much use? Or maybe there's an element in the atmosphere here? Could be because the scientists don't know all the facts about crystal. Even the Ki's—who own an entire planet of crystal—don't know everything about them. They know some crystals affect us but may not know in what ways. I mean…if we stay here too long, would we get like an overdose?"

"Guess we'll find out. By the way, this is good stew."

"Thanks. Figured we may as well enjoy the food while our supplies last." He grinned wryly. "I sure hope we can either get rescued or find a source of food soon. Do you need any analgesics?"

"No. I'm actually okay. And I'm glad I'm with you."

"Yeah. Me too."

After they ate, they went about setting up camp a little better than the helter-skelter way Zack had dumped all their gear. "Hey, I didn't have a lot of time for niceties," he said as he moved several bins.

"Actually, I'm surprised you were able to do as much as you did. Especially against that wind."

He spun around and stared at her, a frown on his face. "You went out?"

"Yeah. Brought in a few more items." She got quiet, sadness for her ship flooding through her, then anger at Ben. "If I ever see Ben again—"

"You'll have to wait until I'm done with him. And I can't promise there'll be much left."

"Why would he do this, Zack? I thought I knew him. I mean, he's my godfather. I've known him all my life. And we've been business partners for the last five years. I trusted him."

"Yeah, I know." Zack took her empty bowl and dropped it into a bucket of water he had near the hot stones. "I don't know, Cass. There had to be an important reason for him to turn like that."

She stared into the fire circle of hot rocks. "I mean, he was always trying to get me into one scheme or another. Him and his get-rich-quick plots. Sometimes I went along, but most of the time, I smiled and just shook my head."

"And what happened those times?"

She looked up at him. "What do you mean?"

"I mean, when you said no, what happened to you?"

Cass had to think hard. "I don't... Wait. The last time he sent me out on one of his crazy trips, I went after that statuette. And Ian showed up just after I figured out where the piece was and then tried to take what I found away from me."

"Who were the buyers? Why that particular item?"

"I...don't know. I thought the Throquins. Ben never

told me specifically who the buyers were, but he must have sold the figurine because he put the credits in my account."

"Uh-huh. But Ian showed up. What about the time before that?"

"Um…I was out doing some recon on a derelict I had heard about. Not much to find. The ship was in bad shape. Engine blown. Full of asteroid holes. But there were some decent component upgrades and… Oh! There was this cache of Aboolean weaponry that I found. Beautiful stuff. I managed to get most of the items to my ship before…" Cass chewed her bottom lip.

"Before Ian showed up, right? Did you ever meet Ian?"

"Once. Though I didn't know who he was at the time."

"How did you meet?"

"At a party." She blew out a long breath.

"A party Ben threw, right? Ben introduced you."

"Yes. Has he been playing me this whole time? Why?"

"Because you're Cassandra Brennan. And the owner of *Seeker*. Even I'd heard of the two of you before we ever met. You find ships and objects nobody else can. Hell, you're almost better than Hopper—when he was Hopper and not Hopper-an. I'm not sure what he is now. But you're well known as someone who can find the best salvage. I've been to other star systems, and no one is as good as you."

Cass silently preened a little in the praise but then sobered. "So he was playing me the whole time. But he knew my folks. He worked for them."

"He kept the books. The inventory, right?"

"Yes."

"I'll bet if you had a forensic accountant go over those books back to when your folks were active, there'd be discrepancies. He's probably been working your family for years."

Cass felt tears sliding down her cheeks, her heart breaking. "Why, Zack?" She knew she kept asking the same question, and that he didn't have answers, but she couldn't seem to stop herself. Ben was...Ben. As close to her as anyone. His betrayal just didn't make sense.

Zack moved over to sit by her and drew her into a sideways hug. "We may never know all the reasons why, but we will ask when we see him. And he will answer."

She gave him a side-eye stare. "That sounds like a threat."

"A promise," he firmly stated. "While I can't be absolutely certain, I'm pretty sure Ben was in on the raid on my parents' farm. He has a lot to answer for."

"And he will."

"That sounds like a threat."

"A promise." She leaned into him, and they sat like that, quietly, for a few minutes, just taking strength from each other. "Zack, you didn't explore beyond this cavern, did you?"

"Not really. I haven't had the time, or the energy, for much else. Why?"

"Because this doesn't look like a miner's chamber. If there isn't a camp outside—and we both know there isn't—they would have one a lot more elaborate than this set up inside." She picked up the lantern and shone the light around the space. "There. See that darkness back there? I'll bet there's a tunnel leading to better quarters."

He nodded. "I guess we should check the tunnel

out."

"Let's go."

Zack gently grasped her arm. "Wait a sec. What if we go down farther and there's a bad quake? We could be sealed in."

Cass closed her eyes, then opened them and glanced at him sadly. "Do we have a choice?"

His shoulders dropped, and he shook his head. "No."

Chapter Eighteen

Hopper-an laid his hand against the wall in his quarters. The material softened and flowed around his hand, feeling like a soft caress. "Amaya-an? What can we do?"

"A lot more than they are aware of, as you know. We need time to get ready, but I feel a hesitation in you."

"I just don't want anyone getting hurt."

"Injuries may occur, but we have done much to keep them to a minimum, especially for your friends."

"What about Cass and Zack?"

"According to my long-range sensors before we jumped, they were heading for the second moon of Kilner. Taking Ben's sabotage into account, if they were able to land safely, they should be all right. Even with damage, there are several mine sites where they can shelter, though we should probably send help for them once we are able to."

Hopper-an blew out a frustrated breath. "That's a lot of possibilities, Amaya-an. If they got to the moon. If they landed safely. If they found one of the mines…"

"This assessment is the best I can do with the information I have. I am sorry, Hopper-an, that I cannot be more specific."

He patted the wall with his free hand. "Your assessment is fine. I'm sorry I'm so worried. Cass has been a good friend for many years. She…accepted me even when I was broken. As did the others." He closed his eyes, shoulders slumped, as he prayed everyone was okay. Then he straightened up. "How are we coming with my changes?"

"Your concern is a reason I accepted you as my captain. That, and you had the perfect genetic structure."

"What am I, Amaya-an? Am I Masaaki?"

"You are a hybrid, but there is Masaaki DNA in your genetic makeup. That is why the changes worked so well on you. You are truly one of my people." The wall softened more into a hug, then drew back. "Another twenty-six minutes and we will be ready to act. Are the people ready?"

"Yes. Make sure they're alone, then open communications with them."

"Done."

"Omar? This is Hopper-an."

"We're here. How are you coming with preparations on your end?"

"We will be ready in twenty-five minutes."

Omar chuckled. "Okay. We'll be ready. We were able to come up with basic weapons and even a knock-out gas we can use to take out the guards. Taking them down won't be easy, but we think we can do what's necessary."

"We will speak again at the time."

"Okay."

Hopper-an laid his head against the wall. "I hope this works, Amaya-an."

The wall softened and curled around him once more, soothing him. "It will, Hopper-an. It will. We have formulated a good plan, and our people are strong."

He drew away. "Finish the rerouting, and I'll head

back to the bridge." Hopper-an disengaged his hand and strode away. Ben met him in the corridor.

"Where were you?" Ben demanded. "You're supposed to be on the bridge."

Hopper-an wondered if Ben had tried to sit in the captain's seat and grinned when he saw Ben rubbing his rear. Amaya-an would not allow Ben to sit there and had probably stung him a little. "I needed to relieve myself. Would you prefer I do that on the bridge?"

"Take a guard with you the next time."

Hopper-an stopped and turned to him. "Ben, you have taken over the ship. We have the McClarens on our tail and all our friends—my friends—are either missing or imprisoned in the *Raider*. The guards prevent me from accessing any vital parts of the ship. What do you expect me to do?"

"I expect you to be on the bridge."

"Which is where I am heading." Hopper-an could see the frustration in Ben's face, but he kept his smile to himself.

Once there, Hopper-an resumed his seat in the captain's chair while Ben berated the guard, then strode away. Hopper-an counted down the time in his head. When the time for action neared, he switched on the private com signal.

"Are you ready?" he whispered.

"Yes," Omar answered.

"Three… Two… One… Go!"

Hopper-an leaned back as the seat completely enveloped him, and he released a series of commands. Alarms sounded all through the ship. His guard spun around. "What is that? What's going on?"

The guard stomped over to him. "Hey, you. Freak.

214

What's—"

"Now, Amaya-an."

Blue lines of sparks covered the guard, and he went twitchy-stiff. When they stopped, he dropped to the floor, and the seat released Hopper-an. He stepped down, pulled a length of thin, strong binding fiber from under his suit, and tied the pirate up, then hauled him to the side so no one entering would see him.

Hopper-an sat back down and waited, smiling when Ben came storming in. Hopper-an lifted the little finger on his right hand, and Amaya-an locked the doors.

"What the hell is going on?" Ben screamed at him.

Hopper-an just smiled. "We are taking back control, and you cannot stop us."

Ben snorted, but Hopper-an could see beads of sweat on his forehead and the doubt in his eyes. "You can't. I have control of all your vital systems. This ship is mine." He dashed for the door, slamming into the solid panel when it failed to open, and he fell to the floor.

"Actually, Ben, *we* have control of all our systems." To prove his point, the alarms stopped.

Ben tapped the com unit on his wrist as he struggled to stand. "Guards! Is anyone there?"

Hopper-an strode over to him. They were almost the same height, but unlike back on the station, Hopper-an now stood tall and with a dignity he didn't have before. "We also control communications."

"But I…"

"You attempted to sabotage this ship. Amaya-an and I have rerouted around all your little surprises. You were treating this ship as a container. She is a sentient being and watched what you were doing so she could undo your sabotage, which she has."

215

Ben reached for him, but he stepped back. "Amaya-an."

A column of bright sparkles encased Ben. "That is a contained forcefield. Unlike the guard over there, I want you to see exactly what is happening and know that we are in control." He turned to the view screen at the front. "Show me."

Scenes from the landing bay, engine room, crystal rooms, armory, and more displayed on the screen. In the landing bay, both guards were down and didn't look like they would move again. Annie was tending someone lying on the floor.

"Annie?"

She glanced up, then back down at her patient. "Paul is hurt pretty badly. I need to get him to the med-bay. June too. Katie said she'd get an anti-grav unit. Donnie went with her."

"Just tell her to bring…" Hopper-an shook his head. "No. I'll tell her what to get. Do what you can until she gets there."

"I will."

Hopper-an glanced at the other scenes. In each one, his team members had secured the guards and were hauling them back to the bay. "Katie?"

"Yes, Hopper-an?"

"I know Annie sent you to get an anti-grav unit, but here's what else you need. In the med-bay, go to the third cabinet on the left and open the top drawer. In there, you'll find a specialized scanner. Annie knows what to do with the apparatus. But beside that, you'll find a type of syringe. Take that as well. I will tell Annie what to do with that."

"Got you."

Hopper-an watched as Katie got the required tools, and she and Donnie headed for the landing bay. He turned back to Ben. "As you can see, you are done."

Ben stared at him. "Not yet, Hopper. Ian still has a few tricks in his arsenal."

"That's Hopper-an. And whatever Ian McClaren can throw at us, we can handle. You are finished, Ben. I don't envy you when Zack and Cass see you next." He went back to the captain's seat. "Amaya-an, change course. We're going back for Cass and Zack." He looked at Ben. "I need to know…why?"

"Why what? Why take over this ship and all the crystals? Why else? For the money."

Hopper-an shook his head. "Not from what I discovered."

Ben peered at him. "What do you mean?"

"I mean, I found out that, although you have been working for Ian for years, you've also been thwarting him where you could. To keep Cass safe. You were also in contact with your father for much longer than you led anyone to believe. He was your go-between with Ian, wasn't he?"

Ben's shoulders dropped. "Sometimes. I had to do what they wanted, or they'd hurt Cass."

"Ben, what you've done is horrible, but maybe you did so for some of the right reasons."

"So you'll let me go?"

"That will be for the others to decide."

Ben nodded, his shoulders slumped, and his face holding a sadness that Hopper-an knew went deep.

Chapter Nineteen

Cass stared at the unappetizing mess in her bowl. She closed her eyes and forced herself to take a bite. When she opened her eyes, she glanced at Zack, who looked about as enthused over his meal as she felt. "What I wouldn't give for some of Katie's nachos. Dripping with melty cheese, spices, sauteed veggies."

"I'll take that. Or a big steak and all the trimmings," Zack said as he took another bite.

"What is this supposed to be, anyway?" Cass held up her spoon and let the viscous liquid drip back into the bowl.

"The package said, 'Nutrient Stew—a flavorful broth full of body needs and taste.' "

"Sounds like someone from the backlands of Jovani not only made this mess but wrote the description as well." She set the bowl aside.

Zack shook his head. "Come on, Cass. Awful as this crap is, you need to eat. We got a lot done, but we still have a lot to do." He moved over to sit beside her and wrapped his arm around her. "We have to try to get some sort of signal out. Or do whatever we can to get us off this rock."

"I know." Cass laid her head on his shoulder. After two days, they were awake and rested, their wounds nearly healed, but they both tired quickly in the thin atmosphere. The first day, they'd assessed the damage to

Seeker and determined that there wasn't enough left to fix. Her little ship was truly salvage. Cass spent most of a day coming to grips with the decision. A freezing snow and ice storm had settled the matter, nearly sealing them into the cave and dropping the temperatures to below levels they could handle. So they'd started exploring deeper into the caverns. They'd looked through a couple of tunnels, but none of them had really panned out until the last one. Plus, exploring took a lot of energy.

They'd finally found the old mining quarters several hours walk in and set up camp, then spent the next two days moving all their stuff down. Being underground wasn't too bad if you didn't mind the lack of sunshine. At least, they weren't fighting gale-force winds or the freezing cold anymore. Not that the temperature was balmy, but they weren't shivering. The place was a squared-off room with old tables, benches, tiered bunks, and some shelving units. The accommodations weren't much, but they were better than what they'd had previously. Another exit on the far side from where they'd entered led downward to a second, much smaller space with a clear pool fed by a stream coming from a crack in the wall. They'd tested the water and found the liquid mineral-tasting but drinkable, but they had to haul buckets up to the room every day. They hadn't had time to explore farther, but that was on their list.

"I'll eat mine if you'll eat yours." Cass pointed at Zack's bowl sitting next to where he'd been.

Zack chuckled. "All right. All right. Come on, let's finish this wonderful repast. I'd like to see if we can get these old power cells up and running and maybe work on the com unit we found. With a lot of luck, we might be able to get a message out."

219

They both picked up their bowls, saluted each other with their spoons, and gulped down the soup. Unfortunately, they both knew that their supplies were running low. A few more days and they'd be down to a handful of nutrient bars. They'd probably have lasted a little longer energy wise if they'd stayed in the first cave, but they'd have frozen to death even quicker. Before they moved deeper, they made sure to set up markers and etch arrows on the cavern walls for any rescuers to follow.

Cass gathered the bowls and spoons after they finished. "My turn to wash up. What's first on your list?"

"The power cells. You need help getting the water?"

Cass moved her shoulder around. "No. The shoulder feels as good as new. So's my leg. Shouldn't take me long to haul a few gallons up."

"Okay." Zack leaned over and kissed her, and she held him for a moment. She broke away from him before their kiss could go deeper. "You. Power cells. Me. Water."

"Yes, ma'am!" He grinned at her as she gathered up the bins and power sled they were using to haul water from the spring they'd found. Cass flipped on her battery torch and headed out of the cave. Their lamps and heater were growing dimmer. If Zack didn't get the cells juiced up somehow, they'd be in the dark—literally. She didn't want to think about their food supplies. They were down to one meal a day, and that, barely palatable. She really hoped they'd be able to get some sort of signal out soon or these caves would be their tombs. At least, when the end came, she'd have Zack with her. Zack who had become her heart. She really wanted to live, especially with him, but if the gods determined otherwise, they would be together at the end.

She rinsed their bowls and spoons in the outflow, then filled the water bins with several gallons. Before heading up, she glanced around. There was a large pile of rocks right about where she thought a tunnel might be. She went over and studied the formation. A cave-in from seismic activity? She looked down to see the water from the pool seeping under the rocks, then studied the pile closer. The mass didn't look like a normal rock fall. Not that she had a lot of experience with them, but there was an oddity about this one that didn't look natural.

Cass paced the width of the fall, studying the stacked rocks intensely. To the far right, where they met up with the cave wall, she noted that the edge looked too straight. Too unnatural. "A door? Disguised?" She felt around all the edges, frustrated when nothing happened. Finally, she just shoved at the one side…and a crack opened. Excited, she shoved harder, and a space opened enough for her to squeeze through. Zack wasn't expecting her back right away, so she headed through the opening.

A smooth slope, bordered on one side by the stream from the pool, led downward. Cass followed the descending path, her light barely cutting the darkness a few feet in front of her. She stopped when she entered a large cavern—this one nearly as large as Amaya-an and as amazing.

Her light picked out crystals of all shapes, sizes, and colors in bands and columns. That was amazing enough, but the fact that there were…buildings. Or constructs that looked like buildings at the base of the cavern and reaching up to the ceiling was what stopped her. Unfortunately, some of them had toppled over, and several were leaning against one another.

One pyramid-like building that was still intact almost looked like a temple she had seen in pictures on Amaya-an, with large cats carved from black crystal guarding the enormous door. Water splashed in several pools surrounded by walkways and smaller buildings. She counted the steps leading up to the doorway of the temple—nine sets of nine. Could this be where Amaya-an's people ended up?

The desire to go down there and explore almost overcame her safety instincts. She wanted Zack with her. Reluctantly, she turned and headed back up to the water and to Zack.

"Zack!"

He looked up from the table where he worked, wires and components of several cells scattered across the surface. "What's wrong? Are you okay?" He rose and came over to her, checking her over as if she'd been hurt.

"No. I'm fine. But you have to come with me. You've got to see what I found! It's amazing!" She grabbed his hand and hauled him through the caves and tunnels toward the opening. "Watch your step. The ground is a little slippery."

"What is this? How did you find this tunnel?"

"The rockslide wasn't a rockslide. Well, not a real one. The rocks hid a door. And the door led here." They reached the end of the tunnel, and Cass tugged Zack to a stop. "Look." She shone her light around.

"What the...? Cass! This looks like a small town."

"I know. I think this might be where Amaya-an's people took shelter. The construction and layout matches up with what we saw on Amaya-an about her people."

"Except from the damage, I think something bad happened."

"Maybe a quake of some sort? I'm not sure. Most of the buildings look to be intact, but some of them, especially the ones along the outer edges, aren't."

"I'm guessing these tremors we've been feeling did that."

"Probably."

They found steps to the side and took them down to the bottom of the huge cavern. Set in the wall at every other step, they saw a series of white nodules. Cass shone her light on one, and the node sparkled. Barely, but there was a sparkle. "Zack, I think these are lights, but they need light or energy to power them. I wonder if there's a power reactor somewhere."

"Let's find out!"

Laughing like kids, they scampered down the remaining stairs, their lights barely making a dent in the darkness. They reached the bottom and stopped at the conjunction of three paths.

"Left, right, or middle? If you were putting in a power station, where would you put one?" Cass asked.

"Depends on the kind. But knowing the way these beings used crystals, I'd say a central location."

"Agreed." Cass pointed down the middle path. "Shall we? "

He grinned at her and took her hand. "Let's."

They walked past buildings constructed of crystals, rocks, and some substance they couldn't name but looked like some sort of mortar to hold the structures together. They came to a main area from which nine paths radiated away from a single small nine-sided building.

"I'll bet that's the powerhouse," Zack said.

Cass nodded, and they went in the open door. Their

lights showed a central column with a console. Around the outer walls were other consoles. Zack went to the central one. "Cass, give me some light."

She went over and held her light up for him to see. "This looks like the engine room console in Amaya-an. I wonder…" He ran his hands over the sides, and the panel lit up. Cass and Zack grinned at each other. "Can you get the power working?"

"Maybe. Let's see what I can do. I'm glad I worked on Amaya-an."

He moved his hands around the console, touching different spots until he touched one area, and the entire cavern lit up.

"You did it!" Cass stood in the doorway and squinted in the sudden light. "Can you tone the light down a little?"

Zack moved his hands, and the lighting dimmed down to a bearable level.

"Wow. Zack, this is amazing."

"It is!" He joined her. "Shall we?"

They strolled through the town, each building and path leading to a new discovery. Some of the places were obviously homes. Others seemed to be businesses of a sort. "I wonder what happened to the people?" Cass asked as they looked through an empty home.

"Three thousand years. They might not have had enough food. Or the atmosphere wasn't good for them. Or any of a thousand other factors. Who knows?"

"True, but they lasted long enough to build this place." Cass opened a door. "Odd. None of the other places have doors."

They stepped through and stopped. Bright lights shone down on rows and rows of raised beds. Water trickled through the beds.

"This looks like a greenhouse," Cass said. "They would have grown food here."

"All dead now without light," Zack said as he picked up a handful of dirt and let the dust trickle through his fingers.

"Yeah."

They left the greenhouse and went on, heading for the temple. Neither one talked much, the solemnity of the place getting to them.

"All those people. Gone."

They stood at the base of the steps leading up to the temple. "Do we dare?" Cass asked.

Zack sighed. "We've come this far. Maybe there are answers here."

As they slowly climbed the enormous steps, Cass almost felt like the cats were watching them. She shivered as they reached the doorway. "Whatever this is, it's not open like the other buildings, and I don't see a way to get in."

"How did you open the tunnel to get here?"

"I just shoved on the side."

They tried shoving, but the doors didn't budge.

"Zack, look at these symbols on the doors. I wonder if they are the key to opening them."

"How much of the language did you learn from Amaya-an?"

"Not much, but I'll try." Cass studied the symbols. "This one is for birth. The first life. This one is ninth or final life."

"So the rest of these must be for the other levels."

"Yeah, but I don't know what this middle one is for. The design doesn't match the others and isn't one of the life symbols."

"The symbol looks a little like Amaya-an. The ship," Zack said. "Maybe that's what happened to them. With all this crystal around, could they have built another ship?"

"Well, the only way we'll know is if we get in." Cass touched each symbol in life order and finally pushed on the last one.

There was a deep rumbling from underneath them, and both cat statues turned toward them, the spears they held dropping down with Zack and Cass in the middle.

Zack grabbed Cass and yanked her down several steps just as an arc of blue light shot out from the spears, sparking where they'd been standing seconds before and hitting the middle symbol.

The spears rose. The cats turned back.

And the doors opened.

"Well, okay then," Cass said as she dusted herself off. "I guess you had to show...um...humility? Or get zapped?"

"Possibly. Or some sort of security system to keep anyone not authorized—like the miners—out?"

Cass motioned toward the open doorway. "Shall we?"

Zack stared at her. "Are you sure you want to?"

"Damn straight I do. Coming?" She headed back up the steps and entered the dark temple. As she did, interior lights came on, highlighting an even larger cavern. One where a ship like Amaya-an sat. Beside that one was a second—but empty—slip. Far across the space was an enormous, closed doorway. Large enough for the ship to go through.

"Well, I think that explains what happened to the

people," Zack said. "They built another ship and left."

"Building another ship like Amaya would have taken them years," Cass said.

"Decades. Maybe even centuries."

"So what did they do with their…um…dead?"

"We haven't looked everywhere. And I'm not sure I want to. But I'd like to see that ship."

"Agreed."

They found a way down but had to be careful as some of the steps had crumbled away. At one point, they had to creep across a narrow ledge, their backs to the rock wall and toes hanging over the edge. Finally, they reached the ground and looked up at the beautiful ship.

"She's gorgeous," Cass murmured between breaths.

"She is. I wonder why she's still here," Zack said.

"I wonder if we can get on board." Cass walked around the ship one way while Zack went the other, looking for a ramp or opening.

"I think I found a way in," Cass called out, a few minutes later. She waited for him to join her at the opening. "I think this would be one of the airlocks near the docking bays. Shall we?"

He grinned at her. "It would be a shame not to."

They stepped through the opening into the dark. As soon as they did, lights came on, and a voice sounded through the ship.

Unfortunately, the ship wasn't speaking their language.

"I think I caught a few words," Zack said. "I think she's speaking the same language Amaya-an was using before she learned ours."

"Amaya-an?" the voice repeated. Then a string of other words.

"Wait! Stop!" Cass said but the voice continued. "Zack, do you remember what the word for stop is?"

Zack hissed a sound through his teeth, and the chatter stopped.

"Okay, that worked." Cass sighed. "But how can we tell her our language?"

"Do you still have the backups of Delta from the *Seeker*?"

"Yeah, but how…?"

Zack shrugged. "If I were a pilot, saving my AI would be the first action I'd take—and I would have if I'd known where they were. Hopper showed me a lot about *Seeker*, but not that."

"Oh. Okay. Yes, I have them back at the campsite."

"Go get them. I have an idea."

Cass scrambled back through the town and the tunnels, clambered over rocks, skinning her hands and legs on shards of crystals. She skidded to a stop at their campsite, grabbed the backups, and scurried back to Zack and the ship, arriving out of breath and her hands and legs stinging from where she'd cut them. He side-eyed her, chuckled, but held his hand out for the cube.

"What are you going to do?"

"Hopefully insert this into her data stream and get her to connect with us a little. I think I got her to understand what I'm trying to do." He placed the data cube into a slot at the console where he was working. "Cross your fingers."

Lights flickered, and strange symbols flashed across the view screen, finally settling into a sort of language they could follow.

They waited what seemed an interminable time.

"You…are…people…but…not…my…people."

"Yes."

"You know Amaya-an."

"Yes. What is your name?"

"My name being is… My name is Zara."

"Hello, Zara. My name is Zack. This is Cassandra."

"Are my people safe?"

"We don't know, Zara. Nobody knows what happened to them. They disappeared centuries ago." Cass noted that Zara's grasp of the language was quick. Almost quicker than Amaya-an's had been. But then, Amaya-an had been damaged. This was a new ship. Maybe her creators had updated her.

"By your calendar, two millennium have passed since they left this place."

"So you were here a thousand years?"

"No. My people were, but not I. I was built during the last century of their occupation. Everyone left in my sister ship, the Netierie-an. I was not yet finished, so a handful stayed behind to help me to completion, but then the world shook again, and they were…gone. I used bots to finish the building, but I have no captain to direct me."

"I am sorry, Zara. You said the world shook again?"

"Yes. The shaking was…not good. The people had to move from the outside to here, but the tremors continued. That was when they began to build Netierie-an and myself."

"You are not the same as Amaya-an, and yet the same."

"Amaya-an and her sisters, like Netierie-an, are mostly for transportation of people. I am mostly for…"—there was a hesitation, and Cass thought maybe she was looking for the right word—"cargo?"

"Cargo is what we call material objects that are not

people," Zack said.

"Then yes, I am a ship for cargo."

"Zara, if you had a captain, could you leave this place?"

"Yes. Would one of you be my captain? I would really like to leave here. Even though I have been asleep, I have been lonely."

Zack and Cass looked at each other. "Don't look at me," Zack said. "I'm not a pilot. I just work the systems."

"Then you are an *et*," Zara said. "You are Zack-et. One who keeps systems running and follows the captain. What of you, Cassandra?"

"I thought you couldn't be captain of more than one ship?" Cass said. Though she really wanted to run this beauty of a ship.

Zack touched her arm. "Cass, the *Seeker* is gone. Your ship is gone. You are no longer her captain. Just be sure you want to do this. I will support you whatever decision you make."

His words hit Cass hard in the stomach, and she sat down on the rocky ground. She'd known that. She'd seen the *Seeker* and knew there was no hope, and yet... She sighed. "How can I not? We need to get out of here before this becomes our grave."

"We're not dead yet, Cass."

She gave him sad eyes. "*Yet* is the operative word. Our food is almost gone, and we can't live on the surface. Plus, although you're an amazing engineer, how likely is it that you'll get a signal out?"

His shoulders drooped, and Cass wrapped him in a hug. "You know the reality as well as I do. This is our only choice."

"You're right. Go for it, but you'd better not change

like Hopper-an did. I love you just the way you are."

"I love you too, Zack." She laid her hand against a wall. "Yes, Zara, I could be your captain. But does that mean I have to bond with you? Like my friend did with Amaya-an?"

"Yes and no. We would need to bond, but not a full takeover like a ship like Amaya-an. I carry no weaponry. I am not a ship of war or protection. I am just...room."

"You're not *just* room," Cass argued. "You are amazing. And I would be proud to be your captain. But before I do, we need to take care of our possessions." She looked up at the ceiling. "Zara, do you have food we can eat?"

"One moment please."

They waited less than a minute. "As I understand your nutritional needs from your Delta, yes, I believe I can provide what you need. I also have medical facilities to finish healing your injuries that I detect. And you may find clothing and other items of need in the second hold. My people packed items in there before they left."

"Food first," Zack said. "Preferably what we can actually eat. Zara, can you direct us to a galley?"

"And a shower and clean clothes," Cass added.

"Might be better to do that after we get our stuff from our camp," Zack argued.

Cass chuckled. "Okay. Okay. You're right. Food. Then we need to go back to our camp to get our gear."

With Zara's directions, they headed to the upper level to the galley. Even though Zara was mostly cargo space, the living levels were in the same area, just much smaller. Cass counted the tables in the galley. Nine tables for nine people each. And just two tables in the captain's mess.

231

"What would you like to eat?" Zara asked.

Cass grinned. "You have Delta's databases?"

"Yes, ma'am."

"Then I'd like salty chips with spiced protein, melted cheese, topped with my favorite toppings. Delta should have the specifics for you."

Zack cocked his head at her. "Are you sure a meal that spicy and heavy is a good idea? We haven't eaten much for a few days."

"The food of the gods," Cass said. "If I can't handle this, I give you permission to say, 'I told you so.' "

He laughed. "Zara, make that two. And two blue beers as well."

"Five minutes, please, until I have your request programmed in correctly."

They wandered around the area until the catering unit dinged. When they went back, they found a large platter heaped with Cass's favorite food and two large glasses of beer. Zack tentatively took a sip of the beer and grinned.

"Damn, that's good."

Cass grabbed the platter and took the food to a table while Zack brought the beers. She picked up a loaded chip and took a bite. Her eyes closed, and she let out a long breath of satisfaction.

"Good?" Zack asked.

"Don't tell Katie, but I think this is even better than hers."

They dug into the meal, groaning in delight, but could only finish off less than half the platter.

"I simply cannot eat another one," Cass declared, sitting back in her chair and eyeing the still heaping platter sadly.

"Neither can I." Zack sighed. "But damn, that was good."

"Have I overestimated amounts?" Zara asked. "This was similar to what your Delta had in her records."

Cass chuckled. "No, Zara. The problem is with us. We haven't eaten much for several days." With regrets, she took their leftovers to the recycling bin and sorrowfully dumped them in.

"Ah. Your systems need time to reset."

"Exactly," Zack said. "But the meal was delicious. And just what we needed. Thank you, Zara."

"You are most welcome. Will Cass become my captain now?"

Cass glanced at Zack who shook his head. "We need to go back to our camp and get our gear. We will be back, shortly, Zara," Cass said.

"I look forward to being with people again. Even those who are not Masaaki."

Cass laid her hand against the wall and could swear the material warmed up and softened under her touch, like a super-soft piece of foam. "We might need a couple hours to get all our gear."

"I believe if you look in the third bay, you will find mobile sleds. You can use them to help transport your belongings if you wish."

"Thank you," Cass said. "We'll do that, and we will return shortly. I promise."

"Understood. I will continue to converse with Delta and learn more of your people."

"Zara, is there any way I can talk to Delta or her to me?" Cass asked.

"I am sorry, but we have not yet figured that out. We can exchange data, but that is the best I can do for the moment."

"That's fine, Zara. Thank you. We will return as soon as possible. Can you direct us to the bays you mentioned?"

A brightly lit line appeared in the middle of the wall to Cass's right.

"Follow that line to where you need to be. While you are gone, I will prepare for flight initiation."

"Thank you, Zara."

Zack and Cass wandered through the ship, following the line and checking the spaces out. "Zara is easily three times the size of the *Seeker* and much more streamlined." Cass tried hard not to be envious of the ship, but she was.

Zack took her hand. "And you're going to be the captain."

"Oh! Yeah. I guess I am. Wow. That's... I..." She sighed and shook her head. "I guess I hadn't really thought about being the captain, but I am now."

He stopped her and turned her around to look at him. "Cass, if you don't want to do this, you don't have to. We can figure out a different solution."

Cass was shaking her head before he finished talking. "This is an amazing opportunity I can't pass up."

"But the symbiotic part?"

"Okay, I'll be honest, that does freak me out just a little, but..." Another head shake. "If you were a pilot, would you pass this up?"

Zack snorted. "No." He stopped in front of a door that swished open. "I think we're here. And there are the sleds. I think."

"Well, they're flat, but I don't see any controls."

"You need to touch the panel on the front," Zara said from above them. "Then the control panel will appear.

You can also attach two or more in a string through the panel."

"Show me," Zack said.

Various lights lit up, and Zack did as she directed. A column rose from the panel, and the sled rose to float a few centimeters above the floor. Once Cass saw what he was doing, she did the same with a second one. Then they got two more and attached them together. "Okay. Let's head back and get our stuff."

They each stepped up on a sled, and Zack showed Cass what to do with the screen. With a few rough starts and stops, they got them moving and headed toward the bay doors. "Zara, can you please open the doors to this bay?" Cass asked.

The doors opened, and they slid out and headed up through the cave, through the doors and the town, and to their camp. They loaded as much as they could onto the four sleds. Cass watched Zack manipulate the panel as electronic sides rose to keep items secure.

"How 'bout if I take these two back and you finish packing up the rest," Zack said.

"Okay." Cass stopped as the ground shook hard and dust and small pieces of crystal rained down. She grabbed for the wall, but that was shaking as well. Zack, standing on the sled, didn't feel the tremor but could see what was happening. Fortunately, the quaking stopped after a few seconds. "Zack?"

"I'd say that was a bigger one. They're getting worse. I think we need to hurry up. We don't want a rockslide to block us from the cave. You pack up, and I'll deliver and be right back."

"Maybe just drop the stuff off on this side of the town and then come back here. We can move all our gear in shifts."

"Good idea. Be right back."

Cass watched him go and gathered the rest of their belongings. It didn't take long to shuffle the sleds through the tunnel to the town.

From there, they moved to the ship and secured their possessions in the bay. As soon as they did, there was a strong quake that toppled parts of buildings and sent rocks crashing to the ground.

"Zack?"

He nodded. "I'll check."

"Be careful. I don't want to lose you now. Or ever."

She watched him as he crossed the town, climbing over sections of buildings that hadn't been down earlier. Though his trek didn't take more than a half hour, to Cass the time felt more like days.

He did come back, though, and shook his head. "We are definitely not going back that way. The tunnel is completely blocked."

"Well, I guess we have no choice but to go forward, then." Cass picked up a bin containing their clothes while Zack got their E-suits. "Zara, can you point us toward quarters?"

"The captain's quarters are next to the bridge. Zack can have his choice of quarters on that same level."

"Thanks, but we will be sharing quarters—um, if they're big enough for two?" After several weeks with him at her side, she wasn't about to give up their connection now. Especially since they were the only two people on board.

"There is a removable panel between the first two cabins. The expanded space should suffice," Zara informed them.

"Thanks." Cass pointed at the line. "Let's go find our new home."

Zack bowed her through the door, and they headed for their quarters. Cass's cabin was the same size as the one on the *Raider* but also had a small office in the front area. Removing the panel took a little work and some swearing on Zack's part, but he soon had the wall down, and they moved furniture around to make the space suitable for the two of them.

"I'm going to get a real shower and get cleaned up before I do this," Cass said.

"Want to make that for two?"

She grinned, took his hand, and led him to the fresher unit. The cubicle was barely big enough for the two of them, but they made the space work. As Zack rubbed her down, Cass knew she hadn't felt this good in a long time. Well after the sonics closed down, she and Zack finally left the tight space and moved to the bed.

"Cass? Are you sure?"

For an answer, she lay down and pulled him to her. "Definitely."

He stretched out over her, resting his weight on his knees and arms. Cass felt the heat building in her. She wanted him. Loved him. Wanted to make love to him. She wanted him in a way she'd never wanted anyone else.

"Tell me now if you want me to stop," Zack whispered.

"Don't you dare." She reached out and wrapped her arms around his neck, arching her back so they touched.

"You have the most gorgeous body."

Cass felt a blush that spread from her chest upward. Nobody had ever said that to her.

Zack assaulted her mouth with his gentle touch, holding her tightly against him. They spent the next hour exploring every inch of each other, satiating each other until they exhausted themselves.

And Cass had never felt better in her life.

"We should probably move," Cass finally said.

"Yes. Zara probably wonders what's taking us so long."

Cass chuckled. "I have a feeling she can probably figure that out." She smacked him on the ass. "Come on, lazy bones. Let's do this."

They rose and dressed, but when they moved to leave the room, Cass hesitated. Was she really going to do this? Meld with a sentient ship and become the captain?

Zack came to her and engulfed her in a hug. "You got this, babe. And I got you. I will be with you all the way. Where you go, I go. I will be *et* to your *an*. I will be your support when you need one, your lover when you want one, and your critic when you deserve one. You are not alone anymore, Cass. We will not stop looking for your family, and I will always care for mine, but we will be family for each other now too."

"I love you, Zack."

"I love you. Now come on, Captain. Let's get you bonded."

Cass stood at the closed door to the bridge. "I can do this," she whispered.

"Yes, you can, boss," Zara said. "Delta says to get your fardling butt out there and do this."

Cass laughed so hard she couldn't catch her breath. "Thank you, Zara."

She opened the door, and Zack offered her his arm,

and they strode onto the bridge.

Chapter Twenty

As Hopper-an accessed the com unit, he smiled at
Ben still standing in the forcefield. "Omar, do you have
them all?"

"Except for Ben and the other one you have up
there."

"You can come get the guard any time. We will
discuss what to do with Ben. Where did you put the
others?"

"Right now, we have them secured in a bay on the
Raider. But I'd like a better solution. Any ideas?"

"Amaya-an? What did you do with those who broke
the law or harmed others in some way?"

"The punishment depended on the crime. In some
cases, the offender had to work for the person they'd
wronged until the debt was repaid. In other cases, where
the problem went beyond one person but was an affront
to society as a whole, the criminal was banished to a
remote island or even another world. We would give
them enough supplies to last a year. After that, survival
was up to them."

"Did you ever check on them?"

"Sometimes. Sometimes not. Our monitoring
depended on the seriousness of the crime."

Hopper-an tapped his finger on his lips. "Amaya-an,
can you reprogram the *Raider* to a new destination? One
far away from here and so that the program cannot be

undone without your input?"

"I can. But what about Timmons? He is not guilty of the same crimes as the pirates."

"If we remove his components, can you still reprogram the systems?" Hopper-an asked.

"You do not need to remove his components," Amaya-an said. "I can download him to a secure area of my system and reprogram the component as a secure dummy system."

"Okay. Proceed."

"Do you have a destination in mind?"

"Somewhere remote and not in the known shipping and travel areas. I don't want them to get back too easily."

"Understood."

"Omar, did you hear all that?"

"Yes."

"Okay, make sure there are supplies for them on the *Raider*. We'll have to replenish them in a month, but they should be okay until then."

"Actually," Omar said, "with what is probably on Ian's other ships, they should have enough for more than a month. But we can check. Are you sure of this, Hopper-an?"

"If you have any other ideas, I am open to listening. But remember that these pirates have been raiding claims and shipping lanes for years, and they've hurt a lot of people. What will happen if we turn them over to security on the station?"

He could hear Omar sigh in the background. "Understood, Hopper-an. And we're all in agreement. The McClarens own too many security people. They'd probably get off with a small fine, if that, and go right back to what they're doing."

"That's true. So…you agree?"

"We do."

"Okay, Amaya-an?"

"I have finished the programming. Would you like me to do the same with the ships following us?"

That took Hopper-an aback for a moment. "You can do that?"

"The reprogramming is a challenge, but yes, thanks to what I found in the *Raider's* data banks, I can do that."

"Omar? How do you and the others feel about that?"

"She can reprogram all of McClaren's ships?"

"Yes, I can."

There was a pause, then Omar came back. "After what they did to us and tried to do, and what they have done to everyone within several parsecs, we all agree that Amaya-an can reprogram their ships. The vote was unanimous."

"Amaya-an, go ahead with the programming," Hopper-an said.

"The changes may take up to two hours."

"That's fine. How far are we from where Cass and Zack were stranded?"

"Nineteen hours, twenty-three minutes."

Hopper-an smiled. "Thank you, Amaya-an. Have you been able to raise Cass or the *Seeker* yet?"

"No."

That bothered Hopper-an more than Ian McClaren and his pirates did. He prayed that his friends were safe. "Okay. Keep trying."

"I will."

He turned as Omar, Tom, and Meri came onto the bridge. They had an anti-grav sled with them and dumped the still unconscious pirate on it, then turned to Ben. Omar held a gun, and Meri and Tom stood on either side of Ben, then nodded to Hopper-an. He released the force field surrounding Ben, and before he could bolt, they had him secured and on the sled.

"You can't do this to me. I'm your friend. I've known you all for years. You can let me go. I won't bother you." Ben kept pleading.

"Quiet yourself, or I will knock you out," Omar said softly. "You *were* our friend. We trusted you. And you betrayed us. And you hurt Cass. You deserve the worst, but we understand from Hopper-an that there were extenuating circumstances." He turned to Tom, who had been a Fleet advocate at one time and still held his badge.

"Ben Knoble, you have been judged and found by a jury of your peers to be guilty of conspiring to commit theft, piracy, terrorism, and more. All your crimes have been formally listed and recorded and sentence passed. While your fellow pirates will be banished from this area to an unknown sector of space, your sentence will be slightly different from theirs. They will be given enough supplies to last one year. After that time, their survival is up to them. You have your choice. You can join them in their banishment or be turned over to Fleet for sentencing to a penal colony."

"But…you can't do that!"

"Actually, we can," Tom said. "As a sworn officer of the court and a legal advocate, I have the power to become judge and pass sentence when another is not available. What is your decision?"

"But…but I did what I did to save Cass. I had to. Don't you see? I didn't have a choice."

"Which is why you have one now," Tom said.

"Choose."

With Ben continuing to argue, the three of them guided the sled out of the bridge, and Hopper-an sat back with a long sigh. A part of him regretted what they'd had to do, but knew their actions were for the greater good. "Amaya-an, in your former travels, did you run across any uninhabited planets that had appropriate living conditions for our friends to survive?"

"Two had possibilities."

"I guess there's no way to know if they're still uninhabited?"

"I have checked your long-range explorers. One still meets your criteria. The pirate ships will need six months, five days, and sixteen hours to reach the place."

"The world is outside current shipping and travel lanes?"

"Yes. We found the world when we were trying to avoid a warring faction in a nearby system. The planet is a remote one in a binary system. There are five other worlds in the system, but all are uninhabitable by most species. The planet that is habitable did not meet our needs but, I believe, will be sufficient for the pirates."

"What's wrong with this planet?"

"The world was a mostly water-based planet with multiple islands but no larger continents. Although livable, being surrounded by water is not an environment the Masaaki relish. So we kept looking."

"Understood. Set their programs for that planet."

"Yes, Captain."

"Has Ben made his choice?" Hopper-an asked, knowing Tom would have pushed him for an answer.

"Yes. He has chosen to go to a Fleet penal colony."

"Then we'll need to detain him in a room until we

return to station."

"Tom and the others are taking care of that now."

Hopper-an looked up as his com unit pinged an outside call coming in.

"I repeat, Hopper-an and Amaya-an, this is Cassandra-an and Zara-an. Please respond."

Hopper-an bolted upright in his seat. He heard his friend's voice, but *an*? What had happened to her? "Cassandra-an? This is Hopper-an. Can you further identify yourself?"

The view screen came to life, and Hopper-an was looking at his friends. Cass was seated in a captain's chair that looked identical to his, with Zack by her side.

"Hi, Hopper-an! Am I ever glad to see you!"

Chapter Twenty-One

Cass leaned back in her seat, smiling at the startled look on Hopper-an's face. She had to admit she was more than a little happy to see them. She and Zack and Zara had been looking for them for the better part of a day.

"Zara-an, how far are we from Amaya-an?"

"At our current speed, we will reach them in six hours. Though if they continue their current course, that time will be reduced."

"Where are Ian McClaren's ships?"

"They are between the two of us. His ships are moving toward Amaya-an but at a much slower rate."

"Maybe they haven't recovered from the pulse yet," Zack said. "Zara-an, can you contact Amaya-an and finish updating your systems to match hers?"

"My sister ship is already taking care of that. I have also given her access to my records, so she is aware of where I came from and what happened to us."

Cass turned back to Hopper-an. "So, Hopper-an, is everyone okay? And what about Ben and Ian and Ian's crews?"

"We are all fine. Paul and June were hurt during our fight for freedom but are recovering nicely. We have rounded up all the pirates we have here on board, including Ben, and currently have them in custody on the *Raider*. Amaya-an has programmed the ship so they cannot get out or get away. They have all been tried, convicted, and sentenced to banishment according to the laws of the Masaaki and our own courts with Tom as judge. Because of extenuating circumstances, Ben has chosen to go to a Fleet penal colony instead of banishment. This has been agreed upon by all. We are going to reprogram all the ships to go to a distant, uninhabited planet where we will drop them off and then scuttle the ships so they cannot leave."

Cass hated to see that many ships destroyed. "What if you left the *Raider* for them just in case of an emergency but brought the others back?"

Hopper-an raised an eyebrow at her. "Are you sure?"

"Yep. Our people deserve a little reward for what they've gone through on this trip. I'd say six ships should do nicely."

He snorted at her but nodded. "Amaya-an agrees and will see to the programming. Are you and Zack all right?"

"More than all right. Our, um, adventure was touch and go at first, but we discovered some interesting details about crystals, especially browns and blues."

"Their healing properties," Amaya-an said.

"Yes. If not for them, we'd probably still be stuck in our original cave and wouldn't have found Zara."

"Um, yes, about that… You're Cassandra-an?"

"Kind of? Zara and I reached a sort of compromise on that. When I need to be, I am Cassandra-an, but most of the time, I'm still just me. Cass."

"Interesting."

They both turned when Ian popped up on the screen. "What the hell? Where the hell have you been? I

247

haven't been able to raise you for almost a day." His eyes widened, and he got an evil grin on his face. "Well, well. This is a pleasant surprise. Cassie, my darlin', is that you in that nice fancy ship?"

Cass sat up straight. "My name is Cassandra-an, and yes, Ian, this is my new ship."

"Your new ship?" He laughed. "In case you haven't heard, I'm taking ownership of all new ships of this class. They all belong to me now."

"Well, that would be interesting, if this was a ship you could take charge of."

Cass was skating a fine line, and she knew it. They had defensive shields but no weaponry. There was little they could do beyond evasive maneuvers if Ian decided to attack.

"Oh, I can, and I will."

While they chatted, Cass sent a series of messages to Hopper-an and Zack. They both gave her a subtle nod. She also saw a note from Hopper-an telling her that, with Zara-an's help, they were able to finish programming Ian's ships more quickly.

Ian turned to Hopper-an. "Where's Ben? I expected him to be on the bridge."

"Ben is…detained," Hopper-an said. "Cassandra-an, are you ready?"

"I am."

Hopper-an nodded again. "Now, Amaya-an."

All Ian's ships shuddered to a stop. Cass watched as Ian's face went from smug to startlement to anger.

"What the hell is going on? Why did we stop?"

Cass could see his men scrambling behind him, trying to figure out what was going on.

"Ian McClaren. You have been tried by a judge and

jury and found guilty of multiple crimes. Your punishment is banishment from any space, shipping lanes, or planets that are inhabited by known peoples. Your ships have been reprogrammed to deposit you on an uninhabited planet in a distant sector where you will be stranded with enough supplies to last you and your band for one year. In addition, all but one of your ships will be forfeit and distributed to those who have incurred the most damage from you and yours," Hopper-an intoned.

"What? You can't do that! That will never stand up in a court of law. No advocate will agree to that."

"Ah, but, Ian, you know as well as I do that out here, the laws are different. You should feel lucky that we aren't spacing you," Cass said. "I am tired of you stealing what I have worked for. Of you chasing and harassing me. Of you plaguing other fliers and salvagers and stealing their claims. We are all tired of your tactics, Ian. And this time, you won't have the people you've bought to fall back on. Amaya-an and Zara-an are unique ships with sentience who you tried to kidnap and enslave, and you are therefore subject to the laws of their people. Thus, banishment. Be grateful for them. Frankly, I'd have spaced you. Or blown you out of the sky, but I do like your ships. They're quite nice!"

"You can't do that!" He sputtered, his face turning red. "That's…"

"Piracy?" Cass laughed. "Sucks when the tables are turned, doesn't it? Have a nice life, Ian."

She nodded at Hopper-an. "Execute."

She watched as the *Raider* left the bay of Amaya-an and, along with Ian's other ships, spun to the right and took off. Ian's angry tirade was cut off when they went into jump mode.

"Thank you, Hopper-an," Cass said. "I am so happy to see you." She grinned when Omar and the others joined Hopper-an on the bridge. The only one missing was Ben. He would forever be a hole in her heart, but at least he was still alive, and she would see him eventually. Though forgiving him would take a long time, if ever. She could hate him for what he did, but he'd been a big part of her life, one she couldn't forget.

Cass looked over as Zack touched her arm, and she gripped his hand.

"Ben's a survivor. He'll be okay in a penal colony. He'll have challenges, but at least we know he won't be hurting you anymore."

"Hurting us. He did this to both of us."

"Yes, but—"

Cass reached up to silence him. "The length of time doesn't matter."

Zack nodded at her. "Shall we head for home?"

Cass smiled and nodded. "Zara-an? Set course for Pointe Noir."

"Yes, boss."

Epilogue

Two Years Later

"Is everyone ready?" Cassandra-an announced to the crew. She got the go-ahead from everyone. She smiled at Zack sitting on her right, excitement shining in his eyes. Excitement like she was feeling.

"Amaya-an, are you ready?"

"Yes."

"Set course, Zara-an, and convey our route to the other ships."

"Course is set."

"Okay, everyone, let's go."

With the newly upgraded Zara-an in the lead, Amaya-an on her right, and three of Ian's former ships behind them, they headed away from Pointe Noir. Other ships saluted them with light displays as the five ships headed out.

"You're finally getting your wish," Zack said as he gripped her hand. "You're going to find your parents."

"*We're* going to find them," she said as she gripped his hand back. The past two years had been an interesting time. The uproar from Amaya-an and Zara-an appearing at Pointe Noir had been news for months—and continued to create news as Cassandra-an and Hopper-an fought for and won independent status for the ships. As a concession, Amaya-an agreed to hand over information on crystals to the scientists and engineers who'd come to study her.

Cass knew they would spend years sifting through all the data.

They'd also been able to explain the mystery off Pointe Noir where Kataya had *changed*. To Cass's—and everyone's—surprise, Amaya-an and Zara-an had asked their captains to vacate the ships and then flown directly into the lights, then sat there for several hours as the phenomenon grew smaller and smaller and finally disappeared. From what Cass understood, they had absorbed the energy from the singularity, taking the unique properties of the mass into themselves and making them even stronger. That had caused a huge uproar throughout the station and beyond, bringing in all kinds of security to surround the ships. Cass and Hopper had spent months fighting legal battles for the ships. Finally, Amaya-an and Zara-an had taken over the fight and informed everyone that either Cass and Hopper had the rights to the ships, or the ships would simply leave, and nobody could stop them. And to prove as much, they'd flown through the barriers surrounding them, scattering security and science ships alike. There was a short show of force from Fleet, but Amaya-an and Zara-an quickly showed them they were no match. Finally, after a lot of wrangling, Cass and Hopper were granted rights to the ships and all they held.

After several upgrades and refittings, Zara-an was now more like Amaya-an with weaponry and stronger shielding. She was still a cargo ship—which was now filled with enough supplies for a lengthy trip—but she was ready for whatever arose.

The other three ships, one with Omar and Katie in

charge, a second with Annie and June, and a third with Tom and Meri, had been part of Ian's fleet and had showed up, along with three others, just six months earlier. Cass had laid claim to them, as was her right, and promptly gave them to each of the teams that had been with her. She'd sold off the other two. She'd also sold all her holdings to the other team members who were staying behind. Zara-an was her home now, and with all the credits they'd received in bounties, crystal permits and patents, and the claim on the crystal mountain and city where she and Zack had been stranded, they never had to work again.

So she was off. With Zack as her husband and a son—compliments of their first time on Zara—with his nanny back in their quarters, life had finally settled down into a good place. They also had Zack's brothers on board. With Annie and Amaya-an's help, Dan's scars were gone, and he wouldn't stop talking. Jimmy would still need some time, but their new med-tech was also a psychologist who was helping him.

Cass would never forget Ben and what he had done to her, but he had been a part of her life for so long. He had been sentenced to twenty years in the Jovani penal colony, and she'd seen him off with tears and not a little regret. She knew he'd done what he had to protect her, but there was also more than a little greed in his actions.

They had never told the authorities or anyone the coordinates for the land where they'd banished Ian and his pirates. If anyone ever found them, it would be by accident. Amaya-an had had the ships set buoys warning anyone off the place, so Cass was sure they'd still be there. They'd sent a drone supply ship a month after they'd returned home with enough supplies for two

253

years. After that, survival was up to them.

"Let's go find the *Phoenix*," Zack said as he leaned over and hugged her.

"Second star to the right, and straight on 'til morning," Cass whispered, then grinned as she hugged him back. "Let's go!"

GLOSSARY

AI (artificial intelligence) ~*~ basically a computer that can think like—or better than—a human. They are capable of making decisions and can have basic emotions.

Bots – robots.

Cold Sleep – this is where a person is put into a coma-like state and sustained in a "life pod" that enables them to endure lengthy space trips.

Chrystolian Opals – also called Ki Opals or crystals. A special kind of rock discovered on Ki's Planet found to have special electronic properties that can be used as natural power sources.

CP or Cygnian Plague – an illness from the planet Cygnus that is usually deadly. Telltale signs include purple spots on the victim.

Droid – android – a robot that is human-like in appearance and action.

E-suit/environmental suit – space suit, not as bulky as ones worn by Earth astronauts.

Fresher – a bathroom with a sink, toilet, shower (usually sonic).

FTL – faster than light drive, also called a jump drive. It allows ships to cross vast distances in small amounts of time.

Jump systems – a special type of engine in a spaceship that allows the ship to contract space so as to make the trip shorter. There are points in space (like a star or planet) that you can set coordinates for and jump to there. But there are limits, so an extended trip might take several jumps.

Life pod – a single-person sized unit that can sustain

life for extended periods of time.

PAD – basically a tablet computer (Personal Administrative Device).

Thillo-toum – a martial art form similar to Judo.

Toluba – a martial art form similar to karate.

Watch your six – a term used especially by fighter pilots meaning your rear. When sitting in the cockpit of a plane, think of a clock face with the twelve being directly in front of you. Thus, the six would be behind you, to your rear.

Warrior Class – similar to the US Marines, they are highly trained military personnel who work in a wide variety of jobs including fighting, transportation, guardians, and more. Each job has a specific color of beading and clothing that denotes what they do.

White root – a plant found on Ki's Planet with multiple varieties. Most are harmless and have medicinal properties, but one variety—the thorny white root—is highly addictive leading to psychosis and death.

People (in order of appearance):

Cass – leader. Cass Brennan (aka Cassandra, Cassie). Owns and operates a salvage and cargo company. Partnered with Ben Knoble. Runs the *Seeker*, her salvage/cargo ship. Lost her parents seven years ago when their ship, the *Phoenix,* went missing. Uses her job to continue the search for them.

Ben Knoble – Cass's partner and godfather. He was best friends with her parents. Runs the business on the planet – he's the face of the business. Knows who to sell to and who to contact for best prices on what they bring in. He handles the contracts. But he's also a bit of a conman. And often gets Cass in trouble with his schemes.

Zack Anderson – engineer, bartender, electronics expert. Older brother of Dan and Jimmy. Parents died when McClarens burned out their farm to get to crystal caves. Dan and Jimmy were badly injured. Zack pays for their care. Cass's love interest.

Omar Tal – Surian race with shoulder-length gold hair. Mountain big. Owns Omar's Bar on Pointe Noir. Married to Katie.

Katie Tal – Aboolean/Human. Almost as tall as her husband, Omar, but reed slender with waist-length white hair and gold eyes. Expert fighter. Helps run the bar.

Hopper – human. Electronics expert. Old space accident left him nearly idiotic/savant. Doesn't like to be around people. Wears cast-offs of what he can find or scrounge. You want something done, Hopper can do it.

Chief Simon – runs the landing bays and bay security on Point Noir.

Captain Jaylee Kulanie – head of security on Pointe Noir.

Donnie – early twenties, human mix with some Asian characteristics from mother. Six feet tall. Muscular. Works with his father in cargo/salvage. Hard worker. Son of Paul.

Paul – late forties/early fifties, human, red hair, green eyes, six feet tall, muscular, no-nonsense kind of guy. Serious. Salvager/cargo. Good worker.

June – tall, broad, weighty without being fat. Solid muscle. Short salt-and-pepper hair, gruff but kind, mostly runs shuttles/cargo but also does some salvage. Partnered with Annie.

Annie – tiny but feisty. Extremely smart. Good worker. Knows salvage. Life partner with June. Healer/medic.

Timmons – the *Crimson Raider* AI.

Delta – the *Seeker's* AI.

Ian McClaren – former boyfriend of Cass turned pirate. Has a large fleet (six ships) and steals a lot of Cass's claims because he knows she's the best. Tall, light hair, brown eyes, rakish, good looks. Comes from a large clan of pirates and thieves.

Meri – pure Aboolean. Petite (five feet), slender, waist-length white hair, gold eyes, master of several styles of fighting. Married to Tom.

Tom – also Aboolean but from a different tribe. Bronze skin, black hair, dark eyes, tall, fit, also an expert fighter and weapons master married to Meri.

Ty – procurer of information you can't get through legitimate channels.

Mituna-an – captain of the Amaya-an. Masaaki race, feline in facial appearance, biped with arms/legs like humans, but also with a tail.

Ships:

Amaya-an – sentient ship in symbiotic relationship with her captain, Mituna-an.

Netierie-an – sentient ship built after Masaaki stranded.

Kataya-an – Amaya-an's sister ship. Destroyed in war between Throquins and Rujaz. Became a space anomaly near Pointe Noir station.

Zara-an – sentient cargo ship Cass and Zack find in the abandoned Masaaki city. Bonds with Cass.

Seeker – Cass's cargo/salvage ship. Run by Delta, its AI.

Crimson Raider – aka the Raider. Once one of Ian's ships. Run by the AI Timmons.

Sword's Edge – one of the McClaren ships.
Dagger – one of the McClaren ships.

Species:
Abooleans – there are many different races on Aboo, separated by tribes or clans. But all are humanoid. Most belong to tribes or classes that are denoted by their clothing and hair. Some of these include Warriors, Physicians, Merchants, Builders, and more.

Humans – though there are few humans on Aboo, there are a few. And more on other worlds and stations. How they got out into these places has been lost in time.

Masaaki – cat people. Though humanoid (walk upright, two legs, two arms, etc.), their features are feline in appearance, and they have tails.

Orilians – humanoids with blue scales, webbed hands and feet, and nictitating eyes. They mate once a year and prefer to build nest-like structures in cliffs near the ocean.

Rujaz – bronze skin that turns bright red when angered (which happens often). Shorter and heavier than most beings due to their main planets being gravity heavy.

Surians – coal black skin and gold hair, they mostly come from the desert planet of Jovian.

Throquins – part of the mysterious Throquin Dominium. Vaguely bird-like in appearance with sharp, pointed faces and taloned feet.

Places in the series:
Aboo – fourth planet in the Chalian system that is roughly the size of Mars. A mostly temperate island paradise (think Hawaii but circling the planet). A line of

islands marches around the globe at the equator called the Maltric Chain, but there are also land masses north and south that have harsher climates. Each island contains a space dock, some larger than others. The main island, Tyreegel, is where planetary government is located. Amanda Ki owned a compound on this island.

Aino – a small planet, roughly the size of Earth's moon, uninhabitable without special living quarters and environmental suits, important only for its mineral resources for the other planets in the system. Third in the Chalian system.

Aino Station – small station circling Aino. Stopping-off point for miners, ore transfers. Almost no amenities.

Argonia – mountainous area (think northwestern US or western Canada) on the Apitac continent north of Tyreegel. Protected woodlands. Mostly privately owned by the Warrior tribe, they control a large portion of the continent.

Boherea – abandoned ancient city on the southern continent. Mostly taken over by the desert.

Candelot – old Earth-like planet.

Dinarian system – five planets, only one vaguely inhabitable (mostly ice covered), multiple moons that are more habitable. Old mining system but played out.

Jovani – largest planet in the Chalian system, sixth one out from the sun. Mostly desert planet. Most cities are underground with just minor building aboveground due to harsh sandstorms and winds.

Kilner – uninhabited planet, ice covered, multiple moons; in the Dinarian system.

Lanicam – ancient realm on Jovani long since overtaken by the sands. All that's left is the language, like Latin, not spoken by anyone but used by many.

Mt. Pitonas – main mountain on Tyreegel. Old, dormant volcano, largest mountain in the islands.

Pointe Noir – major space station circling Aboo. It is a small city of almost 5,000 people of many species and is the jumping off point for all space travel in the system.

Secundus – fourth planet in the Xy System.

Thexadon – fifth planet in the Xy System.

Udara Station – old station in the Xy System, rarely used anymore.

Xy-One – third planet in the system, Earth-like, but largely unsettled. Two major cities – Delphi station and New Nova. Important for the deposits of Ki opals.

Xy-Three – also called Ki's Planet. Much smaller than Xy-One, but where Amanda's parents originally found the opals and white root plants. Volcanically active in the southern hemisphere.

Yalla – northeastern part of the Apitac continent on Aboo. Like Maine in makeup.

A word about the author…

Vicky has been married forever to the one person who accepts that she lives in a fantasy world most of the time. She's even been seen at the beach building worlds for her stories. In addition to creating fun characters, fantasy worlds, and suspenseful situations, she also enjoys and is very good at things like writing policy and procedures manuals and setting up continuity and organizational spreadsheets, both of which she has actually earned money doing. She has a master's degree in library science so likes things organized. Okay, so her family thinks having the spice rack alphabetized it a bit much, but she has no trouble finding what she needs when she needs it. And just because her extensive library is cataloged and organized, that doesn't mean she's obsessive. Honest.

When not writing, Vicky can be found in the kitchen whipping up gluten-free, lactose-free, other allergy-free meals. Or watching the world go by from her front porch swing.

http://www.vicky-burkholder.com

www.ingramcontent.com/pod-product-compliance
Lightning Source LLC
Chambersburg PA
CBHW060534260626
47161CB00003B/896